E. L. YOUNG

MACMILLAN CHILDREN'S BOOKS

First published 2007 by Macmillan Children's Books
a division of Macmillan Publishers Limited
20 New Wharf Road, London N1 9RR
Basingstoke and Oxford
www.panmacmillan.com

Associated companies throughout the world

ISBN: 978-0-330-44640-2

1 3 5 7 9 8 6 4 2

A CIP catalogue record for this book is available from the British Library.

Printed and bound in Great Britain by Mackays of Chatham plc, Kent

For James, Joy, Peter, Clare and Alastair

It wasn't the bang that made Vassily Baraban afraid.

In fact, he'd barely noticed it. At his desk in the small, untidy laboratory at Imperial College, London, Baraban was staring at his computer screen. Around him was a jumble of papers. A journal of astrophysics, with handwritten scrawl in the margins. A manuscript on an unusual gamma-ray burst. A request from a professor at Sweden's prestigious Karolinska Institute to visit London to discuss Baraban's research.

The professor sounded excited. He had reason to be, Baraban thought. His latest work was ground-breaking. Earth-shattering. 'Space-invading,' he muttered under his breath.

Baraban's eyes flicked to a photograph tacked to the wall beside his desk. A spectacular shot taken by the Hubble space telescope, it showed the voracious death spiral around a massive black hole. Baraban shivered. Beneath the photograph was another, yellowed at the edges, marked by creases. A beautiful woman with cropped dark hair was cradling a baby in her arms. A grand building rose behind them. The Hermitage Museum in St Petersburg.

Baraban reached out and touched the picture gently. His son was now fourteen years old. He had never returned to the city of his birth. None of them had been back to Petersburg. One day, Baraban thought. One day, when my work here is done . . .

. . . And then there was the knocking. Insistent this time.

In his first few years in London, Baraban had leaped at every knock. His nerves had been on edge – with good reason. Annoyed now at the interruption, he turned to the door.

Behind a glass panel was the sallow face of the night janitor. Baraban glanced at his watch: 2 a.m. He waved a hand angrily, to indicate he was still immensely busy. Time meant nothing to him. Only ordinary people, he would often tell his son, are governed by the clock. As the janitor shuffled away, Baraban let his eyes return to the computer screen.

His gaze barely had time to settle . . .

This noise was sharp. A scraping. It had come from behind, to his left, and it had sounded like fingernails on glass. Baraban's head shot round. Now his irritation turned to fear. The sound had been made by a glass cutter. The glass cutter had removed a square section from the generous laboratory window. And there, in the room, were two hefty men.

They were Russian. Baraban knew this in an instant, even before they opened their mouths. The first man was well over six feet tall, skin the colour of dirty snow, tiny blue eyes lost in the rough fleshiness of his face. His head was shaved. Even the black stubble on his scalp looked dangerous. From an inside pocket in his canvas jacket, he now produced something that resembled a taser. But while there were electrical sparks, the weapon appeared to have no darts. Baraban froze, transfixed. Sweat sprang from his palms.

'Sergei, I shoot now?' the first intruder asked. His voice was thick.

He was stupid, Baraban decided, but it didn't make him feel much better.

'. . . W-who are y-you?' he managed to stutter.

'My name is Vladimir—'

But the man called Sergei stepped forward and silenced them both with a wave of something more conventional. A black handgun.

Sergei had blond hair, gelled into tiny spikes. There was a tattoo of a laughing woman on his bicep. It bulged as he lifted his arm, and levelled the gun.

'You do not talk,' Sergei said. 'You come with us.'

'That is impossible,' Baraban said quietly. Fear made his voice shake. Only ordinary people felt fear, he reprimanded himself. '*Who are you?*' he said, with defiance. 'What do you want?' And he peered at the chunk of black plastic in the shaven-headed man's hand. Scientific curiosity for a moment overwhelmed his fear:

'Is this a new weapon?' he enquired. 'I do not think I have seen such a thing before . . .'

The man grunted. 'We have no time for this.' He lifted the weapon – and fired.

Twin flaring pulses leaped across the lab. Baraban's chest was pierced by a fierce shooting pain. His limbs felt paralysed. His flesh was cold and hot, burning and numb. His vision blurred. He had read of such a thing, after all, in a memorandum from a colleague in the Ukrainian military. But he had not realized the device was beyond the prototype stage. It was intriguing. These thoughts blasted through his mind in a split second.

'Electric bullets,' he murmured. 'Very advanced . . .'

And then the photographs on his wall seemed to merge, his wife into the black hole, a supernova into his son. He began to sway.

'*Pridurok!*' Sergei hissed. 'Idiot! Do not let him fall! Quick, protect his head!'

These were the last words that Baraban heard before he slipped towards the ground – and before he was knocked unconscious as his ample head collided with his desk.

Central London, 28 hours later

It was still dark when the alarm went off. The sound sent shock waves blasting through the sleeping boy. He'd put the clock underneath the duvet, so it wouldn't wake the woman in the room next door. She was a light sleeper and she took a strong interest in his activities. This morning, he had no desire to explain himself.

Will tumbled out of bed but was instantly alert. Within five minutes, he was dressed. Jeans, T-shirt, jumper and jacket, and trainers with the new soles. He pulled a rucksack from the top shelf of his wardrobe and a plastic storage crate from underneath his bed. From the crate, he took the reason for the 6.30 a.m. start: a coiled length of ten-millimetre climbing rope and a harness. In the bottom of the crate, wrapped in a sheet, he found the spear-fishing gun, an old birthday present from his father, which he'd never used – at least on fish. Will stuffed the lot into his rucksack and slung the device on top. 6.45 a.m. His heart was pounding. He was ready.

The third stair down was the one to watch for. One hand on the banister, he skipped over it. Then he was out of the front door and into the freezing fog of the early December morning. Will closed the door gently. He glanced up at the window of the studio. No light. Natalia was still asleep.

Will knew the way well. Left out of the house, across the square, telling himself to slow down, though his feet were itching to break into a jog. Dawn was breaking. Grey colour slowly crept over the buildings. To his right, a red double-decker rumbled past, spewing out exhaust. Through the dim light, a black cab followed it, veering off towards Tottenham Court Road. Will hoisted the pack higher on his back and pulled his scarf up across his mouth. With numb fingers he reached into the pocket of his jacket and touched the smooth soft leather of a cricket ball. A ball his father had given to him, for luck.

Seven minutes later, he was there. Will paused outside the gates. There were two security cameras. One over the double front doors to the school. The second around the back, overlooking the car park. They were a few years old. And obvious. Will had timed the narrow arc of the front camera from a few metres on one side of the front gate to roughly a metre on the other side. He glanced at his watch – another present from his father. A barometer, thermometer, altimeter, wind sensor, bug-sweeper and timepiece rolled into one. Ten seconds. Eight seconds. Five seconds. And he ran.

Eight seconds later, he was crouching to one side of the main entrance. The camera had missed him by a mile. He was breathing hard. It wasn't the exertion. It was excitement. There wasn't much that he liked about the school but the building itself was perfect. Three storeys high – an ideal testing ground for the prototype.

Will glanced around the yard, but it was far too early for any teachers. They wouldn't arrive for more than an hour. The cleaners worked at night. The caretaker had Thursdays off.

Quickly, he slipped around to the rear of the building and looked up. The school was old, Victorian. To Will's left, an iron fire escape zigzagged its way up the solid, red brick. The walls seemed to soar. But Will had confidence in his design. He'd been over it countless times. The mechanism would work, he was sure of that. At least, he thought he was sure – but there was nothing like a trial run for throwing up oversights or errors.

Will took a deep breath. He checked his watch: 7.12 a.m. He had plenty of time. He lowered his rucksack to the ground and pulled out the device. It needed a name, but this was Will's only superstition: name nothing until it works. Then he hauled out the rope, and the climbing harness. The harness slipped easily over his jeans. Next came the speargun. It was low-powered, running on pressurized gas. It should be all right, he hoped. Deftly, he tied one end of the rope to a metal rod to which he'd soldered a grappling hook – a replacement for a spear.

The fog was clearing, but mist still swirled around the roof. Will grabbed the speargun and closed one eye. It was psychological. He felt it would help his aim. The base of the gun close to his chest, he fired. Rope whizzed past his ears. And, to Will's relief, the grappling hook caught in the old iron guttering that was fixed just below the tiles of the roof. He gave a quick tug. The hook moved. Then it held. Two more tugs. He attached the device to his harness, then the rope to his device, and tried his entire body weight. It didn't budge.

Two quick breaths, and he took the device in his hand. Inside the black casing was a motor, powered by batteries, which turned a series of cogs and wheels. How many movies had featured gadgets like this? he thought. How many people knew that all were phoneys. Special effects. All faked. But this . . .

He pushed.

The response was instant.

Excitement flooded through Will's body as it was lifted off the ground. The cogs turned so quickly that to anyone else the sound would have been a seamless whirr. But Will could visualize every turn, every spin of every wheel that was necessary to hold against the rope, to move it through, to pull him up.

He'd intended to time the ascent, but it was too late. Already he was three metres up in the air, and he could see across the roof of a low house on the other side of the road. He turned back to the wall and blinked up, as the mist parted and the pale yellow sun took the chill from his face. Will could make out the shape of the lichen on the tiles. In an instant, he reached the guttering, and swung his legs up and over. For a few moments, he just crouched there, up on the roof. To get to the fire escape – and so to get down – he'd have to edge a few metres across the tiles. It had been raining but his soles did not slip. Slowly, each muscle in his legs tense, Will stood up. The wind cut across his face, but it did not matter. Nothing mattered. Except that he was there, on the roof, his school beneath his feet. Will clasped the black plastic casing against his body.

'Rapid Ascent,' he whispered to himself.

After two months of creation, at last it had a name.

Will did not know it, but it was his trial of Rapid Ascent that secured his invitation to join STORM.

STORM. A secret organization. A group that would change his life.

He had been wrong that early morning, when he'd believed he was alone. Someone else had been watching. A girl, called Gaia.

It was a Monday, four days after the triumph of Rapid Ascent. Will was walking along a glass-walled school corridor, on the way from double chemistry to theoretical astrophysics.

He was thinking about the device, and the sense of achievement, which had not lasted. Perhaps it wasn't surprising, Will thought. Pleasure and excitement quickly faded. A few hours, nothing more. Natalia had told him it would take time. *A little time*, and he would adjust. The words built an awful pressure in his chest.

Will was about to turn the corner towards the physics labs when he felt a tap on his shoulder.

He looked around. Gaia.

'Have you got a minute?' she said. 'I want to ask you something.'

Will was curious. They barely knew each other, though they were enrolled in the same annexe to the main school, a unit dedicated to exceptionally gifted pupils. There were twenty students, from all over

London. Will had taken a dislike to most of them. In part, because they had such a high estimation of themselves.

Only the previous day, there had been laughter when a new girl could not solve a quadratic equation. His classmates liked nothing more than a chance to demonstrate their brilliance, if at all possible at someone else's expense. Will didn't sympathize. He'd always taken his intelligence for what it was – something he was born with, not something he had earned. It was nothing to feel superior about. But he seemed to be the only one who felt that way. Three months at the school, and he had made no real friends. He generally kept himself to himself, like Gaia. And yet she'd been there for two years.

He knew this about her: she'd been kicked out of seven schools already. She spoke fluent French, Italian and Mandarin. She'd won a prize in last year's international science Olympiad. And while he came top in every other test, she always beat him in chemistry. She was tall and skinny and she had dark, curling hair and brown eyes.

Will wondered what she wanted. Perhaps she needed his help with the homework. The Birch and Sinnerton-Dyer conjecture was difficult. There was a one million US dollar prize for its solution, after all.

He nodded.

She looked him straight in the eye. It was an intense

gaze, and it made him uncomfortable. But the last thing he would do was look away.

'You're very good,' she said.

Will frowned.

'I mean,' she said quickly, 'you know you are. You come top in everything.'

'Not chemistry,' he said, slightly bemused.

She gave him a smile, which quickly vanished. 'I'm serious,' she said. And she hesitated.

Will wondered where this was going. If she wanted help with the homework she only had to ask.

'I heard you talking to Naresh yesterday,' she said. 'You were telling him about that new lock you invented.'

Will was surprised. He and Naresh had been eating lunch in the cafeteria. He thought they'd been alone.

'It's got two keys?' Gaia said.

Will nodded slowly. 'Yeah, two keys.'

'And last week, when you got on to the roof, I saw how you did it. I saw you shoot up the rope. Then that *device* pulled you up. '

Will stared at her. He hadn't seen Gaia. He hadn't seen anyone.

'How does it work?' she said.

Anger blazed. 'What were you doing at school? *Where* were you?'

'It doesn't matter,' she said. 'Tell me: how does it work?'

'We're going to be late,' Will said. Had she been

following him? But *why*? The thought was strange. He made to turn away. He tried to swallow the anger.

'Please, Will. Tell me.'

Will stopped. Her voice had not been imploring. '. . . It's got a motor in it, powered by batteries,' he said, with irritation, 'that turns a series of wheels and cogs, and they pull the rope through.'

'I've seen that in movies.'

'That was fiction,' Will said quickly. 'I made it work. The US military—' And he stopped himself. The last thing he wanted to do was brag about his achievements. If he did that, he was no better than the rest of them.

'We're late,' he said again. The building was silent. Classroom doors were closed, the corridor was empty. He started to walk towards the lab.

'Just one thing. The thing I wanted to ask you,' Gaia called.

Will wanted to keep walking, but he paused.

'I want you to meet a friend of mine. His name's Andrew. He's got an idea. It will change your life.'

Will turned. Gaia was standing rod-straight in the middle of the corridor. Her brown eyes were gleaming. 'It won't only change your life,' she promised, 'it will change the world.'

And so, the following afternoon after school, Will let Gaia lead him through the streets, towards Andrew.

Will walked with his head down. Gaia had tried to make conversation, but he hadn't seemed keen. She'd given up five minutes ago. Now they walked in silence. Will followed her rapid stride. She was guiding him, after all. He didn't know where they were going – except that it was to a house in Bloomsbury. And he didn't know what to expect – except that the meeting was secret.

As they walked, Will thought about her words in the corridor: *It will change your life* . . . But already, his life had changed.

The night before, Will had lain awake, unable to sleep. In his mind, he saw his mother's dark eyes, swollen from crying. It was three days after the news. A man in an expensive suit had arrived at their farmhouse in Dorset. Will had overheard the whole thing. His father had been killed in action, somewhere in eastern China. And he'd watched, afraid, as his mother had flung herself on a chair, shaking with grief. She was an emotional person. She always blamed her Russian mother. And, she'd told Will, as he sat on the sofa in the stricken, silent house, now she felt she couldn't cope. She needed to spend some time with her mother, back in St Petersburg. It would be good for Will, she felt, for him to get out of Dorset, to go somewhere else. Like London, she'd said. To stay with her old best friend, Natalia. It was best for both of them, his mother had promised. And Will, too stunned and miserable to speak, had only nodded.

His father was dead, and his mother had sent him away. He had no brothers or sisters, no uncles or cousins. Three of his grandparents had been buried before he was ten. He was alone.

Desperate sadness had overwhelmed him. But three months had passed, and some of that misery had turned to anger. Those first few weeks, Will had read his mother's emails avidly. Every few days, they had talked on the phone. Until she'd made it clear she still wasn't ready to come back. Hurt, Will had deleted her emails and ignored her calls. Now, they no longer came. It wouldn't be for long, she had promised him in the car on the way to London. She needed just a *little time* to sort herself out, or she'd fall apart and she'd be no use to him. There had been a strange note in her voice. Will wasn't sure what it was – but he hadn't quite believed her. And three months wasn't *little time* in anyone's estimation, Will thought. It certainly wasn't to him.

'It's not far now,' Gaia said.

Her voice jerked Will from his thoughts.

The sun was low in the sky, about to dip below the roofs. The air was cold. It bit through his jumper. They were close to the British Museum. Ahead, coaches from across Europe were sucking up their tourists.

To their left was a sunken garden, almost hidden behind walls. And then an office block. Will caught a glimpse of his reflection in a window. His longish brown hair was flat over his ears. His narrow shoulders were hunched. He'd lost weight since coming to London. Through his jumper, he could feel his ribs.

And he wondered what lay ahead. He was curious about Andrew. For the first time since Rapid Ascent, he felt a trace of anticipation, warm in his blood.

'That's it,' Gaia said.

She was peering across the road, at a two-storey Georgian house with dense ivy clinging to the walls. It stood on its own, surrounded on three sides by trees, imposing and gabled, a country house in the heart of London. The sun had vanished. Smoke rose up from twin chimneys, through the dusk.

'Andrew can't wait to meet you,' Gaia said. 'You're just what he wants.' And she coloured slightly. 'Don't take that as a compliment, I only mean it as a fact.'

Gaia quickly crossed the street, into shadows. She was a strange girl, Will thought. But then she probably thought he was strange. Most people seemed to. At least, they did now, here in London, where he felt so strongly that he did not belong.

Gaia glanced back. 'Come *on*,' she said.

She led the way to a back door, overhung by a vast, leafless oak. There was a stainless-steel intercom, with an old-fashioned phone handset. No button to press, Will noticed, and yet a green transmission light had flicked on as they'd approached.

Gaia picked up the handset and pressed it to her ear. She waited a moment and then replaced it.

'No one there?' Will said.

'Ear-print recognition. It recognizes the shape of my ear, and—'

'Yes,' Will said quickly, impatient to skip past his misunderstanding. 'I know what ear-print recognition is. But it's a gimmick. It's nowhere near as accurate as iris checks, or fingerprints.'

Gaia shrugged. 'Andrew likes gimmicks.'

Will glanced up. Drilled into the lintel above the door was a tiny hole. Containing a miniature camera, he guessed. This was primitive security. And obvious. But perhaps it was designed more to impress most guests than to keep undesirables out.

At last, a boy's voice cut in.

'Yes, good Gaia, you would have been in automatically but the camera picked up someone else. Will Knight, I presume?'

'Yes,' she said.

The intercom crackled.

Gaia shivered.

She slapped the intercom. '*Andrew, hurry up!*'

There was a click, and the door opened. It revealed a boy of about their age. He was small and skinny, dressed in red trousers and a white T-shirt embroidered with an elephant. A gold watch hung heavy on his slender wrist. Bright-blue eyes smiled at Gaia and scanned Will up and down. He wore thick, frameless glasses, and an expression of assured sincerity. Fourteen, but more like forty, Will thought. The boy held out his hand.

'Pleased to meet you, Will,' he said. 'My name's Andrew. Welcome to STORM.'

Expectation.

If Will was honest, it had eaten into him.

Gaia had given only the name, and dropped few hints. Andrew wanted to reveal the detail himself, she'd said, as they'd stood together in the school yard, after double astrophysics. But she'd known how to tempt Will. The very latest technology would be available. Any piece of kit that he might reasonably need would be his. His capacity for thinking of useful kit was pretty infinite, Will had told her. It would be no problem, she'd replied, her eyes shining.

Now, Andrew led the way into his house. They passed through a darkly lit hallway. It was heavily wall-papered, in embossed green. Greek busts were illuminated in niches in the walls. At the end of the hall, Andrew opened the door to a spacious drawing room. The first object Will noticed was a yellow chaise longue, angled towards the open fire. And then a skull, on an antique card table. Beside it was a photograph of the British astronaut, Esmee Templeton, with the words *To Andrew, keep reaching for the stars, Esmee* scrawled in biro at the bottom. Prints of exotic birds and horses with hounds were hung in vast gilt frames on the walls. Will blinked.The scene was lit with a thousand brilliant shards of light from a crystal chandelier.

Will's heart was beating fast. It irritated him. He pressed his palms to his trousers.

'Please, sit down,' Andrew said with formality.

But Will had already crossed to the skull. Softly, he touched the rough edges of a hole about a centimetre across, halfway back along the cranium. The bone was cold.

'Human,' Will said.

'Trepanned,' Andrew said, his back to the fire. Gaia was on the chaise longue, beside him. 'He had a hole drilled into his head to release an evil spirit. That was before effective anaesthesia. I imagine he must have needed rather a lot of *evil spirit* to help him cope with the pain.'

Will glanced at Gaia. Andrew even told forty-year-old jokes.

'But Gaia could tell you all about it.' Andrew turned and plucked a dusty book from the shelf beside the fireplace. *Journey to the Bismarck Archipelago* was printed on the spine in faded gold ink. 'Dad used this one, didn't he?' he said, waving it at her, a smile on his lips.

She read the title. '*Andrew.*' It was a word of warning.

'No, really – Will, listen to this.' And Andrew flicked the book open to an apparently random page. '*It was close to dusk when we arrived at the encampment. My legs ached, sweat burned in my eyes. There was a beauty in the half-light. But, barely a moment later, there was horror . . .*' Andrew peered at Gaia over his glasses. 'What comes next?'

'*Andrew.*'

'Come on, Gaia – what comes next?'

'Andrew, please!'

But he was smiling. 'Come on, I know you know. Don't you? Don't you, Gaia?'

'You know I do,' she said, exasperated, and she turned her eyes to the flames.

'So tell me the next sentence.'

'Shut up, Andrew. Please.'

And Andrew raised an eyebrow at Will, who was confused. *'It was the scream of a man inhabited by demons. The scream of a man who, as we watched, had his scalp peeled back, and his skull spiked through.'*

'Skull *pierced through,'* Gaia said, unable to stop herself.

Andrew beamed at Will, triumphant and proud. 'The wonders of a photographic memory. My father's a psychiatrist. He used this book to test her . . . Didn't you know?'

Will glanced at Gaia. She looked embarrassed, more than anything. 'No,' he said.

'And you go to school with her. I'd have thought it was obvious.'

Will shrugged.

'Andrew loves talking about other people,' Gaia said, her exasperation fading. 'It's one of his faults.'

But Andrew only smiled at her. 'I don't see how it can be a fault when I point out a strength. So, Will,' he said, and he replaced the book, 'Gaia tells me you're the best student in the class. That's quite an achievement, given your company.'

'It is what it is,' Will said. He hadn't meant to sound cryptic. 'That's true,' he said, seeing no point in false modesty. 'Except for chemistry. No matter how hard I try, Gaia always beats me.'

Andrew placed a friendly hand on her shoulder. And Will watched with interest as she turned to the fire, apparently warming her hands, but at the same time shrugging Andrew off.

'Right,' Andrew said, and he pushed his glasses back up along the bridge of his nose. A nervous gesture, Will thought. 'It's been nice making your acquaintance. Now give me a few minutes then come down to the basement. I'm going to make sure everything's set up. Caspian's already down there.'

Andrew gave them a brief wave, and he vanished.

As soon as he had gone, Will checked out the room more thoroughly. Along with the antiques and the sinister curios there was a lot of high-tech gadgetry. Nothing too innovative. All off-the-shelf. A metre-wide LED TV screen, the latest Apple iBook, open on a spindly legged writing desk. On the richly woven carpet were two halves of a wireless keyboard, which were designed to sit on each knee, to remotely control a computer.

'It must be useful to have a photographic memory,' he said, without looking at Gaia.

'Sometimes,' she said.

And a firmness in her tone encouraged him to change the subject.

'All the stuff in this house must cost a fortune. Do you make that much from psychiatry?'

Gaia looked surprised. 'It's Andrew who's rich. Andrew Minkel, I thought you'd have heard of him. The software millionaire? He made his first million by the time he was ten. Now I think he's up to about two hundred.'

'*Two hundred million?*'

She nodded. 'He owns this house. His aunt lives here, but she's on holiday somewhere in Scotland. She goes away all the time. Andrew prefers it. His parents are overseas.' Gaia glanced at the gold clock on the mantelpiece. '. . . We should really go down. The door's in the kitchen.'

And Will followed her into the hall and through to the basement steps.

At once, his full attention was seized by the room below. It was cavernous, with black-painted walls. At the rear, Andrew was fiddling with something on a low table. Three plastic-moulded chairs were arranged in a row, their backs to the steps, facing the table. In one corner of the room was a stainless-steel bench, topped with kit. From the steps, Will recognized an electron microscope, equipment for DNA sequencing, even a gun whose spark could catalogue the precise make-up of a sample of rock.

A tall, well-built boy with a loud, deep voice and a shock of black hair leaned against one wall. He and Andrew appeared to be arguing.

'We must blame the solar cycle,' the boy was saying. 'Radio emissions from the Sun confirm that the peak of activity is approaching. The danger will increase—'

'But didn't Delacroix contradict—' Andrew started to say.

'Nonsense,' the boy shouted, angrily waving his hand. 'Delacroix has the brain of a dog.'

'Animal intelligence—' Andrew began, before once more he was silenced.

'Delacroix has the intelligence of a foetus. It is the failing of mankind. Without geniuses, where would humanity be? In the Stone Age! We are the ones who must carry life forward.'

'Forward to where?' Andrew said, and he stopped fiddling and stood up.

'To perfection! We must mirror the objectivity, the efficiency of space. Think of the precise *absence* of the vacuum, the unthinking devastation of the supernova, the hunger of the all-consuming black hole! Why should humanity not have at least a taste of that perfection? *We* are of space. Our molecules belong to the universe. To pretend otherwise is to waste our time—' He seemed to check himself. 'To pretend otherwise is to waste what we can be.'

At the top of the steps, Will shook his head. 'He's insane,' he whispered to Gaia.

She shrugged. 'In some ways.'

'*We are of space?*'

'He's right – in a sense.'

'He's mad.'

She gave a tight smile. 'He's supposed to be very brilliant.'

'So who is he?'

'His name is Caspian Baraban. Son of the famous astrophysicist.'

Will thought for a moment. He'd never heard of an astrophysicist called Baraban. But he didn't want to admit this to Gaia.

'How do you know him?' he asked instead.

'Andrew's known him for years. I don't think they're close friends. But they went to primary school together.'

'In England?'

Gaia nodded.

'So why does he still talk with a Russian accent?'

Gaia shrugged. 'I think he spends most of his time with his father – maybe that's why. I only met Caspian a couple of weeks ago.' She hesitated. 'There were only going to be the three of us to start with, but then I told Andrew about you.'

'What about me?'

She looked round. 'He wants the best people.'

'At *what*? Solving the Birch and Sinnerton-Dyer conjecture?'

'You solved it?' Gaia's eyes were wide.

Will almost smiled at her astonishment. 'Not yet,' he conceded. He switched his gaze to the scene below. 'Does Caspian know what's going on?'

'He knows as much as you.'

'And you?'

'I don't know everything. When you know Andrew better, you'll understand. This is important to him.'

Andrew must have heard them talking, because he looked up and waved.

'Excellent timing!' Andrew called. 'Please, come and sit down.'

Caspian Baraban stared up suspiciously at the new arrivals.

'Caspian, meet Gaia and Will,' Andrew said, as they took their seats. 'Will, Caspian is an astrophysicist. Caspian, Gaia is a brilliant chemist. Will is . . . well, apparently Will is an inventor.'

Will glanced at Gaia. '*Inventor,*' he mouthed.

'How else would you describe yourself?' she whispered.

'Not only an astrophysicist,' Caspian announced. And Will felt Caspian's cool, black eyes lock on to him. 'I also have interests in quantum physics and nanotechnology.'

'Of course,' Andrew said.

'In fact, only last month I was with my father in Cambridge – you will have heard of my father, of course – he pioneered research into strangelets—' And

Caspian bit his tongue. Thoughts were tumbling through his mind. Thoughts and fears. He could not let them out.

'I think,' Gaia said, 'that Andrew is ready.'

Gaia had noticed Andrew's faintly nervous impatience. Now he flashed her a grateful smile.

'Right,' Andrew said. And he pulled a keypad from his pocket and pressed a button.

The lights dimmed. He pressed another switch and a cloud of mist descended from the ceiling. Will guessed what it was at once. For the first time that evening, he was impressed. He'd read the patent only the previous month. Sandwiched between two layers of flowing air, the fog became a screen.

'I got this last week,' Andrew was saying. 'The company wants me to test it.' And he composed himself.

Will sat back in his chair. All eyes were now on the skinny boy with the bad clothes and more money than Will could even comprehend. Maybe at last he would discover what STORM was all about.

'Imagine,' Andrew said.

He waved his hand towards the fog. Instantly, the hovering screen was illuminated. Pale light danced across the walls. Andrew pressed another button on the keypad and an image of a mushroom cloud appeared and rotated.

'The atomic bomb,' Andrew continued. 'August 1945, it killed more than two hundred thousand men, women and children.'

Another click.

Will recognized the shape of a chemical plant.

'Bhopal. 1984. An explosion in India. Poisonous fumes filled the air and more than fifteen thousand died.'

Another click. A coal-fired power station, blasting out dark smoke.

Another click. Birds dripped with oil from a slick.

Another click. An emaciated man lay on parched ground. Flies clustered around his mouth. A child was crying nearby, his belly distended.

'The world is full of nightmares,' Andrew was saying. 'The *same* world has money. We have science. We have international funding bodies, we have committees to do this and committees to do that. And yet malaria kills a child every thirty seconds. Megacorporations pollute the atmosphere, so global warming threatens us all. AIDS wipes out more than eight thousand people every single day.'

Andrew's face was taut, his expression intense. He was behaving, Will thought, as though he was talking to a conference hall packed with eminent listeners, rather than three other kids. Andrew must have been thinking about this day for some time. Caspian, Gaia and him . . . Was Andrew pleased with his audience? Will wondered.

'We have a choice,' Andrew was saying. 'We sit back, we wait, we hope that one day we can grow up to do something about the bad in the world. Or we act.'

Another click. The fog went blank for an instant. A logo appeared. STORM. In red letters, rotating.

'S.T.O.R.M. Science and Technology to Over-Rule Misery. We might be young, but we are not impotent. We *can* act. We *can* change the world. The only real challenge is for us to believe it.'

He let his gaze focus on each of the three members of his audience. Andrew's words had been drenched in belief. His blue eyes were alight with passion.

'My vision is this,' he continued. 'That we come together, and we recruit others who have talents, and under the banner of STORM we work to tackle the problems in the world. Why not? We're geniuses. We *can* take on HIV. We *can* take on global warming. We have the brains. I have the money. I say: let's do it!'

There was a stunned pause. After a few moments, Caspian Baraban began to clap. Gaia put her own hands together. Her head was bowed and nodding, apparently in deep agreement. Will looked at them in disbelief. And his anger surprised him. Who did they think they were? It was typical, he thought – exactly the warped idea of reality of his classmates. He hadn't known what to expect from the evening. But he hadn't expected this. It was all so worthy, he thought. And naive. Disappointment, and three months of frustration, rose to the surface.

'Don't you think—' Will said loudly, and the clapping stopped. He stood up, and stepped towards Andrew. 'Don't you think you're expecting a little too much? We haven't even left school. You want to take on global warming when the best scientists in the world are already working on it? You think you can beat *HIV*?'

Andrew looked at him impassively. 'Yes,' he said. 'With others, I think we can.'

'Working here in your *basement*?'

'Why not?' Andrew said.

Will shook his head. 'You've been successful and it's done something to your head. You think because you can make money out of *software* you can solve the world's problems? I can't believe how arrogant you are.'

There was a tense silence. At last, Andrew nodded slowly. 'And I can't expect everyone to share my belief from the start. Most of us are so used to living within confinements we can no longer even dream of what truly is possible. We *accept*, because we are taught that we should not *expect*.'

'What you're talking about is a dream,' Will said. 'That's all. You want us to waste our time on things we can never achieve. I have better things to do.'

Andrew shrugged. 'If you feel that way, Will, you may of course feel free to leave.'

Will's next sentence froze in his mouth. He glanced back at the three seats. Baraban was sneering at him in scorn. Gaia was looking at him gently, a slight frown on her face.

And Will instantly felt heat in his cheeks. Perhaps he should have kept his mouth shut. He could have left and simply not said a word.

He turned away from Gaia, and he leaped up the steps, out of the door, and into the blackness of the night. He walked quickly, and he didn't look back. His mind was racing. It was odd behaviour for him. In the past few months, he'd learned to keep his own counsel. But what he realized was this: he'd been curious about STORM. He'd begun to think that Gaia might be all right. He'd let himself hope that something new could be about to change, even to improve, his life. And life as usual had let him down.

Will sighed and angrily shook his head. It was no good thinking that way. It would get him nowhere. What would his father have said?

And Will brushed a tear from his cheek. The trace of moisture that remained was evaporated by the night breeze. It chilled his face. He wrapped his arms tighter around his chest. It wasn't far to Natalia's house.

A few minutes later, he was outside her gate. The first-floor window was lit. Her studio. Will could see the outline of her plump body at her desk. He could even see the fine brush in her hand. Natalia. His mother's childhood best friend. Natalia would look after him, his mother had said, as she'd packed up her house and packed off her son.

Will reached in his pocket for his key. The second key, for the one lock. It was true, he had invented it . . . Double Entry. It was simple. Natalia could switch the setting, so, with one key, she could give access to the builders who were always working on the crumbling terrace, but with the switch turned, a different key was required – and any builder who might be tempted to come back and help himself to some of her art would be kept out. It was better security than Andrew's, with his useless ear-print recognition and his mail-order miniature cameras. And Will thought of Gaia in the corridor at school, and all she had seemed to promise.

He glanced at his watch: 6.30 p.m. He'd told Natalia he had extra science classes after school. She believed him, of course. She seemed to believe everything he said. It wasn't so much that she was trusting, Will thought, more that she didn't seem to live quite in the real world. The key turned. Will pushed open the door.

Russian folk music was playing on the old stereo in the kitchen. From upstairs there were voices. Natalia's – and a man's. Her friend, Roden Cutler, Will presumed. Then his pocket vibrated. He pulled out his phone, frowning at the name of the person who was calling. *Gaia*.

Will stopped the call and put the phone back in his pocket. He didn't feel like talking to her. He felt like going up to his room, lying down on his bed, trying to forget about the past few hours. But then the song changed.

. . . As you sleep, I hold you dear
As you dream, I'm always near . . .

The song stopped Will in his tracks, one hand on the

polished wooden banister, one foot on the first stair. *As you sleep, I hold you dear. As you dream, I'm always near . . .* His mother had sung in Russian these words, from this song, when he was a young child, as she'd led him to bed. Those lines meant all was well. Meant she was there. Will's stomach turned. Nausea made his body weak. He wanted to go through to the kitchen, to switch off the music. But he seemed unable to move. And then:

'William!'

The strange spell was broken.

'Hello, Natalia.'

She had appeared at the top of the stairs, a beam splitting her plump face in two. Natalia had bobbed blonde hair and storm-blue eyes. She was wearing a flowing Egyptian galibeyah and leather sandals in the style favoured by Ptolemaic pharaohs. Her work clothes.

'I thought I heard the door!' she cried. 'How was school?' She descended the stairs as rapidly as her bulk would allow. 'You look so pale. You have been working so hard.'

Will shrugged. Natalia resisted the temptation to touch him.

'Come through to the kitchen,' she said. 'I have made beef bourguignon. And I have had Roden drooling, because I insisted we wait for you.'

Will nodded. He changed the music and Natalia did not blink. She lifted the pot from the Aga. Her black cat,

Dmitri, was forced from his spot in front of the stove and started to arch around Will's legs. At once, he felt a little better. The anger had subsided.

'Where's Roden?' he said.

'Ah, he is coming,' Natalia replied. 'He was in the studio, looking through my new drawings. Mmm.' She beamed at Will, a half-empty spoon in her hand. 'Delicious! Some French chef would kiss my feet for just a taste.'

'Not in those shoes.' And Will tensed. He had meant to sound light-hearted, but he didn't really feel it. He hadn't meant to offend her.

But Natalia smiled. 'Ah, you are right!' She looked down at the battered suede. 'What was I thinking? Roden tells me I must buy new ones!'

'Did I hear my name?'

Their heads turned. Roden Cutler had stepped into the kitchen. He smiled, but it was a cool smile, Will thought. Hard to be warm with such thin, bloodless lips, and such eyes. They were yellowish, flecked with grey and green. Animal eyes. Roden was in his mid-forties, probably the same age as Natalia, but grey was thickly streaked through his hair. He was thin, angular, and edgy, and he looked misshapen in his suit.

Roden was in London for a week, on business. As an old friend of Natalia's, he'd been invited to stay.

He brought Will gifts. The first night, a football. And then a penknife that concealed a one gigabyte memory stick among the blades. Will had been confused. Roden was only trying to be friendly, Natalia had told him. At first, Will had been wary. But Roden certainly was making an effort. And he knew about all sorts of things – the history of submarines, ancient Chinese warfare, surgical techniques in the time of the Crusades. Roden liked to talk. And what he said was mostly interesting. Which set him above most people, Will thought.

'Quick, quick!' Natalia said. 'To the table. Tonight we can all speak in French. We can pretend we are in a provincial bistro.'

'I can't—' Will began.

'Then Russian,' she said. 'You speak Russian, William, your mother told me – I know.'

Will looked down at the pile of stew on his plate. Yes, he could speak Russian. His mother was fluent. His father, who was English through and through, spoke it equally as well. Will had grown up with two languages. And he remembered, from years ago, the voice of his father, through the sunshine haze in their garden, telling him he loved him . . . *Ya tebya lyublyu.*

Will woke up aching. There was a pain in his right arm, a cramp through his legs. For a few moments, he lay still, staring up at the ceiling, forcing his breathing back under control.

It has been a bad dream. The same dream. He reached out to the bedside table and picked up a photograph that had been lying face down. It was torture to look at it, and torture not to see it. The faces of his parents, who, only a few minutes ago, had inhabited the living room in their house in Dorset. His mother with a novel at the oak table she herself had built, his father pulling on his boots, preparing to head out to burn the garden waste that had been gathered in a pile in the orchard, beyond the lawn.

Will opened the drawer in the bedside table, slipped the photograph inside. The day before, memories of his parents had been thrust back at him.

He'd been walking home from school, and he'd almost collided with a boy carrying a football, followed by his father a few steps behind. Will had watched as the boy grinned and kicked the ball high in the air. For a moment, the ball seemed to slow through space . . . And Will's mind blanked.

Instead of London, he saw the village cricket green a few miles from his home in Dorset. Surrounded by yews, it was next to the church. Here, his mother and father had taught him physics. From the thwack of the ball on the bat, Will had learned about force, and from the ball's arc, gravity and momentum. On a blanket spread out beyond the crease, his father had taught him the theory of spin bowling – about slow, steady *laminar* air flow, and the critical speed at which the air becomes turbulent . . . In the process, Will had become a competent batsman and excellent bowler – but that had not been the point of those summer evenings.

As the boy jogged past him, Will had felt in his jacket pocket and touched the ball that he kept with him always. It was smooth and cool, worn by the touch of Eric Hollies on the day he became the last man to bowl the legendary Donald Bradman out. Will could clearly remember the look on his father's face as the Christmas-paper wrapping had fallen away.

And Will pressed a hand to his head. It had clouded. That old dream was resurfacing, tumbling out in vivid detail right up to the point . . .

What point?

There was a blackness. It wasn't so much that he'd forgotten. Rather, it was something even his dreaming brain refused to remember. Something from the past so dangerous, locked up so deep, his brain would rather wake him than submit him to the memory. It was pointless trying to find it. All Will could feel was a strange black spot, not devoid, but concealed, throbbing away in his head.

Now, Will sighed. The aches were still there. He turned to look at the clock: 6.30 p.m. He'd lain down on his bed an hour ago, tired after a wakeful night.

It was a Saturday. Three days since the meeting in Andrew's house. Will had done his best to avoid Gaia. For classes they shared, he arrived a few minutes late, seeking out a place by the door and barely waiting for the bell before he slipped out. At lunchtime, he ate like one of the pigeons that plagued the school grounds, alert and fast. How could he talk to her? What was there to talk about? STORM was a waste of time. Not only that, he felt embarrassed. Not because of what he'd said – which he still believed – but because of the way he'd said it and the way he'd left. Andrew didn't need him. And he didn't want Andrew. That was the end of it.

But at last, Gaia had cornered him. As he was leaving the biology lab, slipping on his coat.

'Will, can I talk to you?'

Will frowned. He avoided her gaze. 'There's nothing to talk about.'

'I think there is.'

'What? You're going to talk to me about STORM. No offence, but I think it's a waste of time.'

'If you'd just listen to me—'

'I won't change my mind.'

'Then we can talk about something else.'

'What, Gaia?' And he met her eyes. 'Four days ago, you'd never talked to me. I'd never talked to you. It's not as though we were friends.'

She looked away.

Will sighed. He felt frustrated. What was the point in pretending? They weren't friends. They never would be. He no longer had any friends, and he didn't need any.

'Forget it,' he said. 'Let's go back to how we were.'

Her head jerked up. Her mouth was set, taut. 'We weren't anything.'

Will said nothing, let his silence say 'exactly'.

Now, as he lay on his bed staring up at the ceiling, Will couldn't stop himself from wondering what Gaia and Andrew were doing. Were they in Andrew's basement? Was the crazy Russian boy with them, discussing his latest ideas about quantum computing? Had he been unfair to Gaia? At his school in Dorset Will had been popular enough, despite his brilliance. He hadn't talked that way to anyone. Now he didn't want any friends, and he didn't want to talk to her, but he wasn't totally blind to his old, real self – to how he had been.

Will squeezed his eyes tight shut. And he heard Natalia's voice calling up the stairs:

'Will, the Aga is not working! Roden is back. He says

he will go for takeaway. I was hoping you would show him where to get fish and chips?' And he listened to the thud of her footsteps on the stairs, up to his room. She pushed the door open a little. And she whispered in: 'I am not invading you, don't worry. But I am hoping you will go with Roden. He says there is something he wants to show you.'

Vassily Baraban could not stop a shiver. It wasn't down to cold. Though the temperature outside was minus twenty, the laboratory was warm. All the heat generated by his vigorous mental activity seemed to make it stifling, in fact, and Vassily had peeled off his sweatshirt and thrown it on to the floor. Now he sat at the desk in only his old underpants and a black lab-issue T-shirt.

Vassily looked with disgust at the yellow-white of his flesh. Bruises from when he'd been shot to the ground in London had left ugly purple patches like stains across his legs. But perhaps some good had come out of the past week: he'd eaten next to nothing and the stomach that had been threatening to fall out over his belt had gone crawling back to his ribcage.

The dark, miserable morning of his arrival, he'd been briefed by his new 'boss' via a videoconferencing link. Afterwards, a scientist had come in to discuss the plans for the 'test'. She hobbled, using a crutch, her right ankle in plaster. Her eyes were dark, intense as a black hole. But Baraban had barely noticed. He was too afraid.

Again, Vassily shivered. He glanced over his shoulder. In the far corner of the lab was a camp bed, made up with white sheets and a grey army blanket. To his left was a bathroom. Within five minutes of being bundled into the base, Vassily had been fitted with a GPS-equipped, radio-frequency identification tag. Wherever he went, he could be followed from the Surveillance room. And it had been made quite clear that if he did try to enter one of the forbidden zones – that is, within five metres of the Operations room master controls, or out of the building – the radio-tracking bracelet would automatically punish him with a 500-volt shock. It was like being an animal. Like cattle, Vassily thought.

But, with or without the bracelet, where could he go?

The answer was: three places. To the terrible heart of the laboratory complex: twin concrete tunnels that stretched on as if forever, twenty metres underground. To the canteen, to get what passed for food. And outside: into the wastes. Into snow that would grasp his body in a freezing death grip.

But it wasn't even this thought that sent the tremble racing along Vassily Baraban's spine.

Rather, it was the papers that were spread over his desk.

It was the reason he had been brought here.

His thoughts filled him with horror. He was terrified of failure, because he'd been told exactly what would happen to him and to his family. But perhaps he was even more terrified of success. Strangelets were one thing. This was quite another.

No – no – he had no choice. He had to complete the task. Yet he had tried – and so far failed. Time was of the essence, and on this occasion he, Vassily Baraban, was its slave. If he could not solve the problem, he must go to someone cleverer. And who else, but Caspian, his own son.

On the desk in front of Vassily was a heavy-based Anglepoise lamp and his Personal Digital Assistant. To the side, a blank pad and a pen. His PDA was equipped with a phone, a web browser, and email software – but these functions did not work here, inside the lab.

Vassily had noticed the copper mesh incorporated into the glass of the one small, high window as soon as he'd been thrust into the room by the guards. That mesh also ran through the plaster of the walls and the ceiling. It formed a Faraday cage, which stopped electromagnetic signals – like those from a mobile phone – from getting in or getting out. But somehow . . . somehow, Vassily knew he had to reach his son.

Hastily, he composed an email.

'I have been abducted. They want me to solve the problem – attached. Act with speed, Caspian. Our lives depend on it – your loving father.'

Vassily added a file, encrypted the email, and hit send.

Now, he needed to breach the cage. Then he could

transmit the message. He would find some other way to receive Caspian's reply. Above all, he wanted to protect his son from the people behind this madness.

Vassily had built his own Faraday cage once, in his laboratory in St Petersburg. He knew that the wavelength of the signal produced by his mobile phone was thirty centimetres. A mesh size smaller than this would block his signal effectively. And the holes in the copper mesh in the window were only about ten centimetres across.

Quickly, Vassily formulated a plan. He took a tissue from his pocket and scrunched it up on the desk. The winter sun that drifted in through the window was weak, but somehow it would have to be enough. His hand trembling, Vassily held his glasses above the tissue. The lenses were cracked, but still they would magnify the weak rays.

Vassily waited. Sweat dripped from the end of his nose. And then – at last – a tiny spiral of smoke. The tissue smouldered, and caught light. Vassily reached for a sheet of paper from his pad. He used it to feed the gentle flame and he carefully carried the paper to his bed.

At once, the dry blanket ignited. Vassily backed to the far wall, and he grabbed the Anglepoise lamp from the desk. Unsteadily, he got up on the chair, and then on to the desk itself, until he could reach for the window. The smoke was starting to billow now, and Vassily coughed.

Gripping his PDA in one hand, he grasped the lamp in the other and he brought the base smashing against the window. The first thrust shattered the glass, but it did not break. With all the force Vassily Baraban could muster, he slammed the heavy metal base once more against the mesh – and the glass gave way. At last! Vassily thrust the antenna of his PDA through the mesh . . . And he got a connection!

A moment later, the guards burst into his room, to find Vassily gasping at the window. 'Fire!' he called, his PDA safely back inside his pocket. 'You did not hear my cries! I had to smash the window to breathe!'

Sergei glanced at Vladimir, who was using the pillow to try to put out the fire. He scowled at Vassily. 'You!' he said. 'You will explain yourself to the boss!'

Two thousand kilometres away, in the front bedroom of a flat in Covent Garden, London, the Russian boy with the shock of black hair stared at his computer screen with a mixture of joy and dread.

The joy was at receiving a message from his father, who had been gone more than a week.

Twenty-four hours was not unusual, nor even forty-eight. His father would not answer his phone, would not come home, would 'vanish' so he could devote himself entirely to his work. But then Caspian had noticed the police car parked outside their flat. The university had been tardy in alerting the Metropolitan Police. They'd hoped Vassily Baraban would reappear, *despite* the sinister hole in his window. Or so the inspector had told them, as Caspian's heart had blanched and his mother had turned her desperate eyes to him.

And now this email. It had arrived hours ago! Caspian had been wandering the streets, hoping to glimpse his father on a park bench, or at a table at a cafe. He searched, though he *knew* his father had been seized. Vassily Baraban, the great astrophysicist and his beloved father, was gone.

At first, he had tried to deny the truth, Caspian realized. He had tried to go on as normal, and encouraged his mother to do the same. He had gone to the meeting in Andrew's basement because it had been arranged. He had gone to his tutor's office as usual because he did not know what else to do. Perhaps the hole in the glass meant nothing, he'd whispered to himself. And immediately, he'd felt the pain of the lie.

It is in the hands of the police, he had told his mother. *They will find him.*

And now! His father had tried to reach him – and he had been wandering the streets!

But if Caspian felt joy at a message from his father, the attachment triggered dread. His eyes staggered as they scanned the words . . .

An unbelievable responsibility lay with him. His hands trembled. His heart palpitated.

Were these really his father's words? Was this truly what he wanted?

Caspian dashed to the window and he stared up at the white-black night. To him, the snow tainted the sky like bacteria across a Petri dish. Why this lack of purity *tonight* – of all nights – when he most needed the heavens' help?

Caspian did not look down. But if he had, he would have seen Will walking.

'There's something I wanted to show you,' Roden said.

Will looked round. For the past few minutes, they'd been talking about the latest NASA deep-space probe, the global shortage of cod and fish and chips. The snow had got heavier. It did more than swirl. It was careering through the fog, settling thickly on the pavement. But Will let his jacket hang open, glad to be talking and walking, clearing away the unpleasant closeness of his dream.

Now Roden was reaching into the pocket of his jacket, and he produced a photograph, lined with two sharp creases.

As Will took it, he stiffened. The photograph had clearly been taken in St James's Park. The spires of Whitehall gleamed in the background. In the foreground, smiling, he was astonished to see himself, aged about three, with his mother. Her hair was black, in sharp contrast to the bright summer sun. Will's head jerked up.

'*Where did you get this?* From Natalia?'

'No . . . Actually, I took it.' And Roden hesitated, taking in Will's surprise. 'When Natalia invited me to stay she mentioned you were living with her, so I brought the photo . . . A long time ago, I was friends with your mother – actually it was through her that I met Natalia. I worked with your mother. When she was at University College. I didn't mention it before because I didn't want to—' and he hesitated, struggling for the right word. 'You know.'

Will frowned. Natalia had told Will only that Roden was an old friend, in London for a week. So far, he'd disclosed little personal information, except that he was an engineer who worked for a satellite-launch company. He'd talked about all sorts of things, except himself.

Now, questions formed in Will's mind. *When did you last see my mother? When did you last talk to her?*

'I . . .' Will hesitated. 'I haven't heard my mother talk about you.' This sounded rude, Will realized, but he didn't mean it that way.

Roden seemed to tense. But then he nodded. 'I've been abroad for many years.'

'. . . Why *are* you in London now?' Will asked, his eyes still on the photo.

'I'm looking for new contracts.' And Roden fixed Will with his animal gaze. 'By training, I'm an engineer. But I wish I knew more about astrophysics, like your mother. She was always impressed with the great powers in the universe – as am I. And with the gap between the theoretical and the practical . . . theories are one thing, aren't they?' He raised an eyebrow, his yellow irises now gleaming. 'But it takes courage, Will, to pursue a theory to its end.'

'And that's what you do?'

Cutler stared for a moment, and then he smiled. 'I won't deny it. I have vision, Will. I see the future. I see changes. Great developments. Man proving his power. Space itself will be transformed. We will do it – people like you and me . . .'

'. . . Like me?'

'Yes, why not! Mediocrity rules, Will, and we must not let it. We must change the rules. Think beyond the obvious. Aim for leaps, and leave the little steps for others.' Roden's cheeks were becoming flushed, his words coming thick and fast.

First Andrew, now Roden, Will thought. Was the world full of overambitious people . . . or were they right?

'Your mother would understand,' Roden said. And there was a trace of bitterness in the sigh that followed. '. . . Your father was different.'

Will bristled.

'. . . He was away a lot, wasn't he, Will?'

The tone was sympathetic. But confusion lurched suddenly through Will's chest. Cutler's eyes were fixed on the pavement, on his black shoes as they stomped through the snow. *Don't talk about my father,* Will wanted to say.

'Your father believed in serving his country. Even if that was at the expense of his own wife and child.'

Now Will could hardly believe his ears.

'Your father made some . . . unusual decisions,' Cutler persisted.

'You have no idea,' Will said darkly.

And suddenly, he had no interest in walking with Roden Cutler. He didn't care about the fish and chips. No one could talk to him about his father. Not in this way. Will veered away, heading back in the direction of Natalia's house.

Cutler caught up with him quickly. He reached out, touched Will's shoulder. Will jerked it off.

'Will – Will, I was only trying to help. Really.'

'*I don't need help,*' Will said. He bent his head against the swelling wind. Why hadn't he stayed in his room? What was wrong with Roden?

Now Cutler had to quicken his pace to keep up. It was hard going, through the snow.

'Will, look, I have to go away for a few weeks,' Cutler was saying, his thin voice suddenly taut with urgency. 'But when I get back, I want us to become close. Really. I'm sorry. I want you to think of me as someone you can talk to. Someone you can trust.'

Will stopped dead. He faced Cutler. Painful thoughts sliced through his mind. 'Like a father?'

Cutler's expression went blank. In slow motion, the

thin lips parted into a smile. '. . . Yes,' he said, 'like a father.'

Will turned away in disgust.

He broke into a jog. From behind, he could hear Cutler's steps, almost silenced by the snow. Suddenly Cutler seemed a predator, stalking his prey through the streets, and all Will could think about was getting away – away from Cutler, from Natalia, from well-meaning people who couldn't hope to understand . . .

But where could he go?

And then a figure that had been almost hidden as it hurried along the street in his direction resolved itself. Will was overwhelmed with surprise. But then anything was better than this.

Cutler came up hard on his heels. He stopped beside Will, who was facing the girl.

Gaia glanced at Cutler. She was wearing a thick overcoat and a brown woollen hat. She smiled at Will.

'There you are!' she said. Her eyes were shining. Her lips were very pale. She had been walking hard and she was out of breath.

Will frowned at her.

'I went to your house, and your aunt told me where you'd gone. I can't believe you aren't ready. Will . . .' And she faked – quite badly, Will thought – disbelief. 'Don't tell me you'd forgotten our date.'

She smiled again, this time at Cutler. 'Are you a friend of Will's? Does he really have a bad memory? Or was he trying to get out of our date? What do you think?'

Cutler looked at her in astonishment. 'Will didn't tell me he had a date,' he faltered.

'Well, we do.' She stepped forward, slipping one arm through Will's. 'There's no time for changing – either you or your clothes – you'll just have to come as you are.'

'You still have my photograph,' Cutler said, matter-of-factly.

Will glared at him. He thrust the picture in Cutler's outstretched hand and Gaia started to pull him back towards Covent Garden, away from Cutler. 'I so love the opera. Nice to meet you,' she called.

And then they were around the next corner, and Gaia's smile fell away.

'What's going on?' Will said.

'Don't get angry, Will – you can drop all that,' she said. 'I had to make you come with me.'

'I'm not angry.'

She looked at him. 'Good.'

Will opened his mouth – and stopped himself.

All traces of Gaia's amusement had vanished. 'Look, you have to come with me.'

'To the *opera*?'

'What? No! To Andrew's.'

'*What*?'

'I'm serious, Will. Forget STORM, if you like. Tonight it doesn't matter. Really serious things are happening.'

'What things?'

'Come with me,' she said. 'I'll show you.'

'*Gaia—*'

'Just shut up. And come with me.'

As they turned away towards Bloomsbury, a man in a woollen hat, black jumper and jeans huddled into the doorway of a shop. He pulled out a secure mobile phone and speed-dialled a number.

'Target has gone off with the girl. She just appeared on the street. They're walking fast.'

A deep voice replied. 'Yeah, yeah, skip the detail. *Just do not lose him.*'

Gaia pressed the earphone recognition unit to the side of her head. Will stared up at the camera in the lintel. They waited.

'He's probably in the basement,' Gaia said.

'He can't open the door remotely?'

Gaia shrugged. She hugged her arms around her stomach. The snow still fell thickly. Will's shoes were soaked, and yet the soles gave good traction on the developing patches of ice.

At last, the door was thrown open. Andrew looked tense. He wore a tartan dressing gown over a Thai beach top and a pair of designer combat trousers. If Andrew was surprised to see Will, or felt any displeasure at his presence, he did not show it. Will felt awkward, of course. But clearly Andrew wanted him, or Gaia would not have come to find him.

'I'm sorry you had to wait,' Andrew said. 'I was talking to Caspian. Come in.'

Will's flesh tingled at the warmth of the hallway. His

chilled fingers seized and he flexed them painfully as Andrew led them through the kitchen and down to the basement.

At once, Will saw that it had been transformed. The walls, which had been bare and black, were now fitted with LED screens. An antique dining table with matching chairs upholstered in green leather was topped with half a dozen new notebook computers. Whatever he was, Andrew was clearly serious about STORM.

'Where's Caspian?' Gaia said.

Andrew pointed to a screen that showed a webcam image of a bedroom. Will could make out a poster of the Horsehead Nebula, glittering on the wall.

'He's at home,' Andrew was saying. 'He said he'll be back with me in five minutes. Apparently he's working on something else.'

'Something *else*?' Gaia frowned.

'What's going on?' Will said. 'Gaia said something serious is happening.'

Andrew raked a hand through his hair. 'Yes, you could say that. Take a seat. I'll fill you in.'

Will and Gaia pulled out heavy chairs from the dining table. Andrew grabbed a remote and stood in front of his monitors. He assumed the attitude of the night the previous week when he'd revealed his plans for STORM. Will watched him doubtfully. In his mind, he still heard Roden Cutler, and saw the hopeful shape of his mouth as he said the word 'father'. Cutler was gone.

And Will hated clichés. Still, he couldn't help wondering if he was out of the frying pan and into the fire . . .

'As you no doubt know,' Andrew was saying, 'we are now at the solar maximum, which happens once every eleven years. Our Sun is at the peak of its activity.'

He pressed a button on the remote. A close-up image of the Sun flashed up on one of the monitors. 'It is *pustulating* with sunspots – here and here. What we're looking at are concentrated magnetic fields. The surface is *raging*. This is an image taken at sixteen hundred Greenwich Mean Time. At sixteen zero five GMT, our Sun did this . . .'

Andrew clicked again. An Mpeg kicked in. A huge burst of plasma jetted from the surface.

'It emitted a solar flare – a burst of hot electrified gas. But this is no ordinary flare. It is the biggest in recorded history. For one whole minute and twenty seconds, the amount of light produced by our Sun *doubled*.'

Andrew paused for a moment. With gravity, he said: 'But this is not the real problem. The real problem is on its way. At the same time as the flare, our Sun let loose a coronal-mass ejection or CME. This is a massive cloud of magnetically charged plasma. This storm is heading right at us. And it's travelling fast. It's forecast to hit at zero six hundred tomorrow morning. What will happen then is simple: *chaos*.'

Will glanced at Gaia, Cutler banished from his mind. He'd studied solar flares in astrophysics. But he knew much less about CMEs. 'What sort of chaos?'

Andrew bit his lip. 'Gaia's read the textbook. Why don't you explain?'

'It won't hurt us on the surface,' she said. 'But it could mess up our satellites. Mobile-phone satellites could be disrupted or knocked out. The Global Positioning System will be hit.'

Andrew nodded. 'Communications and location devices could go haywire. All kinds of things could go wrong. And the people in space – they're at risk from all the radiation.'

'How do you know about the flare?' Will said. 'I haven't heard anything about it.'

'Have you checked the US Bureau of Meteorology's website lately? Do you hang out in Galactica, a chat room for space-weather scientists?'

These were rhetorical questions.

'It was Caspian who got the alert from a friend of his who hosts Galactica,' Andrew said. 'He was the first to find out about it.'

At that moment, the face of Caspian Baraban reared on the monitor behind Andrew. The Horsehead Nebula was obliterated.

'I am here,' Caspian announced. 'But I must go back to my work. There is something very important that I must do.'

Andrew shot him a quizzical look. 'More important than this?'

Caspian ignored him. 'You must monitor the situation. STORM must stand by. There is nothing like this before in our history. Earth will stand in awe of the power of space.'

Will glanced at Gaia, raised his eyebrows.

'What exactly are we supposed to do?' Will called.

Caspian's eyes narrowed. 'Will Knight,' he said. 'So, you have come scurrying back. I suggest you scurry on into a corner and leave Andrew and Gaia to work. This will be the best thing for us all, I think.'

Will's thawed fingers curled into fists.

'*I* think,' Andrew said quickly, 'that we have a long night ahead of us. Caspian, if you hear anything important, please get in touch. I will keep an eye on the bureau transmissions. Thank you.' And he cut the connection.

'So,' Andrew said, 'that's the situation. The magnetic storm is set to reach us at zero six hundred.'

'Until then?' Will said.

'Until then I suggest we do some calculations on the burst – work out which satellites are likely to be affected, study the impact of the last CME. There is a lot to be done.'

For the moment, Will kept his mouth shut. It was all very well to predict and to monitor but what could STORM actually do? There were space-weather scientists out there, with access to the raw data and the historical files, who could provide advice to the operators of space instruments and satellites. Perhaps some could be turned away from the storm. Certainly nothing could stop it.

Andrew took a chair at one of the computers on the dining table. He started tapping at his keyboard. Gaia sat down beside him. 'The flare's hit an American power grid,' Andrew murmured. 'The space-station crew has been inside the shuttle. Good. It's better protected.'

And Will sighed. Was there any point in arguing with them? Perhaps it was better to join them. And it wasn't as though he had any other plans for the evening.

Will pulled out his phone, texted Natalia: *Staying night with friend. Working on school project. Back first thing. W.* And he thought of what Roden would say when Natalia got the message. He glanced at Gaia and now he almost coloured.

'I'm going to get a glass of water,' he said.

Andrew's head shot up. 'There should be bottles in the fridge. I'd like one too. Gaia?'

She nodded, but didn't look at Will. For an odd moment, he wondered if she could feel what he was thinking.

On his way to the steps, Will paused. He'd noticed a new trestle table topped with yet another notebook. Will thought it had been switched off but as he passed the screen a web page suddenly burst into view.

Andrew had been watching him. 'It's just been released,' he called. 'The screen's designed so you can only read it if you're facing it head on. Stops people reading over your shoulder on the train.'

'Do you ever get the train?'

Andrew's expression hesitated midway between a frown and a smile. He let the frown give way. 'Stops someone who might break into the back of my car while I'm being driven reading what I'm working on.'

'A common problem,' Will said.

Andrew's faint smile broadened a little. If Will could have translated Andrew's expression into words, he would have read it like this: 'I really wasn't sure, but welcome back'.

Will took the steps two at a time. The kitchen was warm. It was much bigger than Natalia's, with stainless-steel equipment, smoked glass and wooden benches. Andrew had an Internet fridge, Will noticed. He remembered what Gaia had said about him liking gimmicks.

He turned at a noise from behind. Gaia.

'Actually I'd rather have Coke,' she said. 'I need the sugar.'

Will opened the fridge, pulled out the bottles. Gaia took hers and didn't immediately turn away. He was glad, because there was something he wanted to say.

'I wanted to ask you—' and he stopped. It seemed harder than it should. But Will didn't like shirking anything, even an apology. 'I'm—' and he stopped again. He didn't *like* shirking. But somehow the apology just didn't come out. Instead, he said: '. . . Why did you come to find me? I was rude to you at school.'

She levelled her gaze at his. 'I don't like many

people. When I find someone I like, I don't let surface stuff put me off. I could see right through you.'

And she turned, and headed back down to the basement. The unexpected answer left him confused. To his own shame, Will realized 'you're brilliant, we need you' was more what he might have anticipated. But what did she mean, she could see through him? She didn't know anything about him – nothing about who he was or who he had been.

Grasping the bottles of water against his chest, he followed her. As he left the kitchen, he glanced at the window, at the solid grey denseness of the sky. It was hard to imagine that right at that moment a devastating storm was racing through space. Hurtling through the vacuum. Straight at Earth.

In the basement, Andrew cleared his throat.

'You know there is in fact quite a lot to do,' he said. 'I think maybe we should call a meeting. We can draw up a list of tasks and distribute them according to volunteers and expertise.'

Will glanced at Gaia. 'Andrew, no offence, but that sounds like a waste of time. And there are only three of us. You start on the history. I'll concentrate on what's likely to happen.'

Andrew opened his mouth to protest.

'I'll get on to the GPS satellites,' Gaia said.

'But—' Andrew said.

But no one was paying any attention.

And so Andrew was overruled.

His lips pressed tight, Andrew turned back to his computer and he started to pull up information on the last five major CMEs. The site of the Space Environment Center at the US National Oceanic and Atmospheric Administration was a good place to start. But it was hard to concentrate. Hovering right in the front of his mind was the discovery he'd made quite by accident, in one of the secure space sites. He might share it with Gaia, he thought. But Will? No. At least not yet.

One hand manipulating his wireless handwriting-recognition stylus, Andrew started to detail past impacts on communications satellites. But he kept open the secure website that contained ongoing comms between a floating HQ and Earth's very latest satellite . . . a different sort of object altogether. A *space hotel*. A secret module, launched from the equator only the previous week. Andrew had read about it earlier that day, when he'd hacked into secure space sites after the CME. Quite why the launch should be a secret wasn't clear . . . He would tell Will and Gaia later, he thought.

While Andrew was occupied with monitoring hotel communications, and with the past, Will and Gaia plotted the satellites likely to be most affected by the incoming storm. Mobile-phone coverage certainly would be hit, as would GPS. Andrew had been right: radio-communications systems would go down.

This was slow-going and methodical. The sort of work Will didn't much like. He preferred immediate problems – but for that they would have to wait. The clock ticked slowly, steadily notching up the hours.

At two-thirty a.m., Will could no longer stop his yawns. Tiredness swelled in his brain. And there were still three and a half hours before the serious threat would arrive.

From across the table, Andrew noticed him yawning. 'Grab some sleep,' he said. Andrew's own face looked pale and drawn, his blue eyes shrinking behind the thick glasses. 'Really. I think we've done pretty much all we can. Now we can only wait. You too, Gaia – you do look tired.'

'I thought you wanted to keep track of the bureau communications,' Gaia said.

'I can do that while you sleep.' He looked at Will. 'I don't need it. Some nights I don't go to bed at all. Really – both of you, get some rest. I'll wake you as soon as anything happens. There are bedrooms off the hall upstairs, or you can sleep in the drawing room. The fire should still be going.'

'I don't know,' Gaia said.

'You're worried I might let you sleep through the storm?'

'It's not that,' she said. And yet the thought was there. All the groundwork had been done. And for all his talk of group meetings and collaboration, Andrew could be as competitive as the next person. Gaia was well aware of that.

'Go on. Will, you too. I'd rather you slept now and

were fresh for six. That's when the world will really need you.'

This was too much for Will. 'All right,' he said.

In the drawing room, Gaia reached out a hand to the dying fire. She was mostly hidden by the chaise longue, a tapestry throw over her legs. The room was warm, and very comfortable. Will was stretched out on a leather sofa behind the table that supported the trepanned head. Dying flames in the grate sent an eerie shadow flickering against the ceiling – a skull that stretched from one wall almost to another.

'Does Andrew really not sleep much?' he said.

A pause. And she said: 'Some nights I think he really doesn't. But it's not as though I'm usually around to check.'

In fact, Will could believe that Andrew could go a few nights without rest. He had the stubborn energy of the sort of person who would refuse to leave a task until it was finished. His mother had told him stories about some of the scientists she'd worked with, when she had been a professor of engineering and astrophysics at University College London. Most were normal, she'd said, but one of her colleagues had walked out of his laboratory while thinking about a problem and come back only two weeks later, when he'd solved it. In the meantime, his desperate wife had filed a missing person's report and half the waterways around Oxford had been dredged.

Sometimes, stubbornness paid off.

'. . . How did you meet Andrew?'

'At last year's science Olympiad.'

'You competed against him?'

'Not exactly. He was in Berlin on holiday. He gatecrashed the maths medal classes and blew everyone away. He's very, very good at maths. Actually, he's a lot smarter than he looks. People see this half-blind boy. They don't realize he probably has fifty IQ points on them.'

'So, he gatecrashed the maths, showed off, and you liked him?'

'. . . Andrew's a very nice person.'

Will gazed up at the ceiling, at the chandelier that dangled from its thick brass chain. The tiny fragments of glass glinted in the glowing light from the fire. Was he? Maybe. But Will had insulted two people recently and here he was with both of them. So what did that tell him?

'. . . I still don't really see how I fit in with STORM,' he said at last. 'I invent things. I don't know anything about HIV or global warming.'

'I told you,' she said. 'He wants the brightest people. This is early days – there are only four of us. More will join in time, with other skills.'

'Three of us,' Will corrected. And realized he was counting himself as a member of STORM.

A pause. 'I don't know why Caspian isn't here tonight,' Gaia said, and she yawned. 'This is exactly his field. He knows more about space than anyone I know.

He really *cares* about it. All he ever talks about is his father, and his work.'

Will moved his arm, so he could lie flat on his back. He looked up at the shadow, the skull across the ceiling. What was Caspian doing that was more important, he wondered. And what was happening out in space, as that stream of plasma hurtled on its collision course with Earth . . . Will looked at his watch: 2.45 a.m. The watch that had been a present from his father. And something occurred to him.

'Where do your parents think you are tonight?'

No response.

'Do they know you're here?' Then, more quietly: '. . . Are you asleep?'

'Mum's dead,' came the quiet answer, at last. 'Dad wouldn't care . . . And before you say anything else, I don't really want to talk about it.'

On the leather sofa, Will stared at the ceiling, taking in this information. He wanted to ask when her mother died. And what she meant exactly about her father. But maybe Gaia was right. The last thing he wanted to discuss was the loss of his father. The absence of his mother.

Wind made the old sash windows rattle. The weather seemed to be getting worse, if that were possible.

Will closed his eyes. Gradually, questions faded. His consciousness dissolved, down through his body, until at last he fell asleep.

*

'Will!'

It felt as though he was deep underwater, being jettisoned to the surface.

'Will! Wake up! Gaia!'

Will opened his eyes. Andrew was leaning over him, pupils wide behind the glasses. The room was still dark.

'What time is it?'

'Five. Two minutes past five. Gaia, wake up!'

Will sat up slowly, giving his head a few moments to clear. 'What's happened?'

'It's come early.'

Andrew had thrown off the dressing gown. His sleeves rolled up, shirt flapping behind him, he dashed to the chaise longue and gently shook Gaia's arm. 'Gaia! Gaia, come on, wake up, it's come early.'

'*How could it?*' Will said.

Andrew turned to him. 'It was only an estimate. There was a CME in 1859 that was supposed to take four days to reach Earth. It took *seventeen* hours and forty minutes. People get things wrong.'

'That was *1859*,' Will said.

'People are still people. And there are six people right now who need us.'

'What?'

'Get Gaia up. Come down and I'll tell you.'

Andrew vanished. Will got up, feeling a little

unsteady. Gaia wasn't moving. He called her name. She didn't respond. He reached out, touched her shoulder, and her eyelids flickered.

'Wake up,' he said. 'It's arrived.'

And her brown eyes opened wide. She focused on Will, and then the grate. The fire had gone out. She pulled the throw up around her shoulders. 'What's it done?' she said, sitting up.

'I don't know. Andrew's downstairs.'

Three minutes later they were all in the basement. Gaia rubbed her eyes as Andrew leaped to the monitors.

'As you know, all flights into London were cancelled last night,' he was saying. 'ATC – air traffic control – decided it was the safest thing to do. But someone didn't listen.'

'Who?' Will said.

'A private jet took off from a Buckinghamshire airport – before the storm hit. Just before the radio communications went down, the pilot got through to ATC at London City airport to say his GPS system wasn't working, and he only had enough fuel for another forty minutes of flying. *This was fifteen minutes ago.*'

'How do you know this?' Will said.

'I was checking the comms satellites,' Andrew said. 'And I was listening in on the ATC frequency in case something went wrong with planes. They're very vulnerable.'

'But it'll be light soon,' Gaia said. 'They'll be able to see to the ground.'

'Have you looked outside?' Andrew waved a hand at an imaginary window. 'It's thick fog. And it's *still snowing*. Visibility is practically zero. That plane needs GPS to land, but the storm's affecting the readings – they're flickering all over the place. GPS receivers can't latch on to the code.'

'What about ILS – the Instrument Landing System?' Will said.

Andrew raised an eyebrow, mildly surprised. But Will's father had been an aircraft freak. He'd loved planes, helicopters – anything that flew. Some of that knowledge had rubbed off on Will. And even his father's tiny Cessna had been ILS-equipped.

'The ILS at City is down,' Andrew said.

The news just got worse, Will thought. 'So where's the plane now?'

'ATC is tracking it. The Aerodrome Traffic Monitor shows it's circling over central London – look.' And Andrew indicated one of his wall-mounted screens.

'But *why* did it take off?' Gaia said.

Andrew shook his head, expressing his disbelief. 'I heard the last transmission to air traffic control. The pilot said he had some very important people on board, like the banker, Wilbur Rickmann. They couldn't miss a scheduled meeting in London.'

'Then they're stupid and they got themselves into

this,' Will said. 'How could they take off when they were told not to?'

'Some people think they operate outside the conventions that govern everybody else. Don't you agree, Will?'

Will scowled. Was Andrew trying to make some kind of point?

'So what do we do?' Gaia said.

Andrew looked at her blankly. 'I don't know.'

She glanced at Will.

'I don't see what we can do,' he said, with irritation. 'They're going to run out of fuel, and they'll definitely crash. Or they'll try to land, and they might crash. Their phone is out?'

'Yes,' Andrew said.

'Without radio and without mobile coverage, no one can talk them down. Without GPS they can't get down.'

'That summary is correct,' Andrew said.

Will sat heavily on one of the chairs at the dining table. He fixed his gaze past Andrew at the monitor that showed the extraordinary coronal mass ejection that had travelled 149.6 million kilometres, blasting its way from the Sun.

Andrew looked at his watch. 'Twenty-two minutes,' he said.

'Has Caspian—' Gaia started.

'We don't need Caspian,' Will said quickly. Something had shifted in his brain. This was how it happened sometimes. Plans hit him like intuition. Sometimes he knew something would work before he knew how. Now his brain scrambled to catch up with the detail.

He turned to Andrew. 'You said their GPS was flickering. How do you know?'

'I sampled the GPS signal.'

'You still have that sample?'

'. . . Yes.'

'Is there any kind of pattern to it – to the flickering?'

'You mean, does it deviate in a theoretically predictable way from what the genuine readings should be?'

'Yes, Andrew, that's what I mean.'

Andrew sat down at his laptop. He started typing.

'But how—?' Gaia started. She had an idea of where Will's thoughts were going. But she didn't see how they could help.

Will turned to her. 'When will their mobile coverage come back up?'

'I don't know—'

'Can you check it?' Will said. 'We need to know *now*.'

'. . . All right.' And she took her seat next to Andrew.

Andrew glanced up at Will. He pushed his glasses back up the bridge of his nose. 'I understand what you're thinking,' he said.

'Do you?'

'If we can work out the deviation, and if the mobile network gets back up in time, we can tell them and they can work out their genuine position.'

'It will take too long if they have to do it themselves,' Will said. 'It has to be in real time.'

'*How?*' Gaia said.

Will looked at Andrew. 'You're a programmer. You can write a patch to correct the deviation.'

'Maybe. But then what? We wait for the mobile network to come online and then we email it to them – if they have Internet phones?'

'That's an if,' Will said. 'And it would take too long – the data transmission would be too slow.'

'So how could we get it to them?'

At that moment, Gaia shouted out: 'Twelve minutes. The satellites for London have just been knocked a little – they're not out. The latest estimate is twelve minutes to reconnection.'

'But when they get coverage, Will, what are you proposing?' Andrew said.

'You have a wireless network in the house?'

'Of course – how do you think—'

Will interrupted him. 'Then we use it. What's the range?'

'It's just within the house,' Andrew said. 'I set it up like that on purpose.'

'—But it could be rebuilt,' Will said. 'If we could extend it to a few kilometres, we could call them as soon as their satellite-phone coverage is back up, get someone's laptop to connect to our wireless network and we can send up the patch. Give them a minute to transfer it to the on-board computer, and they'll have

GPS for at least . . . ten minutes before they run out of fuel. That'll be enough time to get to City airport.'

'That's if the GPS deviations are predictable,' Andrew said.

'And?'

'Just a second . . .' Andrew frowned.

'They're not?'

'Hold on . . . damn. Wait, I'll have to try some other software.'

'Just *look* at it, Andrew. What can you see? Do you *think* it will work?'

'You want me to guess?'

'I want you to use your brain. Look at the data. Do you think there's a pattern?'

Will watched as Andrew scanned the table of numbers. The tiny black numerals seemed to merge. Andrew lifted his head.

'—Yes.'

'Right. You confirm that and get to work on the software. Gaia, you need to get hold of a mobile number for someone on that plane. Then come and help me rebuild the network. Andrew, you have spare antennas?'

'Under that table,' Andrew said, pointing behind him. 'There should be a high gain one down there – I get sent them. The big one.'

'Where's the network box?'

'Living room,' he said. 'On the bookcase.' But Andrew's expression toughened. He stood up. 'Look, I think we need to talk about this more,' he said. 'There could be other options that we're overlooking—'

'—No,' Will said. 'There's no time.'

'But—'

'—Andrew, you said it: those people need us. You're a brilliant programmer. You can help them.'

'This isn't what I wanted,' Andrew said firmly. His pale-blue eyes blinked back at Will.

Gaia turned. 'What do you mean?'

'For STORM,' Andrew said. 'I want us to work together—'

'And we are, Andrew.' Will was close to shouting. 'At least, that's what I want – and Gaia. But we can't do this without you. Do you understand? Andrew? Isn't this what you wanted? To help people?'

Andrew closed his mouth.

'If you want to help *these* people, *you* have to write that code *now*,' Will said.

'. . . He's right,' Gaia said quietly.

Will forced himself to hold his tongue.

'Andrew, there's no time to discuss this,' she said. 'Maybe next time things can be different.'

Andrew stared hard at the floor. There was a long pause. Will counted the throbbing pulses in his neck.

At last, Andrew turned back to his screen. And he started to type.

Gaia glanced at Will. He raised his eyebrows. And he looked at his watch. The second hand ticked. And he felt oxygen powering through his blood. He felt his muscles fire, felt electricity sparking pathways like lightning through his brain. No matter what he said, time was against them. The people on that plane stood a real chance of dying.

But Will felt desperately alive.

It wasn't difficult to spot the wireless network box. Twin green LEDs shone from a silver unit on the second shelf up of the bookcase behind the chaise longue.

First, Will inspected the antenna. It was standard. Omnidirectional. Chosen by a security-conscious Andrew to ensure his network didn't extend beyond the house. This was another layer of protection, on top of the firewall that was designed to stop anyone accessing his hard drives.

The standard antenna transmitted its microwaves in the full 360 degrees. In his hand, Will had a 70-centimetre-long directional version – a Yagi antenna. By restricting the radiation to a narrow beam, instead of a broad 360-degree sweep, he could increase its power and so boost its range. He knew that wireless links using dish antennas had created networks that reached out 50 kilometres. But Andrew didn't have a dish – and they didn't need that distance. A couple of kilometres would be more than enough.

Quickly, Will unplugged the black stick-type antenna from the box. He checked his watch. Seventeen minutes of fuel.

And he heard footsteps approaching. Gaia.

'I've got a number,' she said. 'I persuaded Wilbur Rickmann's wife I was with air traffic control.'

'How did you get *her* number?'

'I called the *Standard*. I told them if they could get me a home number, I could promise them a great story. If it all works out.'

'Does Andrew know you've talked to a paper?'

'We can always change our minds. Do you want help?'

'No.' Will had the Yagi in his hand. He turned back to the box. 'I'm nearly finished. I'll be down in a minute.'

With a cable, he attached the antenna to the back of the box and he took the unit to the window. Will needed that antenna to point right up at the sky. Luckily, guttering offered protection from the worst of the snow.

Back in the basement, Andrew was pacing up and down in front of the monitors. He stopped when Will appeared.

'Ready?' he said.

Will nodded. 'You?'

'And waiting. I've secured everything on my system that could be sensitive. But you know this patch, if it works – it won't be perfect. The accuracy of the GPS will be less than normal.'

Gaia was at her computer. 'Six minutes until the mobile satellite comes back on track,' she said.

Will focused on the monitor behind Andrew's head. It showed ATC's plot of the plane, going round and round in circles, a small white icon representing six human lives.

'Five minutes,' Gaia said.

Will took a seat beside her. Andrew came back to the dining table.

'We have to get the call in as soon as the connection's up,' Will said.

Gaia widened her eyes. '*Really.*' Sarcastic. She held the phone handset tight. 'Four minutes,' she said.

'Andrew, are you ready to suspend the firewall?'

'I'm ready!'

And then: 'Three.'

And 'Two . . .'

'That's it!' Andrew shouted. 'The satellite is showing normal function.'

Quickly, Gaia dialled the number. A pause.

'What?' Will said.

'. . . It's engaged.'

Will looked at his watch. 'It can't be . . . They have ten minutes of fuel.'

She stopped the call, dialled again.

Will turned to Andrew. 'Are you sure the satellite's OK?'

'That's what it says.'

'Hello?' Gaia said.

Both heads shot round to face her.

'Hello. Is that Wilbur Rickmann? Hello?'

'Let me,' Will said.

Before she could stop him, Will reached out and grabbed the phone. He didn't see Andrew look pointedly at Gaia.

'Wilbur Rickmann,' Will said. It sounded more like an order than a question.

The line was bad. It crackled in his ear. But at last came the words:

'Who is this?'

'My name is Will Knight,' he said urgently. 'You need to listen to me. I know your GPS isn't working properly. My team has written a software patch that will fix it. You need to get your laptop to connect to a wireless network that we've set up. Then we can send the patch up to you, and you'll be able to transfer it to the flight computer and land.'

No answer.

'*Did you hear me?*'

'. . . Yes, I heard you. Who is this?'

'If you want to live, get the pilot to connect to our network now! It's called STORM.'

'Called what?'

'*STORM!*' Will shouted.

'Tell him to put the laptop by the window,' Andrew ordered. 'And get him to bank the plane – they need to make sure they get a radio path through the window.'

Will repeated Andrew's instructions.

'Wait.'

And Will glanced up at the monitor. It showed the ATC radar display. And there was the plane, still circling above them. Still burning precious fuel as Wilbur Rickmann messed around.

'What's happening?' Gaia said.

'He heard me,' Will said, so tense he could have banged the phone against his head. 'Now, I don't know what he's doing.'

'We've got a connection!' Andrew cried. 'They've connected to our network!'

'Are you sure it's them?' Will said. 'It could be someone down the road.'

'We have to presume it's them,' Andrew said. 'At this time in the morning. Don't you think?'

Gaia nodded.

'Send it up,' Will said.

Andrew's fingers were already flying.

'Are you there?' Will said. 'Rickmann, are you there?'

'I'm here,' came the voice. 'I've connected to your network.'

'We're sending you the patch now. Get it working immediately. You have seven minutes.'

'And—' Andrew called. 'And tell them it won't be as accurate. They'll still have to be careful.'

Will felt his heart hard in his chest. 'Did you hear me?' he shouted down the phone.

The line crackled.

'Did you hear me?'

No answer.

'There isn't enough time,' Gaia whispered, looking up at the monitor.

Will heard her. He said nothing. What could he say?

'What are they waiting for!' Andrew cried.

Will's eyes were fixed on the monitor. 'Have you got it?' he shouted down the phone. No response. But the line was still open. 'Do we still have coverage?' Will said.

'Yes!' Andrew shouted. 'What are they doing?'

'Look!' Gaia's voice. She ran to the monitor.

And there it was. The flight path that had for so long been a circle was straightening into a line.

'It's changing course!' she said.

Andrew stood up. 'They're heading for City airport!'

'Four minutes,' Will said. 'Can they make it?'

'They *have* to,' Andrew said. 'They have to.' He sat back at the table, tapped at his keyboard. 'Still no ATC. Their radio comms are still down.'

Will checked the phone. 'The connection's gone,' he said. 'Or they cut it.' He dialled the number again. Engaged.

'Maybe we should call ATC,' Andrew said. 'They could get them on the phone and talk them down if the patch didn't work.'

'If it hadn't worked, they wouldn't have left their circle.'

'Unless they decided they had no choice,' Gaia said. 'They might have decided to attempt a landing, even without GPS.'

Once more, Will tried the number. *Come on,* he urged. If the patch had gone to the wrong person, they could have another go at sending it up to the plane. The second hand of his watch ticked, counting down the moments left in those passengers' lives . . .

And the phone burst into life.

With a trembling hand Will put it to his ear.

'Hello?'

'Will Knight?' Rickmann's voice.

'*Yes, it's Will!*' Will hit speakerphone.

'We got the code you sent . . .' Rickmann paused. '. . . And that was it. We just touched down.'

The phone fell from Will's hand. For a split second, there was stunned silence in the basement. Then Andrew leaped from his chair. He punched the air.

'*Yes!*' he said.

Gaia grinned at Will. 'We did it,' she said.

Will nodded, exhilarated and then leaden with relief. Andrew dashed around the dining table. Beaming, he held out his hand to Gaia.

'Shake,' he said.

Smiling, Gaia shook his hand.

Andrew turned to Will.

'Shake, Will – we did it.'

'We did,' Will said, feeling stunned.

And Will took Andrew's small, dry palm in his. The pressure surprised him.

'What a *Sun*day,' Andrew said.

Half an hour later, Will's feet crunched as he set off with Gaia towards her flat. The cold stung right through his jacket. But at least the snow had stopped falling. Gaia avoided the ice, her hands plunged into the fraying pockets of her coat.

The plane had been saved, and there had been the rush of jubilation. But then exhaustion, as all that tension was released.

'Go home,' Andrew had said, his blue eyes blinking through those thick glasses. 'Get some sleep. Later we can celebrate. I'll take us to Nebuchadnezzar at Somerset House for lunch. I'll have my car pick you up at twelve thirty.'

'I can walk,' Will had replied. 'It's not far.'

'No, I insist. Anyway, Will, I think you might like to see the car . . .' And Andrew had smiled. 'In fact, perhaps you could bring some of your inventions along to lunch. I'd love to see a few examples.'

Will had hesitated. He wasn't keen on lugging his inventions to the restaurant – even in Andrew's car. But he realized that this was another way for Andrew to extend a hand. To try to mend any broken bridges. And if anyone should be doing that, Will accepted, it really should be him.

Now, as Will walked with Gaia, his brain struggled to take in the night's events. The full analysis would come later. But he was honest with himself. And he knew this:

he had felt more alive, and at the same time more at peace, in these past few hours than he had in a long while. It had felt good to be working on something that meant something – and to be working with other people. Maybe he wasn't really the loner he'd come to think himself to be.

He glanced up. The sky was streaked with grey and a yellow that was clear and pure. Fluorescent strips from shop windows cut through the weak light.

As they turned into Gaia's street, a pigeon fluttered down from a tree. Snow and slush were scattered across the road. The sudden shower made Will blink.

'This is it,' Gaia said.

She was looking up at a first-floor flat, above an estate agent on Charlotte Street. It was neatly painted, the windows screened with wooden shutters.

'Now, don't eat breakfast, because if I know Andrew, he'll be ordering the whole menu,' she said. 'He's thin, but he likes to eat.'

Will watched as she reached into her pocket, found the key, started to turn it in the lock.

'See you later,' she said.

'Wait—' He had to say it.

'What? I'm letting out all the heat.'

'. . . I'm sorry,' Will said.

'I'll close the door.'

'No – I mean, I'm sorry for the way I've behaved. To you, I mean. Like at school—'

And she cut him off. 'Don't worry about it. Really.'

Her gaze was intense and even. 'I'm used to it. If I took offence every time Dad was rude to me, I'd be in a constant state of misery.' She stepped inside. 'Anyway, I knew you didn't really mean it. That's what I meant – I could see through you.' She gave him a tight smile. 'See you later.'

Will didn't know how to reply. Whatever she said seemed to surprise him. So he simply held up a hand in farewell.

He waited until she'd pushed the door shut. Before he turned away towards Natalia's, he gazed up at the first-floor windows, hidden by the shutters. He wondered what she was going back to . . . What her father was like. Suddenly, it touched him deeply, reached right inside his chest. And he felt the truth of his words. He really was sorry.

The emotion hit him. It felt as though a brittle casing he'd built up around himself was beginning to crack – even if it wasn't quite ready to fall away.

As he turned the key in Double Entry, Will heard Natalia cry out. She was wrapped in an old blue blanket, sitting with a cup of coffee by the Aga, which evidently had been restarted. Dmitri was balled on her lap. Her eyes brightened.

'William! I was so worried about you.'

'Didn't you get my text?'

'Yes, but then I couldn't sleep and I watched the news. It said there have been huge flares from the Sun.

My phone stopped working, and I wanted to call you, to tell you. Did you hear?'

Will took off his jacket, hung it on the back of a chair. 'I heard.'

'. . . But did the project go well? Where did you sleep? Who is your friend? Is it the girl Roden told me about? Is she from school?'

'Yeah, from school. I'll tell you in the morning. I'm really tired.'

And Natalia's expression softened. 'William, I am sorry – you have been studying all night? You have that look. You look exhausted. Go to bed. What time shall I wake you?'

Will was already in the hall, one hand on the banister. 'It's all right,' he called.

'By the way,' she shouted, 'you know it is already the morning!'

In his room, Will dragged the curtains shut, kicked off his shoes, pulled off his clothes and fell into bed. When he shut his eyes, he saw plasma bursts, the blink of the ATC tracking screen. Andrew's air punch. Gaia's closed expression as she turned to walk up the stairs to her flat. And then his consciousness faded and his brain was invaded by dreams.

Will could not have known it, but this was the last time he would ever fall asleep in this house.

Unlike Will, Gaia barely slept. She'd thrown her coat over the duvet to try to keep herself warm. But the room was icy. Then there was the noise. Through the window she could hear buses up and down on the road outside, their brakes squealing.

But most of all, there were the thoughts that raced through her head. They whirled, but it was as if she herself was spinning, her brain struggling and failing to find a point on which to fix. It was a sensation she hated. Most of all, she tried to be in control. Of herself, if nothing else.

Every so often, the thought of the night's success burst through her body. It would not let her rest. Perhaps now, she thought, Will would finally be convinced. STORM had to happen. There was no way around it. She needed it, even more than Andrew. What else did she have?

At eleven, she heard her father get out of bed. He staggered through to the bathroom, feet thudding on the carpet. She heard the sound of vomiting. Curling up, she pulled the duvet over her head.

STASIS Headquarters, Sutton Hall, Oxfordshire, 11.30 a.m.

Shute Barrington yawned. He'd been up all night, in his primary office in a remote stately home. He had a desk in London but he rarely used it.

On the screen in front of him was a list of the casualties. One Japanese space probe. A couple of French comms satellites. It wasn't too bad.

'Phone,' he said, activating his secure communications system. Only his voice could do it. 'Rubidium.'

A light flashed as 'Rubidium' responded. When contact wasn't face-to-face, employees mostly went by code-names from the periodic table of elements.

'How's the "hotel"?' Barrington pronounced the word 'hotel' distinctly, to indicate inverted commas.

'All good, sir.'

'Cutler?'

'Ah. Hold on. Yeah, Argon has just checked in . . . They lost him.'

Barrington pressed a hand to his forehead. He raked it through his thinning brown hair. In one sense, it was to be expected. In another, it was an unmitigated disaster.

'Anything from Sir James?' Barrington barely kept the strain out his voice.

'Nothing, sir. He's quiet.'

'. . . Beryllium?'

'Sorry, sir.'

'Any good news at all?'

'Not really, sir.'

'Then I'll take a nap. Disturb me only if there's good news.' And he cut the link. A moment later, he reactivated the connection. 'You do know I was kidding, don't you, Rubidium?'

'About only calling about good news, sir . . . ? Yes, of course.'

Liar, thought Barrington, and he threw himself on to the sofa beneath the window and yanked the curtains shut.

The car arrived right on time.

At 12.30, and feeling refreshed after a few hours' deep sleep, Will was waiting on the pavement outside Natalia's house, a small rucksack slung over each shoulder.

He had considered not going. He'd told Andrew and Gaia he had no interest in STORM. And Gaia had practically tricked him into returning to Andrew's house last night. But . . . the good feelings overwhelmed any intellectual opposition.

Will glanced up. The snow and fog had given way to sun. But the rays were so weak, it was hard to believe that something so benign was also such a threat. Will squinted at the Sun with defiance. When he looked back at the street, there it was.

Not what he'd expected – which might have been a Bentley or a Rolls-Royce – but a huge black military SmarTruck. It looked almost ludicrous parked between a blue Ford Focus and Natalia's 1969 Mini.

Will gave it the once-over. It was a Mark II, he noticed. Again, off-the-shelf. Or rather, off the Internet. Solid, but agile, with easy off-road capability. Gleaming electrified handles. Space for an electric unmanned vehicle on top. A communications module, which, Will knew, would conceal thermal imaging, 3D mapping, and radar that could detect a moving object within seven kilometres.

The SmarTruck could be configured any way the owner wanted it. Will had read about it on a military blog. And he knew you could opt for a weapons module, which could house sixteen missiles and fire two independently at separate targets. He knew the potential spec. Fine for Somalia or Sierra Leone. He could just imagine one bouncing over scrubland, blasting at a hostile helicopter. But who'd need one here, in Bloomsbury, in the middle of London?

For a moment, Will looked at his own reflection in the mirror-treated windows. It didn't interest him much. Still, he hesitated before touching the near-side handle. The door opened. Gaia smiled.

'It's all right,' she said. 'They're deactivated.'

'Are you sure?'

'I was first in. No one opened the door for me and I'm still here.'

The surprise of the SmarTruck overwhelmed the slight awkwardness Will would have felt at seeing Gaia after their parting earlier that morning. Walking home, he hadn't been sure whether he should have said something, maybe asked her about her father . . . Instead, he took in the surprisingly luxurious interior, with its leather seats and personal monitors. An opaque glass screen separated the invisible driver from the passengers in the back.

'Who's in front?' Will said.

'Hello,' came a voice.

Instantly, Will glanced at his watch. The LED that flashed if there was a bug in the vicinity was still. So either the timing was coincidental or the driver could hear him through the glass. Usually the simplest explanation was the right one.

'My name is Sean. Welcome to the SmarTruck II, customized to Mr Minkel's requirements.'

'Mr Minkel doesn't require electrified handles?' Will said, smiling slightly at Gaia.

'Not every day, lad.' There was a trace of sarcasm in the voice, which had a soft Yorkshire accent.

'Or the missile module?'

'Generally not on Sundays,' came the voice. And the truck eased away from the kerb.

'This doesn't seem like Andrew,' Will said quietly to Gaia. 'I had him down as a Bentley type. It would match the gold watch.'

'Andrew loves gimmicks. I told you,' she whispered.

And Will recalled a snatch of conversation from the previous night. No one could break into the back of this truck to try to screen-steal Andrew's secrets, that was for sure.

'We're getting a lot of attention,' Gaia said.

She was right. People were pointing. A straggly school outing stopped to observe, kids and teachers staring.

Will nodded. 'This is one-up on a Hummer.'

'Somethin' more than that,' came the voice from in front.

Will tapped the screen.

'Can you clear this?'

'It's possible. In theory.'

'*Will* you clear this?'

And the glass became transparent. The dashboard resembled a cockpit. Directly in front of Will was a vast man with square shoulders and short brown hair. He was wearing a green military jacket. The angle of the rear-view mirror prevented Will from glimpsing his face.

'Where's Andrew?' Will said. 'Do you work for him?'

'Mr Minkel is already at the restaurant,' Sean replied.

'You drove him there first?'

No answer.

'Where does Andrew keep this?' Will said to Gaia.

'Vicinity of St James's Park,' announced Sean. 'Precise location, none of your business. And now—' he said, as the truck came to a sudden stop. 'We are here.'

'Here' was on the Strand, outside the archway entrance to Somerset House. Tourists mingled with students from nearby King's College. Some didn't even notice the truck. Or they pretended not to. Londoners were expert at nonchalance, Will thought. He could imagine what his old friends at school in Dorset would have made of it.

'Can I have a look in the front?' Will said. But as he spoke, the screen became opaque. Sean vanished.

'Mr Minkel is waiting,' came the firm, disembodied reply.

'Looks like you're out of luck,' Gaia said. And she added: 'Sean let me look under the bonnet.'

'Why?'

'I asked him – I like engines.'

'Do you? Who is Sean, exactly?' Will whispered as he opened the door.

'Someone Andrew trusts,' she said. On the pavement outside, Will was conscious that people now were staring. One Chinese tourist with a camera shaped like a pen even took a picture.

'Not much good for anonymity,' Will said, as they – and the curious tourists – watched the truck swerve away.

'I don't think that's what it's for,' Gaia said as she headed in through the gate that led to the square. 'More for escaping danger or torpedoing an enemy.'

'Very useful in central London,' Will said.

'I don't know. A few months ago, Andrew got mugged outside his bank.'

'. . . So he bought a *SmarTruck*? And hired Sean? Don't you think that's an overreaction?'

She only shrugged. And Will followed as she edged the elegant square.

Another few days, and the fountains that gushed through the remaining snow would be replaced with an ice rink. For now, the ground was covered in shining patches, where the snow had melted and frozen. It was an impressive square, Will thought. Horses and carriages would be at home among all this grandeur. It was a suitable location to lie in state, or to once have come in search of records of births, marriages and deaths.

As they entered the restaurant, Will glanced down at his own clothes. He'd guessed the place would be smart. Instead of jeans, he'd found a pair of plain black trousers, and instead of a T-shirt, he'd put on a school shirt. It still felt all wrong.

'Good afternoon,' said the suave maître d'. 'Monsieur Knight, Mademoiselle Carella, let me show you to your table.'

Gaia glanced back. 'This way, Monsieur Knight,' she imitated.

The dining room was full. Bright-white cloths covered the tables, which sparkled with polished crockery and over-blown glass. The walls were painted an intense, vivid red. Will took in the manicured customers.

Lipsticked mouths were laughing as they engulfed tiny morsels of food. The men were solid in their oak chairs, stomachs vast as their self-assurance. Beyond, through the polished windows, the brown Thames flashed. Will had never been anywhere like it.

Andrew, on the other hand, looked very at home. He rose as Gaia and Will arrived at the table and were seated with a flourish of white napkins and weighty menus.

'I took the liberty of ordering some sparkling water,' Andrew said, in the way one of the men in the room might have said Dom Perignon. 'And a little pâté de foie gras, with a plate of tastes of the sea. I'm told it's mixed sashimi with matched toppings and dressings. For an entrée, the belly pork is excellent. And for a main, I can really recommend the tea-smoked duck.'

'I told you,' Gaia said to Will. 'Andrew is a bit of a connoisseur.'

'I don't like bad food,' he said, a little stiffly. 'That's all.'

'Nice suit,' Will said. Andrew was wearing something that looked very soft. Underneath the cashmere he'd chosen a white Indian-style shirt, collarless, and buttoned right up to his chin.

'Nice . . . shirt,' Andrew said. 'And Gaia, I think this is the first time I've ever seen you in a dress.'

'A mistake,' she said.

'Not at all. You look just right.'

The bottles arrived.

'Do enjoy your water, *sir.*'

Andrew glanced up at the waiter, who was smiling. You might have called it a smirk, Will thought. Andrew pretended not to notice. As soon as the glasses were filled, he raised his in a toast. His expression was intensely serious.

'To us,' he said. And then, in a quieter voice. 'To STORM.'

'To STORM,' Gaia said readily.

Will paused. There was no escaping it. '. . . To STORM,' he said.

Andrew beamed. 'To the first success of many.'

And Will drank. Two toasts seemed two more than enough.

As the entrées arrived – borne by another waiter, with, Will was sure, another smirk – Andrew told them the storm was now officially over. One Japanese space probe was still not responding, and a couple of French satellites were lost for good. But the fallout wasn't as bad as it might have been. He didn't mention the new satellite. There was no need to – it was safe.

'And I had a call from air traffic control at City,' he said. 'They got the number from Rickmann's phone. Apparently we shouldn't have got mixed up in things we don't know how to handle.'

Gaia stared at him. '*What?*'

'Of course, the ATC said they had a plan. But they would say that.'

'Even if they did, we got there first,' Gaia said.

'I don't see what plan they could have had,' Will said. 'If it wasn't for the—'

'—*Exactly*,' said Andrew.

And Will gathered that Andrew didn't want to analyse too precisely where the praise should be laid. It didn't matter to Will.

'I did invite Caspian today,' Andrew said. 'Of course it *was* Caspian who first sounded the alarm.'

'He doesn't like sashimi?' said Will, who wasn't keen on the fish – though the pork tasted good.

'He's busy. He said he was going to his father's lab to work on something.'

'What?' Will said.

Andrew shrugged. 'He's being very secretive.'

'He's refusing to tell you?'

'He just changes the subject when I ask.'

At that moment, a waiter – a third waiter – arrived to whisk away their plates. 'Can I get you anything else, *sir*? More sparkling water, perhaps?'

'No,' Andrew said. 'Thank you.' He glanced at Will. 'This happens sometimes.' And he frowned at the tablecloth. 'They think because I'm fourteen I'm not to be taken seriously.'

And then the main course arrived. No smirks this time. But Andrew flushed.

'I think that was three minutes between clearing the entrées and bringing the next course,' he murmured. His brow was dark, but he occupied himself with the food.

Will picked at his. His stomach was baulking at its richness. He was used to stews and vegetables. This, while undoubtedly delicious, was all sauces and jus. Gaia, who was vegetarian, left half her ravioli.

When the dessert menus arrived, Andrew asked if he could choose for each of them. He whispered his order. Before long, two waiters brought a raspberry granita for Gaia, a sticky date pudding for Will and a chocolate mousse for Andrew.

'Andrew, did you order this because I'm a girl?' Gaia said. And she took his plate.

'But you weren't eating,' Andrew protested. 'I thought you'd had enough.'

She ignored him. Andrew simply shrugged at Will and ordered another mousse. Will looked down at his dessert. Even the custard didn't taste like custard. But then it had been introduced by the waiter as crème anglaise.

'Now,' Andrew said, when the coffee arrived, 'I noticed those bags, Will. What can you show us?'

Gaia turned to him expectantly. 'He was very careful with them in your truck.'

And Andrew blinked at Will. 'I thought you might like the car. I bought it last month.'

'I was surprised,' Will said, as he reached into the first rucksack. 'It seemed a little . . . aggressive.'

Andrew looked taken aback. 'I can do aggressive.'

'Of course you can,' Gaia said, with a faint smile.

'Really—' he protested.

But his attention was instantly gripped by the speargun that Will had laid on the table.

'Put it away!' Gaia said. 'You'll get us arrested!' She turned to Andrew. 'I can vouch for that one.'

'Rapid Ascent,' Will said, as reluctantly he slipped the gun back inside the bag.

'Oh yes, Gaia told me. The marines thing,' Andrew said. 'For scaling walls.'

'Except that the marines don't have it,' Will said, annoyed. 'At least not yet.'

Andrew nodded briskly. 'OK. What else?'

Determined not to rise to Andrew, Will reached under the table and unzipped the second bag. Inside were four of his latest gadgets. He'd made them all with his mother's supervision, in the garage in Dorset. And for a moment he squeezed his eyes shut, trying to suppress memories that threatened to erupt.

His fingers clasped around a chunk of metal. Quickly, he scanned the room.

'See that waiter?' And with his head he indicated a man with slicked black hair positioned near the door. He'd been the first to serve them. The first to smirk.

Andrew and Gaia nodded.

Will pressed a small microphone to his mouth. He whispered: 'This is Will Knight on Andrew Minkel's table. We'd like another bottle of water.'

Andrew watched intently as Will lifted a metal pointer, aimed it at the wall behind the waiter, and pressed a button.

'*What is that?*' Gaia said.

'Wait,' Will said. 'Watch.'

The reaction was extraordinary. A moment later, the waiter froze in mid-step and frowned at the air. With his forefinger he touched one ear, and then the other. He stared out across the tables, his face showing absolute confusion.

'What's happened?' Andrew said.

'*Wait.*'

The three of them watched as the waiter's eyes finally rested on their table. He frowned at Andrew, at Gaia – and then at Will.

Will simply nodded.

A minute later and the waiter sheepishly approached the table, a bottle of sparkling water in a wine cooler clasped in his arms.

'You asked for more water, sir?' he said to Will, his voice loaded with uncertainty.

'Yes, thank you.'

And with another nod of confusion, the waiter left the water on the table and backed away.

As soon as he was gone, Andrew reached out to Will for the gadget. 'What is that?' he said with admiration.

'Speak Easy,' Will said.

'What?'

And Will gently retrieved the device from Andrew's hands and placed it back in the bag.

'It's simple. You hide a bit of audio – like my voice – in a burst of ultrasound, which you can't actually hear. The ultrasound bounces off the wall, and whoever's in that reflected beam hears the voice. The waiter heard me ask for more water, only he didn't know where my voice was coming from.'

'That is genius,' Andrew said seriously.

Will was taken aback. 'Not really—'

'No, I mean it. Really. You invented that?'

'With some help,' Will said. He did not want to lie.

'What else is in there?' Gaia said.

'But I want—' Andrew started.

'We can get them all out again. I want to know what else you've got,' she said to Will.

'OK,' he said. 'There's something called Soft Landing, but you can't really see it properly.' He pulled a small backpack halfway out of the rucksack. The straps, the packaging, and the contents were all of silk, so they packed in tightly.

'What does it do?' Andrew said.

'It's based on a Russian idea for lowering a space probe to a planet. You wear the backpack. When you pull the cord, you release an inflatable umbrella. It helps you glide down safely.'

'From what?' Gaia said. 'A plane?'

'I wouldn't use it for that. Maybe a building.'

'Have you ever had to use it?' she said. 'Were you wearing it that morning at school?'

'No,' he said. And something occurred to him. 'I still don't know what you were doing there.'

She shrugged. 'I was early.'

'*Two hours* early?'

'Wait,' Gaia said abruptly, and she looked around for

signs to the toilets. 'Don't show Andrew anything else till I get back, you promise?'

'. . . All right,' Will watched as she pushed back her chair and strode off. If she wanted to avoid that conversation, it seemed she'd done it successfully.

But as soon as she was gone, Andrew bent his head towards Will. 'I know what she was doing there,' he said conspiratorially.

Will looked at him.

'I think she was planning a little *surprise* for the school. Not that she told me. I sort of guessed.'

'What sort of surprise?'

Andrew steepled his fingers. 'You do know she's been expelled from a number of schools.'

Will nodded.

'You'll have to ask her exactly why. But let's say she made rather an *explosive* impression on various members of staff. Ones she didn't really see eye to eye with.'

'You mean—'

'Gaia is a dear friend,' Andrew interrupted. 'And I'm telling you this only because I admire her, not because I condemn her. I think she forgot all about whatever plan she had when she saw you with your abseil device. She came straight to see me afterwards. She told me all about it. You impressed her. And I happen to know that's not very easy to do.'

'You're saying she made *bombs*?'

Andrew raised his head and blinked through his

glasses towards the toilets. 'Time to change the subject,' he said.

'She planted *explosives*? Andrew?'

But Andrew only smiled. His back to Gaia as she advanced across the room, he intertwined his fingers, pulled his hands apart rapidly and mouthed: '*Boom!*'

'I didn't miss anything?' Gaia sat down lightly and looked at Will.

'No,' he said.

'What are you looking at me like that for?'

'Like what?' But Will found it hard to disguise the impact of his new-found knowledge. He'd known she'd been kicked out of schools, but not for something like that.

'Come on, Will,' Andrew said. 'We want to get to the bottom of your bag of tricks.'

His head spinning a little, Will reached down once more into his rucksack. 'Fly Spy,' he said. 'Though really it should be Locust Spy.'

'A *locust*?' Gaia said.

'I'll show you.'

This was Will's favourite. It had been entirely his design. His mother had helped only with ordering and fabricating the components.

First, he pulled out a hand-held tracking screen and remote-control pad, and laid them on the table. Then, from a box that had once held a set of fuses, he removed his device, wrapped up in protective layers of gauze. Gaia leaned over to watch as gently he unwrapped it, like a mummy.

'*What is it?*' she whispered.

Will pointed to two tiny attachments behind the head. 'That is a miniature video camera, and this is a microphone. They transmit wirelessly to this tracking screen.'

'It's got wings,' she said.

He nodded. 'I based the design on a locust. It's the size of a locust, it flies like a locust.'

'But it's a *robot*,' Andrew said.

'That's right.'

'And it really flies?'

'Of course.'

'How does it see?' Gaia asked.

Will pointed to its 'eyes'. 'These are low-resolution cameras.'

'But how do you power it?' Andrew said.

'There is a battery inside the casing. But—' and he paused for effect – Andrew wasn't the only one who could do melodrama – 'it also eats leaves.'

Gaia leaned forward, as though she hadn't heard properly. 'It *eats*?'

'Yes.'

'It *eats leaves*?!' Andrew's voice had been so loud that the two diners at the neighbouring table turned their heads.

'Children today have no manners,' said the elderly lady in a clear voice.

'Ill-bred,' her husband agreed meekly.

'And quite why children should be permitted in a restaurant like this I have absolutely no conception,' the woman said, even more loudly.

Andrew waved a hand at them, as if to tell them to settle down. His pale-blue eyes were staring right at Will's. 'You're serious,' he said, more quietly. 'This is a robot that eats leaves?'

'It's got a stomach. There are microbes in there that produce electricity when they digest the leaves.'

Gaia nodded. 'Does that provide much power?'

'No,' Will conceded. 'You do need the battery. Though I had been thinking about modifying it to eat flies.'

Andrew's eyes widened. 'How?'

'Same basic idea. You'd have bacteria in little compartments inside the robot. They'd feed on the flies. A fly's exoskeleton has sugars in it. When the bacteria break down this sugar, they release electrons. And that would drive an electric current that would power the robot.'

Andrew raised an eyebrow at Gaia.

'So what do you use this one for?' she said.

'I don't really use it for anything. It's just something I came up with. But watch.'

Will couldn't resist switching it on. He set the tiny insect robot upright on the tablecloth and he used the remote to gently lift it into the air. Gaia and Andrew looked on, entranced, as it hovered for a few moments, and then Will sent it buzzing well above the tables, to rest on a top corner of a dresser at the far side of the dining room. He angled the locust's nose so it pointed towards them.

'Look,' he said. And he held up the tracking screen.

Gaia opened her mouth, and her video image gaped back.

'That is amazing,' she said.

Andrew clapped his hands twice. 'Bravo. A bug in all senses.' He hesitated. 'Have you sold this to anyone?'

'Like who?' Will said as he carefully manoeuvred the robot locust back to their table and into its box.

'The police,' Andrew said. 'I don't know – anti-terrorist people. Surely they could use it.'

'They'll have their own stuff,' Will said.

'But surely nothing like this . . .' Andrew looked seriously at Will. 'You need a manager. Have you patented all this? You could be rich. Couldn't he, Gaia? Except of course no one could know your true identity. You could call yourself *The Maker.*'

Will didn't know how to reply. Slowly, he put the fuse box back in his bag. And suddenly he didn't want to show them any more. He felt uncomfortable enough to be exposing these devices – devices that had taken up countless evenings and weekends. That had woken him up hard in the middle of the night, when he realized a problem or had dreamed a solution. He'd put his mind and his heart into these creations. And now he was showing them off in a restaurant. And Andrew was talking about money and pseudonyms. And he wasn't quite sure how serious Andrew really was. Suddenly it felt all wrong.

'That's it,' he said, with finality.

Gaia glanced at Andrew. 'I thought I saw another box in there,' she said.

Will shook his head. 'It's nothing.'

'Nothing?' Andrew said. 'I don't believe it.'

'Really, it's nothing.'

'If it's nothing, it won't matter if we see it,' Gaia said.

That old trap. Will had fallen right into it.

He met her gaze. Her expression had changed. There was a look of sympathy in her eyes. And he had that same odd feeling that she could tell what he was thinking. Maybe he could show Gaia and pretend Andrew wasn't there.

A moment later, a second fuse box was sitting on the table. This had been one of Will's earliest serious inventions. His mother had bought him the miniature radio transmitters the day he turned ten . . .

Inside the box were four of the devices. With some apprehension, he handed one to Gaia and reluctantly one to Andrew.

'What are they?' Andrew said.

'Slot it over your back molar,' Will said.

'My tooth?'

'Yeah, your tooth.'

'Are you sure?' Gaia said.

Will only looked at her. 'Just do it. And then don't

speak until I tell you to. No matter what I do, stay silent until I tell you you can talk.'

Awkwardly, Andrew and Gaia placed the devices over their teeth. Will did the same. It felt as though something was stuck between your teeth, but Will knew from experience that it didn't take long to get used to.

Without saying a word – and miming zipping his mouth shut to emphasize that Andrew and Gaia must not talk – Will got up from the table and left the restaurant. He walked out into the chill sunshine that filled the courtyard. No one else was there. Taking his time, Will crossed to the Cortauld Institute and rested his back against its solid wall. Someone had dropped an old *Standard,* dated from a couple of days ago, and he picked it up, glancing at the front page. He imagined Andrew and Gaia sitting in silence at the table, waiting for his instructions.

He imagined it – but he was wrong.

The moment Will got up to leave, Andrew quickly pulled the tiny device from his tooth and reached for Speak Easy. Gaia frowned at him hard. He ignored her. She removed the gadget from her mouth.

'*What are you doing?*'

'Shh.'

'What? Will would go crazy if he knew you were touching it.'

'I know. That's why I'm doing it now.' Andrew had the microphone in his hand. Quickly, in a high voice, he said: 'This is the grey-haired lady on the table by the window in the blue dress. I ordered a bottle of champagne half an hour ago. Bring it at once!'

Immediately he pointed the ultrasound wand towards a waiter – the second to smirk. He hit send and grinned as this waiter glanced towards the table of the innocent old lady.

'*Andrew*. Don't.'

'What?' he said. 'Revenge? Don't you do revenge – oh now, let me think—'

'Put it back,' she urged.

But the microphone was once more at his mouth. 'This is the table next to the ugly pot plant. It's obscuring my view. Remove it at once.' *Send.* 'This chocolate soufflé is disgusting, take it back and bring out the chef.' *Send.* 'I ordered trout not duck! And clean this window. It's repulsive.' *Send.* 'How dare you serve me such half-hearted swordfish – I'll have steak instead – yes, me, the old fogey sitting with his mother.' *Send.*

'Half-hearted?' But Gaia couldn't stop herself smiling as at once the dining room became a scene of confusion. Waiters rushed around, pressing their hands to their ears, struggling with a pot plant, calling out the chef . . .

Satisfied, Andrew put down Speak Easy. At the very moment they both slotted the new devices back inside their mouths, Will almost dropped the newspaper in astonishment.

On the front page had been a story about a Russian

mafia boss called Illyr Ruskin. According to the article, he'd wrested control of Moscow and St Petersburg and was now in charge of an international crime gang whose illicit activities reached all the way to London.

Beneath this was an article about policing space. The UN was to hold a special assembly to discuss space laws, and methods to enforce them. *'Our world is changing fast. We must keep up with it,'* a British legal expert said.

Then, as Will flicked through the paper, his eye caught a headline in a news in brief column:

SUSPICIONS ABOUT MISSING SCIENTIST

Police are reissuing calls for information about the suspicious disappearance last week of Russian scientist Professor Vassily Baraban. It seems that Professor Baraban was abducted from his laboratory, said DI Charles Abraham of the Metropolitan Police.

Known in the former USSR as the 'king of astrophysics', Baraban fled from Russia to London with his family twelve years ago. His flight followed disgrace, after his experiments led to the destruction of two laboratories and the deaths of seven of Russia's top scientists. Authorities said Baraban's cutting-edge research on so-called 'strangelets' had been gravely irresponsible.

Baraban's wife has issued a statement: 'Please, for my sake, for our son's sake, if anyone knows where my husband is, contact the police.'

The news item beneath was titled: *Solar flare max: disruptions predicted.*

But Will did not notice it.

'I think,' he said, very quietly, 'it's time for the bill.'

Inside the restaurant, the two tiny tooth phones in Andrew and Gaia's mouths vibrated. The vibration travelled up through their jaws, into their inner ears, and they heard Will's voice.

Gaia cried out and Will clasped a hand to his ear.

'Quietly!' he hissed. 'Talk quietly.'

'Can you hear me?' Andrew whispered.

'Yeah, I can hear you.'

'These are microphones too?'

'Yes,' Will said.

'But how can I hear you?'

'The sound's travelling through your jawbone,' Will whispered.

'You are joking.'

And, despite himself, Will smiled. 'Put them back in the box. I'll come in for the bags.' But all he could think about was Vassily Baraban.

Back inside, Will noticed the confusion at once. 'What's happening?'

Andrew kept a straight face. 'I have no idea.'

As Will packed away Tooth Talk, he hesitated. He'd

been about to tell them about Baraban – but he was distracted. He thought he'd put Speak Easy to the side of Soft Landing. Now it was on top.

'You didn't touch anything—'

'Touch your things?' Andrew said as he slung on his jacket. 'Of course not.'

Will turned quickly. He watched two waiters, who emerged from the kitchen with a bucket of water and a cloth. They were heading for the nearest window. 'No one touches these unless I give permission,' Will said. 'I mean it.'

Andrew nodded, without meeting Will's eyes.

'I mean it,' Will said. His tone had been hard, anger underlining the words.

Andrew glanced at Gaia but she just looked right back. 'All right,' he said, and he held up his hands. 'Understood.'

As they walked into the courtyard, out of what had become a tumult of protest from bemused diners, into the sunshine, Gaia thanked Andrew for lunch.

'Don't mention it,' Andrew said, thinking that anyway it was the table next door that had offered to take care of their bill. Thanks to Speak Easy, of course. 'And thank you for showing me your inventions,' he said to Will. 'I didn't expect they'd be so good.'

'What did you expect?'

Andrew shrugged. 'I don't know – nothing like that. I really am serious – you should go into business.'

'I thought STORM wasn't for profit.'

Andrew's eyes lit up. 'So you're happy to offer your inventive services?'

Will hesitated. He thought for a moment of the plane, and the lives they had saved. Andrew irritated him sometimes, but at heart he wasn't bad. And he was smart. Gaia . . . Gaia probably was less straightforward. And that buzz of feeling better about life that had been born the previous night still had not left him. And now – what did his new knowledge mean? What had happened to Vassily Baraban?

'I guess so,' Will said.

Andrew smiled. 'You hear that, Gaia? We have The Maker. I'll call for Sean.'

'No, wait—' Will said. He held up the newspaper, which had been clenched in his hand.

And he looked at Andrew.

'Did Caspian tell you about his father?'

'Tell me what?' Andrew said. His expression was blank.

'. . . He was abducted. Last week.'

Andrew's eyes opened wide. '*What?*'

Clearly it was news to them. Will nodded. He opened the paper and showed them the article. Andrew grabbed it, incredulous.

'But who abducted him?' he said.

'The police don't know.'

'Caspian didn't say anything . . .' Andrew said. 'But when he came to the basement, his father had already been taken. He must have known. He didn't say anything to me.'

'Isn't that strange?'

'Not really – I don't know.'

'I think it's strange,' Will said.

'I think it's strange,' Gaia echoed.

'Has he been acting differently?' Will said.

Andrew raised his eyebrows. 'I've known Caspian for eight years. I couldn't predict him if I tried . . . So what do you want to do? Turn up at the lab and ask him what's happened to his father – and what is he working on? Do you think they're linked? Do you think that's why he didn't come last night – something to do with his father?' He was looking at Gaia.

'We won't know unless we ask,' Will said.

Gaia nodded.

Andrew frowned. '. . . I suppose we could pay a friendly visit.' And he looked uncertainly at the street beyond the archway. In the past month, he hadn't left home without the safety of the armour-plated SmarTruck and the burly Sean.

Gaia took his arm. 'Come on,' she said quietly. 'You're with us. We can get a cab. You'll be all right.'

As they left the gates, a man in a homburg and a brown Italian raincoat bent his head, apparently to read a city map. He'd ditched the jumper, jeans and woollen hat.

This was one of the first rules of surveillance: if you can't change the tail, change their clothes. Change their demeanour. If you walked with a straight back, switch to a slump. If you trod quickly, start to amble.

It worked. Will saw the back of the man's head, registered nothing, and moved on.

The laboratory was small and untidy. Spread across the desk was a jumble of papers. A journal of astrophysics, with handwritten scrawl in the margins. A manuscript on an unusual gamma-ray burst. A request from a professor at Sweden's prestigious Karolinska Institute to visit London, to discuss Vassily Baraban's latest research.

With an impatient gesture, Caspian Baraban swept the papers to the floor. He had been in the lab for twelve straight hours. And he'd got nowhere. At least, that was how it felt. Once more, he ran the requirements through his brain . . .

Two beams of gold nuclei, set on a forty-kilometre-long collision course. To produce what he wanted – what he needed – the speed had to be right, and the intensity . . . but how to coordinate these variables, to model with certainty, to *know* what would happen when the nuclei were smashed together – to make sure they would break down into quarks and gluons, to make a ball of plasma 300 million times hotter than the surface of the Sun?

Caspian let his head fall to his hands. His father needed him. His own life rested on his success. Not only his, but that of his mother, who right at that moment was weeping into her pillow in Covent Garden. Caspian could predict this with some accuracy. Since the moment of the news of his father's abduction, she has assumed this attitude and – bar essential bathroom visits and moments to sip feebly at a bowl of borsch – she had not left it.

Her uselessness exasperated him. But this feeling came and went. He was fond of his mother, after all. She was not clever, but she had borne him into the world. Perhaps his mother's true genius had been to support his father and to give him life. And with STORM, what could he achieve? What couldn't he achieve? But STORM was nothing now, he told himself angrily.

All that mattered was *this* science. *This* problem. And if he could solve it he could save his father . . .

Once more, Caspian said to himself. He took up the pencil and a fresh sheet of paper.

An hour later, he laid the pencil on the desk. He had forgotten to blink, so his eyeballs burned. His body was racked through with concentration, every muscle knotted, every nerve twitching. And yet . . .

Wait, he said to himself.

Furiously, he scribbled for two straight minutes. With pulsating eyes he scanned his calculations.

Perhaps I have it!

At that moment, signals from his bladder that his brain had been suppressing erupted into his consciousness. The toilet was at the other end of the building. Outraged at the demands of his body, Caspian reluctantly rose from the chair and staggered out of the lab.

'There,' Andrew said.

He was peering at the noticeboard at the entrance to the physics building. It showed the general layout, the fire exits, the first-aid cabinets. The names of the professors and doctors and then the post-doc students were listed on a sheet of paper, next to the relevant laboratory numbers.

Professor Vassily Baraban. P15.

'Down here,' Gaia said.

The corridor smelt of cleaning fluid. They passed a series of labs with closed, locked doors, then turned into a corridor where a vat of liquid nitrogen was carefully being manoeuvred into a lift.

The lab technicians were dressed in full protective gear, with masks and elbow-length gloves.

'Could freeze your face right off,' Gaia murmured as they passed.

One of the technicians did a double take. 'Are you

with the school group?' he called. 'Shouldn't you be in the lecture theatre?'

But Will, Andrew and Gaia were already around the corner.

P 11. P 12. P 13. P 14 . . .

'This is it,' Gaia said.

Will touched the handle – and the door responded. He peered inside. 'There's no one here.'

Andrew and Gaia followed him into the lab. It was cramped and dark, thanks to the boards over the windows. On the far desk was a computer and piles of papers. Closer to them, on a steel bench that ran along the back wall was a plastic model of an atom, showing each constituent particle in a different colour, like a child's toy.

A central nucleus held the protons and neutrons, orbited by electrons. And then there was the weirder stuff, the *anti-matter* – like the positron, the *anti-particle* to the electron.

Will put his rucksacks down by the model and crossed to the desk.

'What are you doing?' Andrew said uncertainly.

'Just taking a look.'

Will let his eyes wander across the papers. Individual words leaped out. *Large Hadron Collider. Big Bang. Critical energy.* And then he came to Caspian's notes.

At first, they looked a mess. Caspian's writing was a scrawl. But the notes were mostly in numbers, anyway.

Will was good at maths, but he struggled to make sense of what he saw.

'Can you understand this?' he said to Andrew.

Andrew joined him, pushing his glasses back up along his nose. Behind them, Gaia was leafing through a pile of drawings. Diagram after diagram fell through her fingers. She recognized a few. An old X38 escape capsule. An ion engine. An inflatable sleeping unit. A couple of pages apparently written in Russian, and an outline of what seemed to be a laboratory with two Russian words in red at the centre.

Andrew methodically followed the code. He had more patience than Will.

'He seems to be talking about a collision of gold ions,' he said at last.

Then, as Andrew picked up another sheet of notes, Caspian's PDA was revealed underneath. Will grabbed it. It was switched on. And an email was displayed. From Vassily Baraban.

An explanatory email, before he detailed the problem.

But what an explanation.

Will stared at the words in sudden disbelief . . .

But *how*?

And *why*?

At that moment, he heard footsteps approaching rapidly along the corridor. 'Hide,' Will said urgently and he placed the PDA back on the desk.

Andrew let the papers drop from his hand. 'What?'

'*Hide*,' Will said. 'Now. Under this bench at the back. *Gaia*.'

Andrew was first to duck. Then Gaia. And Will pulled his rucksacks in beside them, into the shadows. Above them, the atomic model was jolted and vibrated.

'Don't even breathe,' Will whispered.

Gaia's eyes were asking what was going on. Will used his to warn her not to speak. If this was Caspian, he didn't want him to realize they knew what he was working on. Will could hardly believe what he had seen.

Caspian's legs felt like weights. It was as though gravity had suddenly doubled in strength. Rubbing his eyes, he sat once more at the desk and he pulled the papers closer to him. Andrew had dropped them, but Caspian didn't seem to notice. Too absorbed in his work, Will guessed.

For a few moments, Caspian was motionless as he scanned through the calculations. Under the bench, Will controlled his breathing so it was noiseless – a technique his father had taught him. He regulated the air through his open mouth, slowly in and out, in and out. Smoke from a candle. Nothing more. Gaia watched him and did the same.

At last, Caspian moved.

'I was right,' he breathed. 'How did I ever doubt it?'

Instantly, he turned to the computer and hit the Outlook icon.

Caspian's fingers hovered above the keyboard. He could simply attach the solution to an email and send it off. But pride reared in his chest. He, Caspian Baraban, had solved a problem that had foxed his father. His genius had saved not only his own life, but the lives of his father and mother. His breakthrough would change the world. Why shouldn't he share in the glory?

From their position Will, Gaia and Andrew could not see what Caspian was doing. Then, very slowly, Andrew withdrew something from his left jacket pocket. It looked like a hand-held scanner. Andrew reached into the other pocket and pulled out his smart phone. He ignored Will's scowl. Andrew wasn't making a sound, but what, Will thought, was he doing?

Cautiously, Andrew lifted the device out from underneath the table. He held it in the air, and angled it towards Caspian at the computer.

A few moments later, Caspian hit a final key with a flourish and he leaped from the desk, stuffing his notes into his pocket. Hurriedly, Andrew withdrew the device. As Caspian headed for the door, Andrew raised the smart phone, so Will and Gaia could see the result. The screen emanated a ghostly white light. But Caspian did not see it. He was already halfway down the corridor.

'It's for screen capturing,' Andrew whispered. 'I

ordered it last week – it's based on radiation from the monitor. I was going to show you at lunch,' he said to Will. 'But then your stuff was so much better.'

But Will wasn't listening to Andrew. He was looking at the words on the screen.

Those tiny black letters that said so much.

Have created Infinity Code. Bringing it to Petersburg. CME affecting planes. Will take train. Your loving son.

'The Infinity Code,' Andrew said. 'What do you think it means?'

But Will was already at the door. 'We have to follow Caspian.'

'Where?' Andrew said.

'Wherever he's going. We can't let him go.'

Gaia was stretching her back and straightening out her clothes. 'Why not?'

'Trust me,' Will said. 'I'll explain later. Hurry up.'

Why couldn't he just tell them? Perhaps he was still struggling with those words. Could it be a *joke*? And why would Vassily Baraban be involved – and Caspian?

Will led the way along the corridor and out of the building.

'Over there,' Will said and pushed Andrew and Gaia into the shadows.

Across the street, Caspian was getting into a cab.

'I knew I should have called Sean,' Andrew said.

Will jumped into the road. Three cars away another

cab was pulling up, letting a passenger out. Quickly, Will rushed to the back door, Andrew and Gaia in tow.

'That'll be eight pounds sixty,' the driver was saying. His passenger was a student. She was opening her purse and starting to count out coins.

Andrew touched Will's shoulder. 'Will, what's going on?'

'*I will tell you,*' he said. 'Now you have to trust me.'

'No, Will,' Gaia said. 'You have to tell us. Now.'

Her brown eyes didn't blink. Beside her, Andrew was looking at Will with alarm. 'What do you know?'

'. . . I'm not sure, exactly,' Will began.

Gaia shook her head in irritation.

'I mean, I don't understand it. I saw an email from Vassily Baraban on Caspian's PDA. It said he's been abducted to work on a new sort of weapon to take down a space hotel . . . And he needs Caspian's help. That's what Caspian thinks he's done – that's what the code's for – he's discovered how to make a weapon to take this hotel out. They – whoever they are – want to launch it.'

'*What?*' Gaia's face crumpled into a frown.

Andrew stared at Will.

'What hotel?' Gaia said.

'I have *no idea.*' Will racked his memory, came up with nothing.

Gaia glanced at Andrew, who had blanched. He looked at Will. 'I know about this,' he said quietly.

Will stared at him.

'I read about the hotel – when I was hacking into secure sites after the CME.' Andrew blinked. 'It launched last week. It's being kept secret, but I don't know why.'

Nausea suddenly curdled Andrew's stomach. Esmee Templeton, he thought. She was at risk.

'Why didn't you tell us?' Gaia said.

'I was going to!'

Will was staring at Andrew. 'But who launched it? And *why* would it be secret?'

'I don't know!' And then Will's urgency seemed to sweep through Andrew's body, like a virus. He reached into his pocket. The student was still fiddling. 'Here!' Andrew thrust a £10 note through the driver's window. 'Get out!' he said to the girl. 'We need this cab!'

Will and Gaia bundled into the back and almost pushed the girl out on to the street. Andrew threw himself in beside them. Light shone from his eyes. Will was surprised, and pleased.

'Where to?' the driver said to Andrew.

'Follow that cab!' he replied, and he pointed through the windscreen towards Caspian, whose taxi was helpfully painted not black but bright yellow and purple, advertising a chocolate bar.

'And put my foot down?' the driver said, a trace of humour in his voice.

Andrew replied seriously: 'I'll double the fare if you do.'

'He must be going to Waterloo,' Gaia said, as the purple and yellow taxi turned away south.

'Paris and on to St Petersburg,' Andrew said.

'Surely he'd go home first,' Will said. 'He'd need clothes and things.'

Andrew shrugged. 'I've never seen him in anything apart from those jeans and that sweatshirt. I think he sleeps in them.'

'Look,' Gaia said. She was pointing out of the window at a sign for Waterloo station.

London swept past them – people, shops, offices, cars – but Will saw none of it. The radio was on. A news report focused on an upcoming UN special meeting on policing space. Delegates would be arriving in New York in two days. But Will did not hear it. He saw only the calculations and only the email, screaming in his mind. But why Vassily? Why Caspian? And why was the hotel secret – and who would want to take it out?

And then they had passed Victoria station and were heading for Westminster Bridge.

'Go direct to Waterloo. Do not pass Go,' Andrew murmured.

The driver winked at him in the rear-view mirror. 'Will you give me two hundred quid if I do?'

Andrew ignored him, peering hard through the windscreen as they approached a set of traffic lights and watched Caspian sail through. The colours started to change. Green to amber . . .

'Go through them!' Andrew urged.

'Are you crazy?' Gaia said.

'I don't care if you triple the fare,' the driver said. 'I can't go through a red light.'

'It's all right,' Will said, as their taxi stopped and they watched the purple and yellow cab zoom away. 'We know where he's going. It has to be Waterloo.'

In fact, he wasn't as certain as he sounded. But at this stage he could not conceive of losing Caspian.

Two more sets of traffic lights, and they pulled up in the drop-off zone.

Andrew did as he'd promised and doubled the fare. With a wave, the driver was off. And they were left outside Waterloo station, with no sign of Caspian's cab.

Gaia was scanning the line of vehicles. 'He's not here.'

'The cab's not here,' Will countered. 'But that doesn't mean anything. It could have been and gone.'

'So what do we do now?' Andrew said. His chest was heaving slightly, his breath catching.

'If he's here, he'll have gone down to the Eurostar platforms,' Gaia said.

Will nodded. 'But we can't let him know we're following him. And if his cab stopped or took him a long way round we'll need to know if he's behind us.'

Gently, Will dropped his rucksacks to the ground. He reached into the second, and retrieved one of the fuse boxes. From inside he took two of the tooth phones. 'Take one,' he said to Andrew. Before he slotted the second into his mouth, he said: 'Andrew, you stay here. If you see the cab arriving, let us know. Gaia, you come with me. Remember,' he whispered, as he and Gaia headed into the station, the membrane-thin plastic feeling dense between his teeth, 'talk quietly.'

'Why can't I have one?' Gaia said as they approached the escalator down to the Eurostar concourse. They'd already scanned the hordes of passengers milling around the main station hall. No sign of Caspian.

'You're right next to me,' Will said, and in his ear, he heard:

'What?'

'I was talking to Gaia,' Will whispered. 'Andrew, if I want to talk to you, I'll say your name first.'

'Roger,' came the reply. And then, a moment later: 'Will, roger.'

Will and Gaia stood at the balcony overlooking the Eurostar concourse. Down below was a cafe. English holidaymakers were eating croissants and drinking cafe au lait, getting into the mood.

'Can you see him?'

Will shook his head. 'We'll have to go down. Andrew: we're going down to look for him.'

'Will, roger,' came the response.

He's enjoying this, Will thought. Maybe that was all Andrew had needed – a reason, a sanctioned excuse. Andrew had made his choice.

Will turned as a noisy group of overweight men jostled on to the escalator. Quickly, he pulled Gaia on with him behind them. Perfect, Will thought. There was no way anyone could see up past them.

At the bottom of the escalator, it took a few moments for the group to stagger off towards the ticket office. Will and Gaia followed them, using their bodies for cover, then as they broke away, Andrew's voice erupted in Will's ear:

'He's here! I mean, Will, he's here.'

'Andrew, talk quietly,' Will hissed, clasping a hand to his head. He wondered what Caspian had been doing. 'He's here,' he said to Gaia. 'Andrew, stay back, don't let him see you. Stay up in the main hall. I'll tell you when you can come down. If he comes down.'

'Will, I'll follow him,' Andrew said.

'No!'

'Will, what if he doesn't go to Eurostar?'

'Where else would he go?'

'Will, are you talking to me?'

'Yes, Andrew,' Will said, exasperated. 'I'm talking to you. Stay back.'

'Will, roger. He's paid the driver . . . He's heading into the station.'

Down on the Eurostar concourse, Gaia and Will moved to sit at a table in the shadows underneath the escalator. They positioned themselves so no one could see them, unless they were entering or leaving the cafe.

'Will, he's getting on the escalator down to Eurostar.'

'Andrew, *stay back*.'

'What's he doing?' Gaia said.

'He's coming down. We'll stay here and watch him.'

'What can I get you?'

The reedy voice seemed to shoot from a thousand miles away. Will looked up sharply. A waitress in a black dress and a white apron was standing over them, a notepad in her hand.

'Nothing, thanks,' Will said.

'What was that?' came the voice in his ear.

'Andrew, nothing,' Will hissed.

'Nothing at all?' the waitress said, giving Will an odd look.

'No, thanks,' Gaia said.

'Then I'll have to ask you to give up the table,' she said, her lips pursed.

At that moment, Caspian appeared. Will could see only the top of his head – but he knew it in an instant. The shock of black hair moved away from the escalator, towards the ticket office.

'Did you hear me?' the waitress said.

'We're going,' Will said, annoyed. He'd spoken too loudly and in his ear he heard a groan, and then: 'Will, too loud.'

'Come on,' Gaia said. She'd seen Caspian too.

Together, they rose and backed around the underside of the escalator. Through the glass walls of the ticket office they saw that Caspian had joined the end of a queue.

'Andrew, if you're quick, come down. We're underneath the escalator,' Will said urgently.

'Will, roger,' came the reply.

A minute later, Andrew was with them, eyes alight, chest slightly heaving. He reached into his mouth and pulled out the tooth phone.

'I think this needs refining,' he said.

'*How?*' Will said, suddenly angry, his ear still ringing. It was the people who used it that needed refining, he thought.

But Andrew didn't reply. He was watching Caspian, who had reached the front of the queue, and who was now placing a small pile of £10 notes on the counter. Maybe he'd got the cab to stop at an ATM, Will guessed. Though there were plenty of those in the station.

'Now what?' Andrew said.

And Will hesitated. He'd known they had to follow Caspian, and he knew that somehow they had to stop him. *The eight deaths will be unfortunate*, the email ran. *But we have no choice, my son.*

What did he mean, *no choice*? And if Caspian really had come up with a new weapon, would stopping him here in London really mean the end of the project? Of course not. If Caspian could do it, so could the father, in time. Whatever the code was – whatever it meant – surely Caspian Baraban wasn't the only person in the world who could create it.

To stop the project once and for all, they had no choice but to go to its source.

Will took the tooth phone from his mouth and

placed it with Andrew's back in the fuse box. 'We have to follow him.'

'Where?' Andrew said warily.

'To *St Petersburg*?' Gaia said.

Will nodded.

'We can't,' she said.

'Why not?'

'. . . What about school?' she said. 'And *why*?'

'Because if we don't stop them, Caspian and his father will *kill* those people. And we have no idea how – or why. None of the notes make any sense – not for a weapon.'

'*Eight* people,' Andrew murmured. 'Including Esmee Templeton. She's British.'

What did nationality matter, Will thought? And then he remembered the photograph in Andrew's house, beside the skull. Nationality had nothing to do with it. 'I saw the photograph – it said, *To Andrew, keep reaching for the stars*. Do you know her?'

Andrew coloured. 'Not really.'

'She gave you her photograph.'

'I wrote her a letter last year. I admire her greatly. She sent me the photograph.'

Will understood the meaning of the stilted words and his matching tone. And she was beautiful, he supposed. And she was an astronaut.

'Why don't we just tell the police,' Gaia said.

'What use will that do?' Will said.

And anger burned. Time was running out. He had to

convince them. There were two main reasons. One, he wanted to save those lives. Two: he wanted to know what Caspian was doing, and why. Caspian had bought into STORM – or at least he'd seemed to. He'd agreed with the need to save lives, not to take them. Perhaps there was a third reason: why was the hotel secret?

'If this hotel is secret, the police won't know anything about it,' Will continued. 'And they won't know where Caspian's going. And he's going to *Russia*. By the time the police even talk to each other, it will all be over.'

'. . . If Caspian really has come up with some new kind of weapon that works,' Andrew said. 'This does all depend on him being right.'

Will didn't quite agree. The father wasn't incompetent. But now wasn't the time for this discussion. 'And you're going to bet he's not?'

Andrew glanced hopelessly at Gaia. 'I want to help . . . But I can't go to St Petersburg.'

Will fixed him in his gaze. 'I thought you were serious when you talked about STORM.'

He had nothing else left. If that didn't convince Andrew, what would? And, he realized, he wanted this. After six months of having no real wants, except for his old life back, now he was *sure* about something. The private jet had made him feel alive again. He didn't want that feeling to go away. And Will remembered one of his mother's favourite phrases: *No risks, no life*. If Andrew didn't have faith, he did.

Then came the announcement over the loudspeaker. First in French, and then in English.

'The next train to Paris is getting ready to depart,' Gaia translated, before the English.

'We have to get on it,' Will said. 'Look – Andrew, forget the plane, this is bigger. If you want STORM to mean *anything* you have to come to St Petersburg.'

Gaia was watching Will closely. She recalled what she'd said about school and she was annoyed with herself. Why shouldn't she go? Put it another way: why should she stay?

'I'll come,' she said firmly. She looked at Andrew. 'Andrew, you have to. You told me you wanted adventure—' and he lowered his eyes, embarrassed – 'you told me you wanted to get out in the world, you spend too much time at home, and if Esmee Templeton—'

'*All right!*' he said. '. . . All right.'

Gaia reached out to Andrew. To his – and to Will's – surprise, she hugged Andrew quickly. Colouring, Andrew turned to Will.

'I'm glad,' Will said. 'But I'm not going to hug you. We have seven minutes. Somehow we have to get on that train.'

'I have an idea,' Andrew said. 'Wait here.'

'Where are you going?' Will called.

Andrew flashed a frown. 'Just trust me.'

Gaia whispered to Will, after Andrew had left: 'You're sure we can do this?'

What could he say? 'We have to.'

'. . . I've never been anywhere apart from France.'

He looked at her, heard the caution in her voice. 'But you speak all those languages.'

'Dad's Italian. I learned French at school, and the rest from dictionaries. I've got a photographic memory, remember . . . Have you ever been to Russia?'

Yes, he had. Only once. For his grandfather's funeral. And the knowledge that he had been suppressing – that in going to St Petersburg, he would be going to his mother – flooded through him. For a moment, he wondered if he was dragging Andrew and Gaia to Russia not for STORM but for him.

No. The threat was real. The email and the fact of Vassily Baraban's abduction told him that.

Will looked up as Andrew strode towards them, three first-class tickets in his right hand, a look of triumph on his face.

'How did you get those?' Gaia said.

He waved a card. 'Platinum.'

'But you're only fourteen.'

'I'm a multimillionaire, Gaia. The usual rules don't apply.'

But there was no time to talk. '*Come on,*' Will said.

'I don't have my passport,' Gaia said as they slipped their tickets through the barrier and joined the queue for the booths at passport control.

Will glanced at Andrew.

'Of course not,' he said. 'Why would I? Do you?'

Will shook his head.

There were twenty or so people ahead of them. A few businessmen, a young couple and two extended family groups. Grandparents, parents, and a horde of young kids. They dragged huge cases. The kids were arguing. Precious time was passing. *Think*, Will told himself. Instinctively, he reached into the pocket of his jacket and touched his cricket ball. And he heard Andrew's voice, brushing his ear: 'I'd say now might be a time to make use of Speak Easy. What do you think?'

Speak Easy. Of course. Will could appreciate its theoretical power. Andrew had witnessed its impact.

An Italian couple pushed past them. '*Fretta!* Hurry!' called the dark-headed man.

Will thought quickly.

'Stay close,' he hissed to Gaia.

'Really? I was thinking of wandering off,' she replied.

With a fluid motion, Will slipped one of the rucksacks from his shoulder, and withdrew Speak Easy. Ahead, the passport-control officer was scrutinizing the Italians' documents. At the next booth, an English family approached. There were three kids, including a boy who looked about fourteen, whose hair was bleached blond.

Bending his head and holding the microphone close to his mouth, Will whispered: 'Mum, we should tell him – he'll see my passport's fake. I shouldn't have bleached my hair.'

'*Grazie!*' the Italian man said with exaggerated impatience.

Their turn. Will hung back a moment, Gaia and Andrew behind him. As the officer looked down at his desk, he seized his chance. Will aimed the metal pointer at the ceiling and hit send. A moment later, the officer's head shot up. He gazed around, his expression confused. And immediately he saw the family at the booth beside him. His eyes fixed on the boy with the bleached-blond hair.

'Hey!' he shouted. 'Wait!' And he leaped from his chair, to run across to his colleague.

'Now!' Will said.

Walking fast, he headed straight for the narrow space between the officer's booth and the wall. He could feel Gaia and Andrew, tense behind him. But the officer was occupied – with his colleague beside him, he was demanding another look at the blond boy's passport. Will allowed himself one glance. *Just a few more seconds . . .*

And they were through. 'Now *run*,' Will said.

They shot up the escalator to the platforms, running together, ducking into the door to the first class carriages just as the whistle blew. Instantly, Will pulled them into hiding behind a luggage rack. He let his rucksacks slip to the floor.

Will was breathing hard, his blood hot with triumph. 'It worked!'

'It was a good idea,' Andrew said, beaming.

And Gaia glanced at Andrew, beside her. 'I'm really glad we got a good chance to see Speak Easy in action, aren't you? Who'd have thought it could be that impressive?'

He tried to look stern, and she smiled. And Andrew jerked and grabbed at the luggage rack as the train pulled away. He moved to enter the carriage.

'Wait!' Will said. 'He could be in there.'

'No way,' Andrew insisted.

'How do you know?' Gaia said.

'I saw the notes Caspian put down. You don't know what first class to St Petersburg costs.'

'What does it cost?' Will said, feeling uncomfortable. He didn't like the idea of Andrew paying for the tickets, though they'd had little choice. If he kept a tally, he could pay Andrew back.

'More than that pile,' Andrew said. He waved the tickets and strode into the carriage. 'Come on,' he said, smiling. 'You'll be all right. You're with me.'

Before long the city gave way to countryside. Will, Gaia and Andrew sat in silence, staring at the wintry brown through the window, each taking in some of the implications of the project. And their decision.

It certainly didn't escape Will that they looked an odd bunch. They were dressed far from appropriately for a mission to St Petersburg in the winter. And they *were* an odd bunch. A girl he barely knew – and what he did know about her wasn't exactly usual – and Andrew, who was totally unlike anyone he'd met before. A week ago they were nothing to each other. Now they were heading to Russia.

There had been no real time to weigh up the pros and cons. If there had, perhaps they'd still be in London. It wasn't as though Will made a habit of dangerous missions to far-flung places. That had been his father's stock-in-trade.

Was he doing this because he missed his father? Because he wanted to see his mother? Or because his success at saving the private jet had gone to his head? Was he guilty of the precise arrogance of which he'd accused Andrew? Was this the reason he'd convinced them to come?

No, he told himself. Though perhaps there could be many different and valid reasons for doing the same one thing.

But, unlike Andrew, he wasn't naive, he thought. At least, not totally. They were fourteen years old. They were going to St Petersburg. If Caspian had come up with a way to blast away that hotel, they had to stop that weapon – somehow, they had to destroy it. But what sort of weapon? What was the Infinity Code? What did they want to launch? And who was *they* anyway?

Enough. There was no point trying to look too far ahead. They'd have to make it up as they went. It suited him. And as the train sped towards the coast, Will realized that for the first time in months, he felt he was setting his own course. He was free. From Natalia, and her well-meaning hospitality. Cutler. School. England. The past.

'I'm going to be freezing in this dress,' Gaia said. She was slouching in her broad, grey chair, opposite Will, by the window, Andrew at her side. She'd been doing her own thinking. Now she wanted to drag herself out of her thoughts.

'We'll try to buy some clothes in Paris—' Andrew said. 'We have an hour and fifteen minutes.'

'How do you know?' Will said.

Andrew eyed him evenly. 'I'll give you a choice: a moment ago I used the classic though admittedly discredited CIA technique of remote viewing to peruse the train timetable in the office in London with my mind, or I asked the woman at the ticket office.'

'You're sure Caspian's booked on that train?' Will said, ignoring his sarcasm.

'I told the woman that we needed the next train through to Paris and on to St Petersburg – which is of course the one Caspian would take,' Andrew said, with a touch of annoyance. 'You know I do have some intelligence, Will. You're not the only brain around here.'

'I didn't mean that,' Will said quickly. 'I just want to be sure.'

'Well, I think that if we're going to get through this all right we'll need to trust each other's abilities. Don't you?'

'He's right,' Gaia said.

'. . . We need to check exactly where Caspian is,' Will said.

Gaia moved to get up. 'I'll go and look. I'll be careful.'

'There's a safer option,' Will said. His rucksacks were on the seat beside him. He unzipped the one that was closest.

'Fly Spy?' she said.

He nodded. Andrew leaned over the table. 'Can I have a go?'

'Next time,' Will said, as he set the robot locust upright and activated the video screen. 'When it's less likely to be lost.'

There was no one else in their compartment. With a deft twitch of the remote control, Will sent the robot into a hover then reduced its height until it flew just below the level of the seats.

A quick up and down movement allowed it to trigger the door-opening mechanism. Then it was through into the next carriage and on into economy class.

Will gazed intently at the screen, on the lookout for danger, as well as Caspian. The camera's field of view was 160 degrees – not bad, but nowhere near enough to give the locust eyes in the back of its head. Worst-case scenario, someone in the blind spot thought it was a real insect and took a swipe at it.

'I can't see him,' Gaia breathed.

The first economy carriage had been cased. She was right. No sign of Caspian. Gently, Will again manipulated the tiny, flapping robot so it triggered entry into the next carriage. He elevated its position, and it flew along the top of the windows. A couple of people looked up as it passed, but they looked down just as quickly. An insect wasn't a problem if it was flying on by.

'Wait!' Andrew said.

Will had already seen him. Gaia leaned over for a better look. And there he was, five rows back on the right-hand side, in a window seat with the curtain drawn. A shock of black hair. A black sweatshirt. A stylus in his right hand, scribbling electronic text on a PDA screen.

'I can't make it out,' Andrew said. 'Can you focus it?'

Will shook his head. 'The resolution's not good enough. I built it to make out large objects, not writing on a screen.'

Needs refinement, Andrew thought, but he held his tongue.

Caspian Baraban seemed oblivious to his observer. But now they knew precisely where he was there was no sense, Will thought, in risking Caspian noticing the odd-looking insect perched on the curtain rail above his head. Will made Fly Spy reverse its flight path, back to the table and into the fuse box.

'Well, at least he's definitely on the train,' Andrew said.

Gaia nodded. 'And we know where he'll be when we get off.'

She glanced out of the window. While the robot had been hunting for Caspian they had passed beneath the English Channel, and into dusk. The French fields were dark and foreign. She could barely make out the trees.

'I still don't get why the hotel should be a secret,' she said. 'And why would Vassily Baraban be involved in coming up with a weapon? What did Caspian's notes say?'

Andrew shrugged. 'They were about accelerating particles together – stripped down gold atoms. That's fundamental physics. It hasn't got anything to do with any weapon.'

'But that's what the code was for?' Gaia said. 'For a weapon?'

Andrew looked uncertain. He took off his glasses and retrieved a tiny screwdriver from his pocket. With a few sharp twists, he tightened the arms and replaced them back on his nose. The routine motion helped him think. 'It seemed to me it was just about colliding beams of gold ions,' he said at last. 'No weapon would do that. Maybe it's a different project. I don't know.'

'We need to find out,' Will said. 'If someone wants to take out the hotel, we have to stop them.'

'But—' With a twitch of his fingers, Andrew pushed his newly adjusted glasses back up along his nose. 'How do you think we'd be able to do that – to stop them?'

'I have no idea,' Will said. 'But we have to . . . *We might be young, but we are not impotent. We can act. We can change the world. The only real challenge is for us to believe it.*'

Andrew gave him a tight smile. 'I had a feeling that speech might come back to haunt me.'

'That's funny,' Will said. 'Because when I was listening to you talk, I had a feeling that just maybe you were right.'

Gare du Nord, 8.30 p.m. local time

Will, Andrew and Gaia had kept a good distance behind Caspian as he strode into a restaurant on the station concourse. A quick reconnaissance flight by Fly Spy showed Caspian was settled with a bottle of water and his notes on the table.

'He's not going anywhere,' Will said, and his breath condensed in the air. The station was freezing. It was also chaotic, echoing with the sounds of voices in assorted European languages and the cries of a small child in a three-wheeled pram by the information booth.

People milled around, waiting for trains, looking out for friends arriving.

'I'm going to find some clothes,' Andrew said. He'd tried to sound confident, but the uncertainty came through.

'At this time?' Will said. 'All the shops will be shut.'

'Maybe a department store will still be open. I'll ask a taxi driver.'

'Do you speak French?' Gaia said.

'Um, well, enough, I think. If not, everyone speaks English. Don't they?'

'Maybe I should go with you,' she said.

Will nodded. 'You both go. I can keep an eye on Caspian. Just don't be long. And get me a hat,' he called, as Andrew and Gaia started towards the exit and the waiting row of cabs.

A hat, thermal underwear, a fleece, fur-lined boots, a Gore-tex jacket, at the very least, he thought. What would be the temperature in St Petersburg in December? Minus ten? Minus twenty?

It had been summer when he had visited for his grandfather's funeral, five years ago. Will remembered long, light nights that drifted through into the days. He remembered solemn music playing on the ancient record player in his grandmother's small apartment, which had been filled with friends with strange smells and with cards of condolence. And he remembered the way his father had gripped his mother's hand as the coffin was lowered into the earth. Will hardly knew his grandfather. He had wept not for any loss, but for himself – at the pain and confusion he felt to see his mother's composure fracture as she seemed to transform into somebody else.

Will let his legs buckle, so he sat on the floor with

his back to the wall. And he remembered suddenly: *Natalia.*

Pulling out his phone, he saw there had been one missed call. And a text, sent an hour ago: *R u ok? u home for tea? N x*

He could have sent her a text. But that wouldn't have been fair. At least, he thought, he had a believable excuse.

'Natalia?'

'Hello? William – are you all right?'

'I'm fine.'

'You are coming home to eat?'

'. . . Not tonight.' He hesitated. 'Natalia, I'm in a railway station in Paris.'

There was a pause. And then an eruption. 'Oh my god, William – you have run away with this girlfriend? Your mother will kill me.'

'*No!* No – and I don't have a girlfriend. It's my mother,' he said. 'I need to see her, Natalia. I'm on my way to St Petersburg.'

'What? When did you decide all this, William?'

'Only today,' he said.

'And you are taking the *train*? But have you spoken to her? She has called you?'

'No.'

'You know where you are going? Your mother told me your grandmother's phone is disconnected – but I have no address, Will – nothing!'

'I've got the address,' Will said. At least his mother had given him that.

'Oh my god, William, I wish we had discussed this . . . You must take care. I know you are smart, but trust no one. And call me if you get in trouble. I will come and get you. You promise?'

'I promise,' he said.

9.01 p.m. Will slipped the phone back into his pocket, thankful that he hadn't had to lie too much. Natalia trusted him. It made it so much harder to tell her untruths. But he was going to St Petersburg, and he did want to see his mother.

9.03 p.m. Will looked up to see Andrew and Gaia frantically waving at him from the station entrance, checking, he guessed, that it was all right to come on in. They clutched large bags. Gaia had already changed into a pair of jeans, a heavy waterproof coat and walking boots.

'We were in luck,' Andrew said as he dropped his bags beside Will. 'We got you some jeans, a coat, a fleece hat, some boots – we had to guess your size.'

'And silk underwear,' Gaia said. 'Andrew's choice.'

'It's thermal!' Andrew protested.

'It's a good idea,' Will said. 'Thanks.' Before he started towards the toilets to change, he turned to Andrew. 'I don't know how much this cost. And I don't have any money to pay you now. But I want you to keep a list. I'll pay you back when we get home.'

Andrew coloured slightly. 'Really – and I mean this

sincerely – don't even think about it. This is STORM business. I said I had the money and I meant it.' And Andrew sat down to pull on his boots before either of them could reply.

9.10 p.m. Will, Andrew and Gaia made rapidly for the platform. Fly Spy had shown that Caspian was packing up his bag, preparing to join the train.

Andrew led the way, all his confidence residing in the fact that Will and Gaia were covering his back.

'Have you called your dad?' Will said to Gaia.

She shook her head.

'Are you going to?'

'He won't even notice I'm gone.'

'. . . Are you sure?'

'He doesn't see me go to school, he's not there when I get home. If he does notice he'll think I've gone on a school trip or to stay with my aunt or something and he's forgotten.'

'He can't be that stupid.'

'Not stupid,' she said. And she hesitated. 'Drunk.'

'All the time?'

'Yeah, in fact, all the time.'

'. . . Still your dad,' he said.

'I'll send him a text,' she said, meaning to put an end to the conversation.

'*Gone to Russia. Lives depend on me?*'

A flicker of a smile. '*Gone on school trip. Back soon.*'

Ahead, Andrew was hanging out of the open doorway, waving them on.

'Come on! Before Caspian sees you!' he said, his whisper almost as loud as a shout.

It was an old-fashioned train, painted brown with a long red stripe beneath the windows. A series of ill-fitting doors opened directly into individual compartments. Inside these were brown, leather-covered bench seats that faced each other. Andrew and Gaia sat down by the window, and slumped, staying low until the train was ready to depart. It was clear by Andrew's expression that he wasn't impressed.

'It takes thirty-two hours,' he said. 'I thought we had a sleeper cabin. I can't believe this is first class.'

'There's plenty of room. We'll be all right,' Will said.

And he took in their new surroundings. To him, the train was anything but disappointing. The smell of it, the scuffs on the leather seats, the knowledge of the journey that lay ahead . . . The Eurostar express had belonged to his own world. This was something entirely different. Adventure.

9.31 p.m. There was a heave and the seats creaked. Metal shifted against metal.

'. . . We're moving,' Gaia said. And she smiled. A little nervously, but still a smile.

'Beyond the point of no return,' Andrew added.

Will reached over Andrew and pulled down the window. Cold air rushed in – before Andrew protested and Will reluctantly shut it back up.

'I'd be more worried if we'd stayed in London and done nothing,' Will said. 'Wouldn't you?'

'. . . I guess so,' Gaia said.

'I'd be less worried if this train had been constructed after 1914,' Andrew said. 'And if there were beds. And an en suite.'

'We're going to *St Petersburg,*' Will said, meaning to encourage them.

'I know.' And this time when Gaia smiled the nervousness had gone.

Andrew glanced out of the window. Parisian suburbs began to speed past. Grey and unrelenting. The sheer foreignness struck him. 'I'd been thinking that we'd work at home,' he said quietly. 'But I suppose that we should look at this as something to test ourselves against. And we take things one step at a time.'

'Exactly,' Will said.

'This is exciting, isn't it?' Andrew said uncertainly.

'We're going to *St Petersburg,*' Gaia said. 'STORM is going to save that hotel.'

'You are going to save Esmee Templeton,' Will said.

And Andrew blushed. 'You know, I'd prefer it if you didn't really mention her,' he said.

Will glanced at Gaia, who raised her eyebrows.

'It's just – I haven't even met her. It's not as though we're friends.'

'You will be when she finds out you saved her life,' Gaia said.

'Now I think you're teasing me.' But Andrew smiled to show he didn't take offence. 'You know, it would be better all round if you just kept quiet and got out the smoked chicken.'

And with those words Will realized he was starving. The barely touched sashimi and the rich pudding had been hours ago. Caspian and the weapon had filled his body – his mind, his blood, his stomach. 'You bought food?'

'Of course,' Andrew said, as Gaia reached into one of the shopping bags.

'If you call some of it food.' Gaia turned up her nose. 'Liver pâté. Pickled things.'

'I've heard about Russian cuisine,' Andrew said, as he took one of the bags from her. And he smiled slightly at Will. 'I'm not sure which is more terrifying. A new type of space weapon or cabbage soup. Now, who would like a *cornichon*?'

After the meal, Will and Andrew stepped into the corridor. Gaia had lowered the window and she was leaning into the bitter wind, trying to make out the new world they were passing through. The moon was full. She saw silvery fields, low houses with red roofs. Spires and barns. Once she even thought she glimpsed a chateau, haunting in all that moonlight. Bats, or perhaps birds of prey, flew high above the chimneys, up above the bare trees.

Andrew had called up a map of Europe on his phone. After France would come Germany, then Poland, Lithuania, Lativa and Russia. *Lithuania. Latvia.* Whole countries about which she knew nothing. Soon she would see them, see their towns and their lands, for herself.

Gaia let her elbows rest on the window. She blinked. Her eyes were dry. It wasn't just the wind. She was tired, she realized. The previous night she'd had little more than two hours sleep. Now, at last, she could relax. For thirty-two hours there was nothing they could do – except make sure they kept track of Caspian.

Out in the corridor, Will had Fly Spy in one hand, for that exact purpose. He was worried about the battery – he had no spare, and they'd have to find a new one – but they had to know Caspian's exact location.

'This time?' Andrew said, his eyes on the robot, with its miniature video camera and its carefully tooled wings.

Will frowned. 'Next time. I promise.'

'Really?'

Will met Andrew's clear gaze. 'Maybe.'

'Thought so.'

'It's not that I don't trust you – it's just—'

'I understand – these are your children. You are their creator, their God, and who can threaten that relationship? Certainly not an outsider with glasses, who might accidentally send them diving through an open window. That's what you were going to say?'

'Not exactly,' Will said. 'But it'll do.'

This train was more difficult to navigate than the Eurostar express. Will had to fly the insect robot along the corridor then manoeuvre it to peer through the windows, at the people who occupied the brown seats.

It was a strange mix of faces. Blue Scandinavian eyes. Young Russian women, their cheekbones high and sharp. Old men with deep wrinkles and swollen noses.

'*Come on*,' Andrew whispered. 'Where are you?'

And then – Caspian. Four carriages away. Eyes closed. Arms crossed.

'How can you sleep?' Andrew breathed. He looked at Will. 'You're going to St Petersburg to join your father. You have the code for a brilliant new space weapon in your pocket. How can you sleep?' And he yawned.

'Only human,' Will said.

'Yeah. I might have to join him. In sleep, I mean,' Andrew added quickly.

Will glanced at his watch. It showed 10.25 p.m., Paris time. He'd woken in London. He'd go to sleep who knew where . . .

'It's all right – go in,' he said to Andrew. 'I'll just get Fly Spy back.'

'OK. Call if you need me.'

Andrew's expression was deeply sincere. Will nodded.

The corridors were quiet. Four or five people in total between Caspian's compartment, and theirs. These people were taking in the night air. Some chatting. Others drinking from heavy glasses. Fly Spy made it back unnoticed.

When Will re-entered the compartment, the light was out. Gaia was curled up on one of the seats, Andrew on the other, slumped towards the window. Andrew snored slightly. Gaia was motionless, silent in her sleep.

Will sat down beside Andrew, letting his head rest against the seat. The leather smelt acrid. He detected traces of body odour and old sweat. But already exhaustion was sweeping through Will's brain, tuning out the world.

Automatically he reached a hand into his pocket. Touched leather. Slowly, he became aware only of the fact he was moving. And that motion was what he needed. He was going somewhere. Which was all that mattered. Because, since his father's death and his mother's departure, the thing he hated most was standing still.

The next day passed slowly. For breakfast, they ate rolls shoved through their open window by a hawker in an unknown station in Germany or Poland – Will wasn't quite sure which. There was no sign announcing the name of the nondescript town. At least not that they could see. And the mouth of the old woman who was doing the proffering was red and toothless.

'We have no money,' Andrew whispered as Will took six rolls. 'Only pounds, I mean.'

'We'll have to give her what we have.'

Andrew pulled a £5 note from his pocket.

'That's far too much.'

'She'll have to change it,' Andrew said. 'It will have to do.'

Will pressed the note into the hawker's hand as the whistle blew. She knew at once, of course, that the money was foreign, but by the time she had started to protest, the train was already moving. Angrily, she slapped at the windows, shouting as Will watched as first she and then the platform disappeared.

'She doesn't know what she's got,' Andrew said, frowning. 'Five pounds for six bread rolls.'

'The bread's warm,' Gaia said. 'It's good.'

'. . . So worth every penny,' Andrew said and he sighed. He took the bag from Gaia.

And he handed Will a roll, then broke his own open. Gaia was right. The bread was warm and soft.

'Here's to our first breakfast on the road,' Andrew said. 'Where do you think we are?'

Will shrugged. He glanced out of the window. The sky was pale. Cloudless. He could see fields, brown and purple, barren until spring. In the distance was a factory, spewing a faint spiral of white smoke into the air.

Gaia rose. 'I'm going to see if there's coffee in the buffet car.'

Both heads shot up.

She held up her hands. 'It's all right. I'll be careful.'

'If he sees you—' Will began.

'He won't. Trust me. I'll be careful.'

After Gaia had left, Andrew stretched out. He picked up his smart phone. 'I've been trying to think about what sort of weapon Caspian could make,' he said quietly.

Will finished his roll. 'And what are you thinking?'

'Well, I'm not sure. At least not yet. I don't get how gold nuclei could help.'

'You know Caspian,' Will said. 'What can he do that his father can't?'

Andrew shrugged. 'Caspian is by far the brightest person I've ever met – at least when it comes to physics.' He let his gaze shift to the scene moving outside the window. 'The first time I met Caspian I had this feeling he'd go on to great things.'

'Like killing people in new ways?'

'This isn't Caspian's idea,' Andrew protested. 'Whoever ordered the abduction of Vassily Baraban – they're to blame. Not Caspian. You can't blame him for being brilliant.'

Will stayed quiet. No, you couldn't blame him for being brilliant. But you could blame him for using that brilliance, he thought. Andrew, of all people, should know that.

'I was thinking something else,' Andrew said.

Will waited.

'Esmee Templeton—' He hesitated. 'I mean, she's famous. So are the others who are up there. I saw all their names. They're really famous astronauts. Why would you have people like that as staff on a *hotel*?'

STASIS Headquarters, Sutton Hall, Oxfordshire

Shute Barrrington's fingers hovered above his keyboard. He had two backgrounders to write. Senior people in the government were taking a keen interest and he was obliged to respond. He'd left them till the last minute, of course.

Quickly he flicked through the last report from the 'hotel'. And Barrington's knowledge tumbled out:

1. The 'hotel' launched from a vessel on the equator at 0300, 2 December. Secrecy around the launch and the module's true function has been tight.

Personnel blasted off from the Baikonur Cosmodrome to join the 'hotel' on 3 December. Commander James McFadden leads the team. 32 years old. Scots-born, raised in Omaha. A top fighter pilot before he joined NASA aged 29. Hobbies: aerobatics, ice-climbing, free-diving, Chinese ceramics.

Barrington frowned. Was this really what they'd want to hear? He'd never been any good at writing reports.

Up there with McFadden are two Russians, three more Americans, a Spaniard and our very own Esmee Templeton.

Initial reports indicate that all is going well. The team's wake-up song today was 'Ring of Fire'.

And Barrington hesitated. He'd finish this one later. He encrypted the file and opened a new document.

To him, this subject was even more interesting. If Barrington had a nemesis – in fact, he thought, if the *world* had a nemesis – it was this man. The back-grounder had been requested by a new MP with space interests. And Barrington was the obvious man to write it.

2. *Sir James Parramore, 62, is a billionaire British busi-nessman. He operates a shadowy consortium of multinationals with bases in Cairo, the Cayman Islands, Uzbekistan, Guernsey, Russia and Nicaragua.*

Educated at Eton and then Cambridge, Parramore's first job was with the Ministry of Defence. He left after two years to set up his first company, Dunelm Enterprises, which manufactured and sold nerve agents to the then Eastern Bloc.

Parramore was tracked down and arrested once, in London, in 1982. Before escaping, he was subjected to a psychiatric evaluation. The report's conclusion: 'a classic psychopath'.

Parramore's current interests include oil, software, uranium, robotics – and space. Last year, he launched 12 satellites and he has plans . . .

Barrington's fingers froze. Yes, Parramore had plans – his own people had intercepted the transmission that suggested . . . and Barrington slapped a hand to his head. *What if . . . ?*

'What Ifs' played constantly through Barrington's brain. That was the way his mind worked. But this one rang out like a siren.

'Sir?'

The calm female voice came from the speaker on his desk. Barrington scowled hard at it.

'What?' he snapped.

'Sir, the meeting is about to start. Spicer is wondering where you are.'

Damn, Barrington thought. But this was a meeting he couldn't miss.

'. . . Sir?'

'*What?*' Barrington's brain was still running away with Parramore.

'The meeting, sir.'

'Yes, thank you, my hearing is functioning. Didn't you register the reaction in my auditory cortex?'

'Sir?'

'Ah – I mean . . . Forget it.'

He shouldn't even have mentioned it, in fact. This was a new project. And Barrington began to stride across the floor. But a fact he'd been trying to ignore somehow forced itself to the front of his conscious mind. The plant on his desk was glowing. It had been glowing for two days.

It was genetically modified. When it needed water, it developed a fluorescent tinge. The aim was to allow even the most inept of gardeners to keep it alive. Cursing, Barrington filled a glass with water from the small bathroom attached to his office.

'. . . Sir?'

Barrington threw the water into the pot and slung the cup in the sink.

'Sir?'

'I don't know why you keep talking,' he called. 'There's no point. I've already left.'

'Sir?'

Another voice. A man's. Barrington was striding down the corridor towards the meeting room. It was in a converted ballroom, complete with chandeliers and ornate ceiling roses.

Spicer. 'Sir, the ambassador is waiting.'

'For me?'

' —Yes.'

'I'm not first up.'

'No, sir. But I think he wants *you* to hear what *he* has to say.'

Charlie Spicer led the way into the ballroom. Three rows of hard-backed chairs were arranged at one end, lost in all that space. An elderly man in a grey suit was standing before the digital whiteboard. Old technology, Barrington noted with a sigh. Why did these government types insist on bringing their own kit?

'Glad you could join us, Barrington,' the man said, with what clearly was supposed to be a withering tone.

Barrington flashed him a beam and took a seat in the back row. 'How long is this supposed to go on?' he whispered to Spicer.

'I believe the ambassador's flight's at ten.'

The elderly man coughed. 'As you know, I called this meeting to outline the position I shall be taking in New York. The truth is this: space is, quite literally, out of control. And we must rein it in. We need tough new laws to police the activities of individuals on our Moon and in our orbit. And we need enforcement of those laws. Certain individuals, known at least by reputation to some of you in the audience, have been making claims about services they can offer in space which are, to be frank, quite outrageous.'

Barrington glanced at his watch. Only quarter past seven. He sighed loudly.

'But my belief is that we must take further immediate,

urgent action. And I believe that I am the best man to take the lead.'

Barrington glanced at the gadget he'd been clasping in his right hand. Unknown to the ambassador, Barrington had been bombarding his face and neck with microwave beams. A tiny processor inside the device analysed the characteristics of the reflected beams. It used this information to calculate the ambassador's pulse, breathing rate and even minute changes in levels of sweat on his skin.

When the ambassador proclaimed: 'I believe I am the best man to take the lead', an LED started flashing.

Barrington bent his head to Spicer. '*Liar,*' he hissed.

On the train, night fell.

Andrew had spent the afternoon working on an update to one of his virus-spotting programs. Gaia had learned Arabic from a dictionary she'd borrowed from a Syrian woman she had met in the corridor.

In the meantime, Will had kept an eye on Caspian, and watched the landscape speed past. Only it didn't always speed. Once, the train stopped for two hours, for no apparent reason. There was no station outside. Only fields and distant hills. Frost, and what looked like an industrial park, in the gloomy distance.

Andrew joined Will in the corridor. Fly Spy's screen showed Caspian's eyes were still closed.

'Maybe he's dead,' Andrew suggested. 'Problem solved. Game over.'

Will shot him a reprimanding glance.

'It was only a joke . . . You know, Will, you're very serious.'

'This is serious.'

Andrew shrugged. In one sense, of course, Will was right.

Later, despite his claims in London, Andrew was the first to start snoring. Gaia curled up in a ball, like Dmitri. Will lay on his back, staring at the ceiling, waiting for the sleep that finally came.

At some point in the night, other people entered their compartment. Will had no idea when. He'd woken occasionally as the train shuddered to a stop in some town or other. Occasionally, he heard the bang of compartment doors being thrown open then slammed shut. Now, in the middle of the night, he felt the prod of a finger in his ribs.

Instantly, he was awake, his muscles contracted, ready for action . . . But what action? Sitting up, Will blinked at the person doing the prodding. It was a vast, amorphous woman, dressed in black. Her grey hair was cut short, a golden cross dangling over the expanse of her chest. She was smiling. With a coarse, plump hand, she indicated what she wanted: for Will to move up, to let her sit down.

'I'd move,' came Andrew's subdued voice, from the opposite seat. 'If you don't they just push you.'

Andrew's eyes were bloodshot, Will noticed. His skinny body was pressed up against the brown wall of the train, his legs crossed. Next to him was Gaia, her eyes closed. It wasn't Gaia who was doing the squishing. Squeezed in beside her were three men with tree-trunk legs, no necks and torsos that stretched the woollen fabric of their coats.

'This was supposed to be first class,' Andrew whispered.

'Where are we?' Will said. He clasped his rucksacks to his chest and took an upright position by the window.

'No idea.'

Will glanced at his watch: 3.15 a.m.

He could see nothing through the window, only the reflection of the people inside. One of the men was reading a newspaper. Three o'clock in the morning, and no one else seemed to mind. Only Andrew, and Will.

'This is torture,' Andrew said.

Will nodded.

'I do hope we'll be heading straight for the best hotel in St Petersburg.'

'Right. Because of course that's where Caspian will be going.'

Andrew groaned. 'Can't we bug him or something and follow him later – surely you've got a bug?'

'No.'

Andrew looked mildly incredulous. 'All that kit in the restaurant and no bug?'

'When I got up this morning, I didn't exactly know we'd be going to Russia. I didn't pack for a surveillance mission.'

'Well, you're one up on me because I didn't pack for anything,' said Andrew. 'If *I'd* known, I'd have brought a pillow. At least you've got the locust. And the other stuff.' Awkwardly, he tried to shift his body to gain just a little more comfort. 'Gaia's out of it,' he said. 'She's lucky.'

Will glanced at her face. She looked peaceful, he thought. He hadn't seen her peaceful before. Unhappy, excited, rueful, contemplative – but not peaceful. He sighed and closed his eyes. The fat of the woman next to him was enveloping his arm and his thigh. Her legs were apart, her arms folded broadly across her belly. But he had to get some sleep. Struggling slightly, he crossed his arms around the rucksacks, holding them tight.

The next time Will woke, the light was being switched on as someone else entered the compartment. The newspaper man was asleep, he noticed – he must have switched it off. Will's first thought was that there was no more room. But his second was more serious. This newcomer wasn't looking for a seat. He was asking, in what sounded like a language related to Russian, for papers.

This guard had an unpleasant face. He'd shaved badly and bristly tufts of black hair protruded from skin the shade of rancid milk. Sunk above the crooked nose, which clearly had been broken if not once then twice, were two raisiny black eyes. A wrinkled cigarette dangled from his mouth. It filled the compartment with dense smoke.

The other travellers were reacting, pulling passports

and documents from their pockets. Andrew's eyes were on the guard. Already, he was reaching in his pocket for the tickets. Gaia was awake now. She glanced at Will, an unspoken question in her eyes. *What do we do?* He shrugged imperceptibly.

'Come on! Hurry!' the guard said, or at least that was what Will guessed he meant as the fat woman beside him poked around with increased urgency in her small black bag.

'I've got an idea,' Andrew said. And he coughed as at last the woman found her papers and the guard threw them back at her, exhaling foul smoke right into Andrew's face.

Will watched, tense, as the guard flicked through the tickets. He threw them into Andrew's lap.

'Passport,' he said, in English, and waved his hand impatiently. 'Passport!'

'They Are With Our Mother,' Andrew said, loudly and distinctly. 'Down The Train.' And he pointed through the wall of the compartment.

'Mother?' said the guard.

Was it lucky or unlucky, Will wondered, that this man spoke a little English.

'Yes,' Gaia said quickly. 'Down The Train.'

'Our Mother Has Them,' Andrew continued. 'She Doesn't Like To Sit With Us.'

The guard's face blackened. He spoke rapidly in his own language, which produced a laugh from three of the other passengers. One of the hefty men beside Gaia leaned over and slapped Andrew on the thigh. 'Passport,' he said, firmly but not unkindly. 'Need passport.'

Andrew nervously pushed his glasses back up his nose, and at that moment, the guard's demeanour changed. He scanned the faces around him. What was he thinking?

Quickly, it became clear.

As Andrew had lifted his arm, the sleeve of his shirt had dropped a few inches, revealing his heavy gold watch. Now the guard leaned forward and grasped Andrew's wrist. With the other hand, he pulled the cigarette from his mouth.

'You give me this, I find your mother,' he whispered, with a harsh smile.

At once Will bent forward. But the guard let go of Andrew and with the flat of his hand shoved Will back. Will felt his body burn with anger.

'But our mother has them,' Gaia cried.

It was futile. Will could see that the guard didn't believe their unlikely story. Once again, the man's wiry fingers contracted around Andrew's wrist.

'Watch,' he said, distinctly.

Andrew glanced wildly at Will. 'What shall I do?'

'You give me watch and is all OK,' the guard was saying. 'You don't give me, maybe I have to take you inside for question. You get some other train. When we find passport.'

And Will's brain scrambled. As the guard was

preparing to flip open the catch himself, Will spoke, in Russian: 'You leave us alone, and I will not tell my father.'

His voice had been low. Distinct. With every atom of strength that he could muster. Will was aiming for anger rather than defiance. At once, the guard froze. Very slowly, he turned his head. Will glared back at him, feeling his chest strain. It was a good thing, he reflected, that the guard had understood.

'*Shto?* What?' the guard said in Russian, but he wasn't laughing.

This was all right, Will decided.

'If you do not leave now, I will tell my father about this. These are my friends. We go to school together, in London. But I know this station. My father has people in this town. He will find you.'

Now the guard glanced at the men sitting beside Gaia. He raised his eyebrows at them, for support. 'Your father?' he said. And he scoffed. 'Your father? And who exactly is your father?'

Will paused for effect. He might not have a photographic memory, but this name, from the newspaper he had read in the courtyard of Somerset House, had stuck. 'My father is Illyr Ruskin.'

It was a gamble. Would the guard even have heard of Illyr Ruskin? Ruskin might be a notorious mafia überboss, with an empire that spread from St Petersburg to London, but would a frontier guard in some remote train station in some unidentified country even know his name?

But at once, Will saw that the gamble had paid off. It was as though the temperature in the compartment dropped twenty degrees. The guard had heard of Illyr Ruskin. Moreover, to Will's secret astonishment, it appeared that he might even have believed him.

After a moment, the guard gave a short laugh. 'Illyr Ruskin!' he said, as though it was a joke. But no one else in the compartment was laughing. The tension gripped everyone like ice. Will could read in the guard's eyes that, with that laugh, he was trying it on. If he joked, would Will break?

Of course not. How could he?

Reluctantly, the guard let go of Andrew's wrist. It fell, like something inanimate, into Andrew's lap. The guard raised his arm and glanced at his own black plastic watch. He made a tutting noise. Perhaps, Will thought, he was pretending that he now realized the train was late. Without another word, he pushed between Andrew and Will and reached through the window to release the door. He stepped out on to the platform and slammed it shut. From somewhere beyond him in the murky darkness a whistle blew. A moment later, the engine heaved, and the seats creaked.

'How did you do that?' Andrew breathed, as the train pulled away.

'Who's Illyr Ruskin?' Gaia whispered.

'Mafia,' Will whispered back, his heart still racing. And he looked up.

The man with the newspaper was reaching into the luggage rack to grab a battered suitcase. A moment later, he left, only to be followed by the fat woman and another of the huge men. The last passenger – the one who had slapped Andrew on the leg – leaned over to them. His face was drawn. Swallowing, he prepared to speak.

'I hope,' he said, in Russian to Andrew, while glancing at Will, 'that when I touched you, you took no offence. I was trying only to help.'

As this man now left, Will translated.

Gaia faced Will, her eyes shining. 'They've all gone,' she said, grinning. 'They're all afraid.' And she shifted into the far corner of the bench seat from Andrew and stretched out. 'I can't believe it – thanks to your watch, Andrew, now we can sleep.'

'It wasn't my watch that did it,' Andrew said, smiling at Will, still slightly disbelieving. 'Though,' he added, 'as an inventor, I might have thought you'd use one of your *devices* to get us out of our spot.'

Will met his gaze. 'Sometimes your most valuable *device* is your brain.'

Grodno. Vilnius. Rezekne . . . The train stop-started its way east. Ever further away from home. Ever closer to St Petersburg, and the unknown.

At first, Will's sleep was dreamless. But as dawn broke, he woke suddenly, ears pounding with his blood. His fists were clenched, the left around a handful of his jumper, the right around the cricket ball in his pocket. That same old dream. It left him feeling confused.

What was there? After his father put on his boots and went outside, *what came next*?

'Bad dream?'

Gaia was lying on her side. Beside her, Andrew was fast asleep, snoring quietly. Through the window came the first early light. Pink and orange. A pale, rosy glow filled the compartment, turning Gaia's skin an unnatural colour. The light, and the regular motion of the train, made Will feel a little better.

'Yeah,' he said at last.

'What were you dreaming?'

He hesitated. He could tell her he didn't remember. That would be easiest. But he felt a peaceful sort of tired, too tired to lie. 'I was dreaming about my parents. I often have the same dream. I'm at home. Mum's reading at the table in the kitchen. Dad's putting on his boots. He's about to go outside to burn off rubbish in the garden. Then it stops. I always wake up.'

'It doesn't sound like a bad dream,' she said.

'No,' Will conceded. 'I think – I think maybe it's a memory and something happens next. But I don't know what it is.'

'Something bad?'

'Maybe.' Will pulled his hand from his pocket, leaving the cricket ball in place.

'Do you always carry that ball with you?'

He raised his head slightly, surprised. He hadn't realized anyone had noticed.

'I saw you with it at Andrew's house,' she said, as though she'd read his thoughts. 'Did your dad give it to you?'

'. . . Yes.'

There was a long silence. 'I used to have a gold chain that belonged to my mother,' she said eventually. 'After she died I wore it all the time. I never took it off.'

'What happened to it?' And Will felt bad for his curiosity, because she said:

'I lost it.' Now she met Will's gaze. 'I don't know how. It must have fallen off, and I didn't notice. I thought it was the end of the world. So the next week, I took all the things she'd left and I packed them up and got rid of them. I gave some to my aunt. I gave some to a charity shop. We'd been hoarding all these things, Dad and I, for *seven months.* And – he was really angry. At first. Then I think he thought I'd done the right thing.'

'You didn't keep anything at all?' Will said. And at the back of his mind, he realized that though it ought to feel strange talking to Gaia about this, about these things, it did not.

Gaia shook her head. 'I thought about my necklace when I saw your cricket ball. If I were you, I'd get rid of it. You think you're carrying your dad with you, but you're not. Not in a *thing,* anyway. And what if you lose it? You'll think you've lost your dad all over again but it'll be worse because it will be your fault, because you'll have lost him, but that won't be true. Really, Will, it won't. He isn't still with you in *things.*'

She'd spoken intently. Perhaps he might have felt anger, but he did not. Will turned on to his back. He gazed up at the roof, which was streaked with dirt, yellow and brown. Andrew stirred, and his breathing eased. A few moments later, the snoring resumed.

Will was thinking about what Gaia had said. There were so many questions he wanted to ask. When did your mother die? Is that when your dad started to drink? What did you do when your mother died . . . Did everything change? Was anything ever the same?

But he knew the answers to those last questions. Yes.

And, No. Nothing would be the same. A year ago, he was a child in Dorset, protected by his parents. And now?

'Have you managed to sleep much?' was all he said, at last, because he wanted to talk to her, but there was a limit to how much he could think or talk about those other things.

'. . . A little.' And she gave him an odd smile, slightly sad – because she'd misunderstood him – and she closed her brown eyes.

'Welcome in Petersburg!'

The old man was drunk. He spun a little, tripping on his laces as he stared up at the roof of Vitebski station.

'Can you still see him?' Gaia said.

They were pushing through the crowd. People jostled all around them. Will's nostrils were filled with peculiar scents. Body odour. Perfume. Damp fur. The stench of something hot and bitter from a brown paper bag. Ahead, through the bodies, was Caspian. Will's eyes were clasped on to his head, his gaze suckered to that boy. He pulled Andrew and Gaia in his wake.

'Wait!' Andrew called, his arm entangling with someone else's bag. But Will only yanked him on, hoisting the twin rucksacks further up his back.

Half past five in the afternoon. The train had arrived eight hours late. Now they entered the main concourse and the cold cut through them, snatching Will's breath.

'Wait,' Andrew was saying, 'I need to find my hat.' His words condensed, swirling around his face. Gaia had his hand, and she pulled him on behind Will, in the direction of the exit.

'*Come on,*' she said.

It was bewildering. Motion, and all that noise. Russian voices, loud and shrill, deep and ringing, solid as the frozen earth. If Will had let himself pay attention, he would have been thrown back through the years. To his grandfather's funeral. To all those memories, of his grandmother, and her flat, his mother, his father . . . But they'd followed Caspian as at last he'd disembarked from the train. And now Caspian was clutching his bag and striding towards the dimness outside, and a line of private cabs. For Will, the lethargy of the long journey had vanished the very instant the train had stopped. The chase was on.

'Come on,' Will urged. He broke into a jog. Caspian was nearing that line of waiting cars.

And then: '*Will!*'

Gaia's voice. From behind.

Will skidded to a halt. His head shot round. The scene drew all the breath out of him. Ten metres back, the drunk from the platform was clutching Andrew's collar. He seemed to be demanding money.

'Shake him off!' Will shouted. 'Andrew – run.'

And he heard Andrew's voice: 'My father is Illyr Ruskin! Do you hear me? Illyr Ruskin!'

Andrew's shouts had no effect on the drunk. But two policemen who'd been buying breakfast from a stall across the concourse turned sharply at the name.

Will glanced back over his shoulder. Caspian was talking to a driver.

'Andrew, *shut up and run*.'

Andrew tried. But the old man must have been stronger than he looked. Gaia threw herself on him and pulled at his arms. Now the two police officers were advancing.

It was useless. With one final, furious glance towards the taxi rank, Will turned away from Caspian, away from their quarry. He ran and he took the drunk's left arm, Gaia his right. Inch by inch, they pulled the gnarled hands from Andrew's collar. A stink of onions filled Will's nostrils.

The drunk reeled – right into the policemen, who grabbed him.

'Come on!' Will yelled. And his feet felt light as he dashed around bustling passengers, hearing the shouts of the drunk. They had to escape now. They'd lost Caspian. But they had to find a cab.

Will threw himself into the first car, a battered grey Audi, and slammed the door shut. Gaia and Andrew leaped in behind. A rapid glance showed the policemen were pushing their way after them, through the crowd, and Will demanded:

'Vasilevsky Ostrov. Maly Prospect.'

To his relief, the elderly driver did not hesitate. As the car pulled out, Will did not look back.

'I'm sorry,' Andrew said. His voice was breaking, collapsed with nerves. '. . . I'm sorry.'

'It's all right,' Will said.

He tried to sound upbeat, but his spirits were suddenly rock-bottom.

St Petersburg was a city of more than four million people. They had about as much chance of finding Caspian as Andrew had of curing AIDS. All that work, all that care not to be seen, to keep track of Caspian, all those hours on the train – and for what? One drunk to ruin everything. One unlucky moment, and *everything* had changed.

'Will, where are we going?' Gaia said.

Will focused on the blocks of Nevsky Prospect. Under harsh streetlights, solid men strode by in black leather jackets, women in elegant white coats, some in furs. Ahead was the river. Past that, St Basil's Island. Things had changed so quickly, he hardly knew how to think. All those hours. All that anticipation, held in check. They'd been in limbo on the train. In suspended animation. Now they'd woken to a world that was shifting away beneath them.

'I know someone here,' Will said at last. 'Maybe they can help.'

'It's me. I have to be quick.'

'Where are you?'

The young man stared out at the view from his cab. He felt tired, frozen and dirty. His clothes itched. He hadn't washed for two days and hadn't slept for what felt like eight. For the past forty-eight hours he'd been on duty, constantly vigilant, afraid his target might alight at any one of the endless stops the train had made through that long day and nights.

But the excitement of the chase kept his eyes open, and his pulse racing. He managed a smile at the grey concrete and slush.

'St Petersburg,' he replied.

'*Petersburg* . . . Really? That's interesting,' came the voice, assured and distinct. It announced a decision. 'I'm going to join you. Stay on him.'

What else? thought the man, but he only flipped his phone shut.

'Wow.' Andrew stood as if struck, staring up open-mouthed at the apartment block.

The dead tone of his voice gave his opinion away. Will couldn't blame him. Here they were, on Maly Prospect, and outside the block that his grandmother called home.

It was grim. The building was old, and once would have been grand. Now it looked as blank and impenetrable as the grey sky above them. Broken glass littered the pavement and was scattered on to the busy road, beneath three dilapidated cars. Two were missing wheels. Beneath the third was a heavy rusting chain and a filthy tabby cat.

Five years ago, it had seemed as bad, Will thought. But the misery of the scene had at least reflected the emotion he'd been feeling. Now he looked up at the fifth-floor window, with its cracks and bars, and he felt disgusted that his grandmother should live in a place like this. But then his mother sent her plenty of money

– he himself had seen the cheques. If his grandmother wanted to, she could move. Following fast after these thoughts came twin surges of hope and fear.

Would his mother be there? Will hoped so with all his heart. But he was also afraid. What if she were, and she didn't want to see him? What if she were, and she told him she would never come back?

Perhaps Gaia had a sense of what he was thinking, because she touched him gently on the arm. 'Come on,' she said. 'We have to go in.'

'Yes,' Andrew agreed. 'Before we get mugged.'

Will caught the sympathetic glance she shot him.

'I don't see any muggers,' she said.

'What about him?' Andrew said, and he jerked his head at a man walking towards them, a bottle of beer in his hand. Andrew kicked at the pavement with his boot. It rang. 6.30 p.m., local time, and the air was bitter.

'I think,' Gaia said, 'that we'd better go in. Will?'

She was right, of course. And yet Will's feet, as he forced them to move, felt bound to the frozen ground. He wanted to see his mother. He was afraid of seeing her.

Again, Gaia touched his arm, but this time she wound hers through it and pulled him gently. 'Caspian,' she said, her breath clouding and freezing in her hair. 'Remember – we have to find him.'

Caspian. The name shocked Will out of his thoughts.

He looked up. A woman in heavy boots and a thick

scarf was emerging from the solid steel front door. Ducking forward, Will caught it before it shut. He led the way into the stairwell, which was covered in green and blue graffiti and stank of urine.

'Come on,' he whispered. 'And don't talk on the way up. If anyone hears you speaking English they'll come out to find out who we are – and we probably don't want that.'

'Why not?' Andrew said cautiously.

'Look around. This area isn't exactly Bloomsbury.'

Will shot up the broad staircase, through stale, freezing air, to the first apartment on the right on the fifth floor. This was the one, he was sure of it. There was a bristly welcome mat on the peeling lino outside. An iron gate. And behind that a red door, a curling sticker of a posy of flowers just below the spyhole. He couldn't forget something like that.

The first knock sounded weak. Annoyed with himself, Will banged hard, three loud raps. From inside he could hear a piano. Played badly, he noticed. The notes were falling all over each other.

'Perhaps she isn't in,' Andrew said. And he glanced nervously behind him. This was about as far from his home as he could imagine. 'We could go to a hotel—'

'—Perhaps she can't hear,' Gaia said. And she reached out, to knock again. At that moment, the door opened. Gaia had to lean on Will to steady herself. She backed off quickly. But Will hadn't noticed. The old woman who answered had thrown a plump hand to her mouth. She fumbled with the lock to the gate, then clasped Will to her body in a ferocious embrace.

Feeling uncomfortable, Gaia glanced at Andrew as the woman kissed Will repeatedly.

She smelt exactly as he remembered her. Dried flowers and washing powder.

'William! William! God in heaven, what are you doing here? And now look, you have made me cry.'

Elena dabbed at her face with her skirt, smearing tears into her wrinkles and revealing her stout legs. Silver hair tumbled down around her shoulders. She had given Will's mother her eyes, black and sparkling. And the neat shape of her face, with her pronounced cheekbones and broad mouth.

'And look, you have brought these two young people,' she said in clear, crisp English. 'Welcome, please, come in, come in!'

Elena stepped back into the narrow violet-painted hall, colliding with a hatstand. Andrew managed to grab it before the coats could pile to the floor.

'Well, thank you very much indeed—?'

'Andrew,' he said, a little embarrassed. He held out a hand, but the old lady grabbed him too and held him tight.

'And this is Gaia,' Will said. But already he was heading down the hall. He passed the two bedrooms, and entered the bright lounge, his mind on other things. Specifically, on the piano music that cascaded through the open door of the little parlour beyond.

Now the voices behind him faded into the background. The colours in the room fell away. He heard nothing but the notes, and his heart, which pounded.

In a moment, he was in the parlour.

There was the piano. But – there was no one playing it.

Will stared stupidly at the instrument. It had been modified by Elena's friend, Vanya. Elena had switched the controls to 'auto', and the keys were moving, playing 'Russia Beneath the Yoke of the Mongols', without the need for fingers. A gimmick, Will thought. Like one of the pianos you sometimes saw in department stores . . . A *gimmick*.

'My mother,' he said, involuntarily. And his grandmother appeared behind him. She filled the doorway with her bulk.

'. . . Your mother, *dorogoi moi*?

'She isn't here?'

Elena frowned. 'Here? No, William, of course she isn't here.'

Her confusion revealed the truth of her words. But Will could only grasp at her meaning.

'She's gone out? To a shop?'

'Shopping? No. Your mother isn't here, she hasn't been here since your dear grandfather's funeral. I haven't laid eyes on your mother in five years!'

Elena had spoken softly. Yet the words boomed like cannonballs in Will's brain. They shattered his thoughts.

She wasn't here . . . And *yet* . . . Natalia had told him . . . She, his mother, had told him *herself* . . .

Will felt all his energy flood from his body. It was as though he'd suddenly been earthed.

'Come, sit down, *dorogoi moi*,' his grandmother said. 'Let's talk about this.'

Five minutes later, Will, Gaia and Andrew were sandwiched together on Elena's old rose-patterned sofa. Elena had insisted on bringing out the piano stool for herself. She said it was good for her back. She had brewed strong-tasting tea in her singing stove-top kettle and turned up the oil heaters, so that the room was now bearably cold. Still, Andrew shivered. The condensation dripping down the small windows made him feel thoroughly chilled. Will did not notice.

Five minutes of discussion had not really clarified the situation. The last time Elena had heard from her daughter was when Will's father died. Then – nothing. On the phone from Dorset, she had told Elena she needed some time to herself, and she was going away.

'Of course, I worried about you, *dorogoi moi*, but then I knew your mother would make sure you were all right. You are the most precious thing in the world to her. It goes without saying,' Elena said.

Will wasn't so sure.

The world, he decided, was cracking around him. Not only had they lost Caspian, but his mother, who he'd felt sure would be able to help them find him, was absent. AWOL. She had lied. *And lied.* But why?

His anger edged into fear. It was unlike her. And if she wasn't with her own mother, then where was she? What if she was hurt? What if someone had harmed her . . . ? But then she had planned her own deceitful departure. As she had driven to Natalia's house, she had told him again: 'I just need to be with my mother for a little while. I won't be away for long, I promise.'

'You know what I think?' Elena said, as she poured another cup of tea. 'Your mother loved your father with all the passion in the world. I think she needed time on her own – afterwards. She always was headstrong. It's the only explanation I can think of. I am sure I am right. Now my dear, tell me, is that why you came? To try to find your mother?'

Will glanced at Gaia and at Andrew. '. . . No,' he said. 'We need to find someone else. Elena, you were a scientist. Maybe you'll understand. I need to talk to you about space.'

It would be a gamble, Will decided, to tell his grandmother. She might insist on going to the police. Or tell him he was crazy and book them all on the next plane back to London.

Instead, as Will, Gaia and Andrew took it in turns to describe their visit to the laboratory of Vassily Baraban, she only nodded. The cosy expression she had been wearing vanished. In its place, her intelligence shone out.

'So you have heard of Vassily Baraban?' Andrew said.

'Of course! My dear, who in Russia has not heard of him? There was disgrace. Trouble with strangelets.'

'Strangelets?' Andrew said.

'Clusters of quarks and strange quarks – particles that make up an atom,' Elena said. 'It is thought these clusters were created in the Big Bang, when the universe came into being. And, without doubt, they are strange. Just one fragment, the size of a grain of pollen, could weigh several tons, and it could travel at one million miles an hour. In 1993, there was an explosion that started in the Pacific and travelled right through the Earth. It appeared in Antarctica *nineteen seconds* later. There are some who believe this was caused by an impact of cosmic strangelets. And you can see strangelets in equipment that accelerates particles to unbelievable speeds, then smashes them together.'

Will glanced at Andrew and Gaia. From their startled expressions, it was clear they were thinking the same thing. The notes in Baraban's lab had appeared to describe a particle collider – twin tunnels that could speed ions along.

'So you can *make* strangelets in a particle collider?' Gaia breathed.

'Yes, my dear . . .' Elena looked troubled. 'So you say Vassily Baraban was abducted – but you don't know who took him?'

Will nodded.

'And this friend of yours, this boy, you think he has come up with a way to take out a *hotel* in space.'

'Yes,' Will said.

'With a laser, perhaps?'

'We don't think so,' Andrew said, glancing at Will. 'At least, we're not sure. But the email talked about launching something. We think it's a new type of weapon. Caspian described two tunnels – perhaps a particle collider. Could it be—' And he hesitated. 'Could you make a weapon with strangelets?'

Elena raised an eyebrow. 'Highly unlikely.'

'But not impossible,' Andrew persisted.

'Who is to say what is impossible.'

Again, Andrew glanced at Will. Will's expression had clouded over. Suddenly, he seemed to be a million miles away. 'Whatever it is, we do really need to find Caspian,' Andrew continued. 'If they're going to launch something, of course they'll need a launch site – and a laboratory – and enough space for the accelerator tunnels.'

'If the collider really is part of the weapon,' Gaia said.

'I think for the moment we have to assume it is.' Andrew turned back to Elena. 'This complex would be vast. There can't be many likely sites. Do you have any idea where it might be?'

'In Petersburg?' The old lady threw up her hands. 'I don't know, but I can make some calls. I have a friend, Vanya. He knows people. Perhaps he will have some idea.'

Will frowned. 'I thought your phone was disconnected.'

'Disconnected! No, my dear – of course not!'

Elena went through to the telephone in the parlour. Will stood up, trying to peer through the window, but he could see only the reflected faces of Andrew and Gaia, the rose-patterned sofa, the violent paint on the walls. Every step forward, it seemed, he was blocked. Where was Caspian? Where was his mother . . . ? She had told him to call only on her mobile. His grandmother's phone line needed repairing, she had said, so there was no point in her giving him the number. Will could still hear her voice. *Lying*. Suddenly, he felt weary. And trapped.

'I have to go out,' he said bluntly.

Andrew's head shot up from his smart phone. He'd been in the process of Googling 'strangelets'. 'Where?'

'Just out,' Will said.

'But your grandmother—' Gaia protested.

'I won't be long. The news will be the same when I get back.'

He didn't look at her, didn't look at Andrew. He needed to get out of that stuffy room packed with his family, with the past. He needed to walk.

'What's wrong with him?' Andrew whispered, when Will had gone.

'What do you think? He expected to find his mother,' Gaia said quietly.

Two minutes later, Elena reappeared. She held up her hands to deflect questions. 'Vanya is contacting friends who might know. He will call me straight back. Where is Will?'

'. . . He went for a walk,' Andrew said.

Will's strides were rapid. He wanted to get back to Elena – wanted to know if her friend had any clues to the location of Caspian Baraban – but first he needed to clear his head.

He glanced up. The sky was murky, sinister black. Even in their boots, his feet were cold. He could feel the chill spreading, like ice, up his legs. Ahead, the warm light of a shop caught his eye. He glanced down into the basement. And he saw sales women in pink aprons, vegetables still half-covered in earth, unappetizing slabs of meat.

Will walked on, eyes now on the pavement, feet moving automatically, almost without his control. He thought of his mother. It was impossible not to. Was she out in this, he wondered. In *this* world?

She had to be. But *where – exactly*? Had she come here because this was her birthplace? A city that was hers, barely shared with his father – so here she could escape when in England she could not? But why avoid her own mother? Why come to St Petersburg and hide out on her own?

And Caspian. Where was he? Was the equipment ready and waiting? Was Caspian already in some lab, his finger on the trigger . . . ? But of *what*? And *why*?

'Hey!'

Will's body clenched. Two young men in trench coats had stumbled into him. Muscled fingers with rings clasped around Will's coat. Will cursed himself. He hadn't been paying attention to the street. Now the men seared Will's face with their aggressive gaze. And their hands crept lower, to Will's pocket.

Andrew sat at Elena's polished dining table, his smart phone in front of him. A muffled argument emanated through the wall from the flat next door, and Andrew did his best to ignore it.

He was impatient for news from Vanya but the discussion about strangelets had got him thinking. Identifying Caspian's location would be only the first step. To have any hope of stopping the weapon, they'd have to have at least a clue to its identity.

Elena might have been some use, Andrew thought, but she'd protested ignorance. She'd been an expert on the physics of fluids, she said – not the Big Bang, or the more outlandish stuff.

The *Big Bang*, he thought. He'd seen those words on the paper in Baraban's lab. And Caspian was talking about a particle collider. The notes had been clear on that.

Of course, particle colliders were used by reputable scientists to probe the origins of the universe. To try to recreate the conditions immediately after the Big Bang, and to try to make various physics theories make a little more sense. Caspian was a brilliant theoretical physicist. He'd know about all these experiments . . . And Andrew sighed.

He'd known Caspian for eight years. He didn't know him well. But he knew enough to realize that Caspian's enthusiasm about STORM was genuine. He'd wanted to use his genius to benefit mankind, not to kill people. Caspian loved his father, Andrew knew that, but was that why he was working on a new type of weapon?

Possibly. Certainly grave threats would have been needed to force Caspian to such a betrayal of his own beliefs. Unless . . .

If the science was exciting enough, if it became a game that pitted his genius against a fundamental problem . . . Yes, he could believe that Caspian might get carried away by his own brilliance. Enough to kill people? Perhaps. If he wasn't the one that had to pull the trigger.

So what are you planning? Andrew thought. He scoured his brain. Somehow, he had to find some answers . . . The equations tumbled through his mind. What was Caspian thinking? What was he *missing*?

And Andrew raked a hand through his hair. He'd tried brute thought on the train, and it hadn't worked. Why should it now? *Calm down,* he told himself. If your conscious can't handle it, let your subconscious take over.

Sighing, Andrew glanced at his watch. He could hear Gaia and Elena talking in the kitchen. And he realized with a start that Will had left more than half an hour ago.

So where was he?

Andrew's back stiffened.

What if . . . What if Will had seen Caspian?

What if someone else had seen Will? Someone who might want to abduct him?

What am I doing here, Andrew thought, at a dining table in a flat with an old lady.

Then another thought struck him. What if Will had decided to go off on his own? Will might have found a clue. Why should he come back for him, or for Gaia?

And Andrew shook his head. They were a team. *His* team. Because STORM was his idea. If Will had gone off without him, he'd remind him of this.

And Andrew slung off his glasses and pressed his hands to his eyes. He was ashamed of his own thoughts. He was misinterpreting his anxiety about Will's long absence and his frustration with the weapon as anger, he decided. The flush of blood to his head, the prickling sweat on his palms. The signals of emotion. But *which* emotion was, to some extent, up to you. He knew this because his own father had told him.

Andrew jumped suddenly. The phone was ringing. He watched Elena hustle through to the parlour. And he went into the kitchen, to find Gaia. She was standing at the window, trying in vain to see out.

'Vanya,' he said.

She didn't turn. 'I hope so.'

'. . . Will's been gone quite a while. Do you think he's all right?'

'Of course,' she said quickly.

Andrew nodded. Of course. Yes, of course he *should* be all right.

And anxiety Gaia had kept in check was released. It coursed through her bloodstream, infecting her thinking. She'd been talking to Elena, but it had been automatic. She'd been thinking about Caspian. The weapon. And then Will.

Half an hour, that was all. *Half an hour* – plenty of time for something to happen. And it seemed strange, suddenly, to be without Will.

'I've been thinking about the Big Bang,' Andrew ventured.

'I see,' Gaia said. Her voice was curt, clipped.

'We really need to think about this weapon.'

'I thought we'd tried.'

Andrew sighed again. In a voice he'd intended to sound more convincing, he said, 'Look, you said it: of course he'll be all right.'

And then:

Bang. And again. Unmistakable. Bone on wood.

Gaia almost ran into the hall.

'*Where have you been?*'

She threw the door open so hard it scraped the paint off the wall.

The relief on her face touched Will. Though he didn't know that at least half of that relief was for herself. In truth, she'd shared some of Andrew's secret thoughts. Will hadn't gone off without them.

'I needed to get out,' he said.

'So you feel better now?' Gaia demanded, her voice on edge.

Will nodded. The walk, and the adrenalin of his encounter with the two men, had cleared his head. His angry shouts, and the attention they'd attracted, had scared off his would-be muggers. And he'd headed back to Maly Prospect, his heart pumping, his blood coursing. He would put his mother to the back of his mind. He had to.

'Where's Elena—' he started. And his grandmother appeared, a look of triumph on her face.

'Vanya says he has news. He's coming here.'

'What news? *When?*' Andrew said.

'Any moment, *dorogoi moi*! He called from the car. He said he wants to meet you all and he wants to tell you in person.'

'But we have no time,' Will said. 'Can't you call him back – we can talk to him now.'

'It will do no good,' Elena said. 'I know Vanya very well. He is as single-minded and stubborn as you. Besides—'

And she was interrupted, by a loud knocking on the door.

The first thing Will noticed about Vanya was his immense size. And then his delicate outstretched hand. It looked all wrong, that hand, stuck on the end of a massive arm, which itself was attached to a slab of a body.

Vanya wore heavy brown hiking boots with fraying laces. Above those were jeans of a bright, almost luminous blue. When his quilted coat and bulging satchel had been cast aside, Will took in the dirty check of his oversized lumberjack shirt. Open at the neck, it revealed a jutting collarbone and an Adam's apple the size of an apricot. His face was equally as striking. Huge red-veined cheeks, a bulbous nose, and eyes half-closed, as though he was sizing up the world and wasn't impressed with what he found.

'He has the look of you,' Vanya said, as he grasped Will's shoulder. 'What do you think, Elena? No one could mistake the grandson.'

Will shook himself free. He noticed, as he did so, a

sudden twitch distort the pocket of Vanya's shirt. Could it have been a muscle?

'So!' Vanya clapped his hands. 'You ask questions. I bring answers!'

Elena glanced at Will and smiled faintly. 'I told you,' she said. 'Vanya knows everyone.'

'I know the right people,' he corrected. 'It makes all the difference.' He collapsed heavily on the sofa, and Andrew dragged chairs from the dining table so everyone else could sit.

'So what can you tell us?' Will asked.

'Well, first I have a few questions,' Vanya said.

'What questions?' Gaia asked.

'You have come all this way – from London? You have trailed this friend? And you think he is making a new type of weapon.'

'We *know* it,' Andrew said flatly.

'And you followed him without him noticing you?'

Andrew glanced at Will. Frustration made him want to shout. But perhaps it would be better to humour Vanya than to protest. Andrew could see that Vanya was not the sort to be pushed.

'Will has this flying robot that sends back video,' Andrew started. 'It's called Fly Spy. It's based on a locust—'

'Yes,' Will interrupted. 'Without him seeing us.'

'A flying robot?' Vanya said, one eyebrow raised. He looked disbelieving.

'He made it,' Gaia said quietly. 'And other things –

like an ultrasound microphone for sending secret voice messages. And a device that lets you abseil up buildings.'

'Or whatever the reverse of *abseil* actually is,' Andrew said quickly. 'We call Will *The Maker.*'

Will glowered at them. 'Don't call me that.' He wished they would be quiet.

Vanya looked at Elena, who shrugged slightly. 'Vanya, you know, is not too bad when it comes to inventions,' she put in. 'And in his pocket right now—'

Will ignored her. Didn't they understand the urgency? Past Vanya's hulking body, past the lights of the living room, was Caspian. And Caspian's father. And the Infinity Code. He faced Vanya.

'Look, what can you tell us about a launch site?'

'Ha!' A sharp laugh. Twin red spots of irritation appeared on Vanya's cheeks. 'So you have had enough of getting to know each other?'

Elena frowned. Will was right. '. . . Come, Vanya,' she said. 'They are tired. They have travelled a long way. I have made you sound good. So tell them.'

Vanya snorted. 'Well, there are a few possibilities. First, tell me what you think this weapon might be.'

'We *don't know,*' Andrew said quickly. 'But they want to launch it. And they might have a particle collider. So there has to be room for those tunnels. Like we said.' And he glanced at Elena. Could Vanya really be any help?

Vanya nodded. For a few long moments, he said

nothing. Then at last he spoke: 'I have been talking to a friend, Ivan. He is a spy – at least he used to be. He says there is a facility, twenty-five kilometres from here, outside the city. It is owned by a private satellite company – or at least that is what they say they are. It is surrounded by electrified fences. There are dogs, armed guards. There are large hangars, a launch facility, even a helicopter pad. There is little traffic by road. Helicopters come in, sometimes trucks. No one has much idea what is going on there – it is private and it is well guarded. But there is the space there, and there has been the activity. If there is a particle collider and a launch site close to the city, it could be here. This is the best bet.'

Will felt relief as a little of the tension flowed from his body. So a likely site did exist. Caspian would be there. He'd have to be.

'Your friend is a spy?' Gaia said.

'*Retired*,' Vanya stressed. 'But he keeps an interest, shall we say. Once you are used to playing a part in the world it is not easy to step down.'

'So you know exactly where this facility is?' Andrew said.

Vanya nodded.

'And there's still activity?'

'I told you. A few trucks come and go. There are helicopters. A food van.'

Gaia looked up sharply. 'This food van – how often does it visit?'

Vanya shrugged. 'I don't know.'

'We can find out, exactly? Would Ivan know?'

'Yes, but why? What good will that do?'

'. . . Somehow, we have to get inside that base,' Will said.

His meaning wasn't lost on Vanya.

'This is a very serious business,' Vanya said at once. 'I told you: there are electric fences, there are dogs. Ivan says two men wandered by late one night, they were drunk. The next morning their bodies were found. What are you saying: you want to try to get in? You children?' He looked at Gaia. 'You are a girl!'

'Unbelievable,' Elena said. 'Sometimes, Vanya Davydenko, I do not understand why we are friends.'

'So you support this, then Elena? It sounds to you like a good idea?' Vanya cried. His face flickered, changing shades like a cuttlefish. His skin settled on a blotch of red and white.

Why do you think we asked for the information? Will thought. Why do you think we wanted to find its location?

'*Oh God,*' said Andrew. His mouth fell open. Blood drained from his face.

Will and Gaia turned to him in alarm. 'Andrew?' Will said.

'Oh God,' he said again.

Gaia was closest. She reached out, grabbed his arm. 'Andrew? *What?*' she said urgently.

'I've been so stupid. I've been so stupid!'

'*What are you talking about?*' Gaia cried.

'I know,' Andrew answered at last. 'I know what the weapon is . . . I know what they're going to do!'

Andrew dashed to the dining table. He grabbed his smart phone, shoved it in his pocket. The notes were all in there. All he could remember of Caspian's equations, all his thoughts, all his attempts at an explanation.

'I missed it,' he said. And his eyes shot to Will. 'I didn't think anyone would dare. A particle accelerator. Two beams of stripped-down gold atoms . . . Caspian even made reference to it – the night of the solar flares. He knew by then, of course, that his father had been taken.'

'Andrew—' Will's voice. 'Take it slowly. What are they going to do?'

'Of course he couldn't know we'd be coming after him. I mean, he didn't say it explicitly, but—'

'Andrew.' Gaia now.

'Gold ions,' Andrew was saying. 'I can't believe I didn't think—'

'*What?*' Gaia demanded.

'What is he saying?' Vanya whispered.

'Shh,' Elena insisted.

'He was talking about the Big Bang,' Andrew said. 'He was asking if I thought we'd ever see its like again – the moment of creation – of matter and anti-matter. The ferocious energy, and all that came after. Planets and suns – vast suns that burn out and collapse. That exert such a pull of gravity that nothing can escape them.' And he paused. '*Not even light.*'

Gaia froze. It felt as though her heart had stopped beating. She was suspended for that second, that fragment of time.

Then two words pulsed in her brain, as they did in Elena's and Andrew's and Will's. Even Vanya's.

It was Will who spoke them, his voice awed:

'A *black hole.*'

A black hole.

Like so many of the pages of her textbooks, the words, the diagrams, the photographs of her physics books were stashed away in Gaia's mind. So too were her old notes:

A black hole. A theoretical region of space-time from which nothing can escape. Not even light. Where the event horizon concentrates an infinite amount of energy into a finite volume. Probably common in the universe. Even thought likely at the heart of our own Milky Way. In theory, usually formed by the collapse of a neutron star . . .

Here her notes ended and her thinking began.

'In theory,' Andrew was saying, 'yes, you could make one in the lab. In a particle collider – by smashing together heavy ions at colossal speed. I didn't even think of it – not a black hole . . .'

'The Infinity Code,' Will said. 'That's what the name means. But if he made one . . .'

'If he made one in the lab, it would be small,' Elena breathed, and a frown split her wrinkled forehead. 'I was not an astrophysicist – but if they make one it will be too small to do any damage? The mass will be tiny – and Hawking Radiation – it will evaporate?'

She glanced at Vanya, who only shrugged.

Andrew shook his head. 'Hawking Radiation is theory – what if it doesn't exist? And what if this code is not for how to create simply a black hole, but for how to create many and to form them into one black hole, which becomes stable – and dangerous.'

'But if someone thinks they could launch a black hole somehow, so that it destroys the hotel, they are insane,' Will said.

Gaia nodded. 'It might destroy the lab.'

'It could destroy *Earth*,' Will said, quietly.

Elena took a deep breath. 'If they create a black hole in a lab, there is a chance it could tunnel into the centre of our planet – and yes, destroy it. Perhaps it *eats* Earth. Perhaps it blows it apart.' She shook her head.

'You really think this?' Vanya said, his voice low. 'You really think your friends are planning something that could destroy us all?'

If this was right, Will thought – if this was really the plan – then the answer to Vanya's question was 'yes': it wasn't just everyone on that space hotel who was threatened with death. It was everyone. Full stop. Who could seriously want this? And how could Vassily Baraban be so reckless? How could Caspian be so *insane*?

'Vassily Baraban – he is the only one who would do it,' Elena was saying. 'No one else. No one with ethics.'

'But Vassily Baraban isn't behind this,' Andrew said. 'He was abducted, remember – someone's forcing him to do it.'

'And forcing his son?' Elena asked.

Will shook his head. 'Caspian left of his own free will.'

'I doubt it,' Andrew said quickly. 'He would have been forced – there would have been threats. Caspian is not an evil person.'

'But he's creating a code that he thinks will kill eight people – and even threaten *Earth*.'

Andrew couldn't argue with the facts.

'So now what?' Gaia said.

'Nothing changes,' Will said. 'We have to stop it. We have to go in.'

'You cannot!' Vanya cried. 'Elena, tell them – they cannot go there!'

'Why not?' Elena said. 'Our world is at risk. What is more important?'

'It is ludicrous! You cannot possibly think it acceptable for three children to go to that base alone?'

'Whoever said they should go there alone? They can go there with us.'

Vanya stared at her. A blue vein pulsed in his temple. 'We are old, Elena. Look at us!'

She shrugged. 'If our old bodies mean we cannot go with them all the way, at least we can help. I have had more time, Vanya, to think about this. When it was a space hotel, with eight people at risk, I thought – this is my grandson. I will help him, and then perhaps we go to the authorities with what we think. But now? Our world, Vanya! Everyone we love! You know as well as I what the authorities will do! This is private property, and we have no hard proof. They will take too much time!'

'*O, chert!*' Vanya glared at Elena, and at Gaia and Andrew, and then at Will, who did not avert his gaze. 'You are sure of all that you have said? This is no practical joke – you are serious?'

'Will is always serious,' Andrew said.

'And you?'

'I swear my life on it.'

'Confound it,' Vanya said. 'Then no more delays. What we need is a plan.'

*

Vanya phoned his friend Ivan at once. Ivan agreed to email over all the photographs he possessed. And they were in luck. The next food delivery would take place at half past ten that night. Which meant they had two hours for preparations then half an hour to get into position to await the van's arrival at the base.

With this detail confirmed, Elena took the phone from Vanya. She set about making a rough plan of the base and its defences, from Ivan's memory.

'Two guards at the gates,' Elena was saying, the phone at her ear. 'One on the roof of the western hangar. Four more patrol the perimeter fence. Four dogs, at least. The food van is always checked before entering the gates. Then it drives to the west, into an unloading depot – and then the doors are closed behind it. Ivan does not know what happens next . . .'

Meanwhile, in the kitchen, Gaia was busy with her own preparations.

At heart, their plan was simple: at all costs, to prevent what would be a hugely dangerous experiment. They would go in tonight. They would collect video footage of the base. And they would sabotage the equipment, to prevent any immediate plan to create a black hole. Then, first thing in the morning, they would take their footage to friends of Vanya. These friends, he said, had their own friends in 'very high places'. One way or another, the base would be shut down.

For tonight, Gaia knew exactly what she wanted.

And all she really needed was kept under the stained ceramic kitchen sink. Andrew was her assistant, finding and measuring. He opened the bottle of hydrogen peroxide and pinched his nose shut. 'What exactly are we creating?'

'. . . Triacetone triperoxide.'

'Which is?'

'Extremely dangerous.'

'. . . But not to us.'

'Not unless you drop it.'

'Then what?'

'It's shock sensitive. Explosive. And highly flammable.'

'Where did you learn to make this? Not in school?'

'Well, I did some experiments in school.' And she smiled slightly. No one had been hurt. 'When it's ready, don't drop it. It'll take quite a hit to make it go off, but don't risk it.'

'I think perhaps you should look after it,' he said.

She nodded. And she noticed the tense expression on Andrew's face. 'Are you OK?'

'. . . I should have thought of a black hole earlier,' he said. 'I didn't even consider it—'

'None of us did. And if you had, what would we have done differently? We followed Caspian, we made it to St Petersburg. We are going in tonight. If we'd known in London what we know now, nothing would be different.' She paused. 'I'm sure Will feels the same way.'

'Who knows what goes through his brain.' And Andrew bit his lip. 'I mean – I suppose so. He's logical. Your reasoning is logical. It's what he'll be thinking.'

'Everything all right?' Elena poked her head around the door.

Andrew nodded. 'Though I wouldn't recommend any sudden movements. Not if you want to live.'

Elena sniffed the air. 'You are making triacetone triperoxide? A neat little compound. But have you seen Vanya's car, my dear? It feels every bump, let me put it that way. The shock absorbers gave up in 1982.'

Outside, Will and Vanya were loading up Vanya's green Lada. They didn't need much – but Vanya wanted food and water, as well as a little bottle of vodka, 'for courage'. Plus a couple of tarpaulins in case it rained hard and the roof leaked, Will's grandfather's old night-vision binoculars, his Kevlar jacket, and cricket bat – 'for protection'. Vanya was going over the top, Will thought. But at least now he was enthusiastic, and he was going to take them to the base. Will wasn't going to criticize him.

Snow was falling heavily. It obscured the apartment block, blotted out the moon. All around them were the noises of the street. Badly tuned car engines. Heels clacking on the pavement through the snow. Men shouting in the distance. Hard to tell, Will thought, if the voices were happy or angry.

Within a minute, Will's fingers were feeling numb. He clenched them. It made no difference. But he could ignore the cold, he thought. His mind should be concentrating on one thing only: on the base, with its particle collider, and what they could do to stop it.

Will deposited his two rucksacks on the back seat and scrunched up his nose. The Lada smelt of cigarette smoke and decomposing rubber.

'Hey!' Gaia was hurrying towards them. She'd left her coat behind and snow settled on her jumper and in her hair. 'Where can I stash this?'

'What is it?' Will said.

'The explosive. I've made it into a sash. I can wear it over my shoulder. Don't worry, it's stabilized. It'll need a hard jolt to set it off.'

'What if you drop it?'

'I won't,' she said, as she opened the rear door and placed her parcel behind Will's rucksacks. Gaia slammed the door and Vanya and Will jumped.

'*Ty chto, s uma soshla?* Are you out of your mind? There is explosive and you slam the door like that!'

'I'm going to make some shock-absorbing fluid,' Gaia said, ignoring his comment, and she started to hurry back to the warmth.

'What do you mean, *make* the fluid?' Vanya called.

Gaia glanced back. 'Starch and olive oil.'

Vanya shook his head. 'You are wrong, girl, that won't work at all. It will be slippery. What good will it do?'

'Not much,' she said. And Vanya raised his eyebrows

at Will. 'Until you pass several thousand volts through it. That fixes it rather nicely.'

Her words made Will smile. She smiled back.

'Well – and where will you find such a current?' Vanya cried.

Gaia glanced again at Will. It was true, she had yet to identify a suitable source. Will thought for a moment. He could always use the TV. Then he remembered the gas grill igniter for his grandmother's oven. These sorts of lighters contained a piezoelectric element. Depress the button, and the bar strikes the element to generate a spark to ignite the gas. In doing so, it produces several thousand volts at a couple of terminals. Enough for Gaia's fluid.

'The oven lighter,' he said, smiling slightly at Vanya.

Will followed Gaia back upstairs. They had only half an hour and still he had to make a timer for her explosives. But, if you knew where to look, the kitchen was a rich source of parts. The broken microwave was a treasure trove.

With an Anglepoise light illuminating the microwave's dusty guts, Will carefully extracted the keypad. A perfect electronic timer. Once the lighter had done its job on the shock-absorbing fluid, he could use the piezoelectric element for the trigger. And he paused for a moment, remembering the long summer evenings he had spent with his mother in their workshop, dismembering microwaves and old computer monitors.

'Will?' His grandmother's voice. 'Everything is all right?'

He nodded.

'Vanya asks if you are ready.'

'Almost.' And his voice was tight.

'You know, Vanya is rough on the outside. But I would not have gone to him if I did not trust him absolutely. He and your grandfather – they were great friends. Now he is involved, Vanya will do all he can to help. You can hold me to that.'

Will nodded. 'All right.'

'All right – come through when you are ready.'

His grandmother left, and Will hesitated. His mind wasn't really on Vanya. It was on the equipment in front of him.

He had the timer. But the microwave was broken anyway, and he was loath to leave behind something that might be useful. So he removed the magnetron tube. Inside this were two powerful ring-shaped ferrite magnets. Surely they might come in handy.

'Hey!' Vanya's voice. He was on the sofa. 'I have the photos through from Ivan. Quickly – and then we go.'

In his oddly delicate hands, Vanya was holding a slender black phone. There was no maker's mark, Will realized, as he sat beside him. He wanted to ask Vanya where he'd got the phone, but then he saw something.

In among the shots of the rocket launch pad, four-wheel drives, and guards with guns.

'Wait. Go back!'

Andrew and Gaia were here now, crouching and craning their heads to get a view of the screen. Gaia glanced up at Will, whose face had gone pale. 'What?'

For a moment, Will couldn't speak. He was staring at the shot. It showed the gates of the base, and, just behind them, a man. He was wearing a dark-blue suit, and his head was bowed. Even so, he was unmistakable.

'You know him?' Andrew breathed.

Will screwed up his eyes at the shadowed face, and then at Andrew and Gaia. 'Yeah.'

'Well, who is he?' Andrew cried.

'His name—' And Will hesitated. This was unbelievable. He trusted his own eyes, and he knew what he had to say, and yet it made absolutely no sense. What was *he* doing here?

'His name,' Will said, 'is *Roden Cutler.*'

Abominable.

It was abominable. Inconceivable. Excruciating. *Insane*, thought Caspian Baraban.

There was a wooden chair in the corner of the room but he could not use it. He paced up and down, up and down, so frustrated he could almost have hit his head against the cement wall – but of course he would do nothing that might injure his precious brain.

Two hours! *Two hours* he had been here! And how much time had he wasted, when the railway-station taxi driver had no idea of the location of the base, but had pretended of course, and they had ended up at a meat-processing plant in the bleakest of all the world's most miserable industrial zones.

For all his brainpower, Caspian Baraban had made two mistakes. First: he'd believed the idiot taxi driver when he'd claimed from Caspian's rough instructions to know the location of the base. Second: he had brought no roubles.

Caspian tried at once to call his father for help, but there was no response. Worse, the irate driver had decided that in lieu of roubles, he would take Caspian's PDA. He had snatched it from the boy's fingers and driven off, leaving him alone, lost in St Petersburg, on the verge (though he would never admit it) of tears.

It had taken another half an hour for him to hitch a lift back into the city. The truck driver might have stopped, but his kindliness ended there. Caspian's attempts in his imperfect Russian to request that he be taken at once to the base – or if not, a taxi rank – were greeted with dull silence. The driver chewed and drove, chewed and drove, while Caspian's anger seethed inside him.

At the precise moment that Will sat on his grand-mother's sofa and said he needed to talk to her about space, Caspian found himself once more abandoned. But this time it was near the Hermitage Museum. Here, there were tourists. And where there were tourists, there were taxis.

The first driver looked criminal, Caspian decided. It was the uneven shape of his head that gave it away. The second was more promising. This man was young. He actually listened.

'Ah, the base?' he said. 'Where the drunks had their throats cut.' And he pursed his lips. 'You *want* to go there.'

Caspian could have screamed. 'Yes! Yes, I want to go there.' He yanked open the back door and threw himself inside. 'Drive!' he ordered. 'My father's life depends on it.'

'You want to go to the base, it is dangerous. I will charge extra.'

'Whatever you like,' Caspian promised. 'Whatever you want, I can pay.'

Or his father could, he thought. As the taxi pulled away, Caspian cursed the Sun. If it hadn't been for those flares, he would have been in Petersburg twenty-four hours ago. He could be with his father right now . . .

His father. And Caspian's chest swelled suddenly as he imagined the look of pride that would light up his father's pale face. His son – the genius. His son – who had produced the greatest code in the history of humanity. The code for something beyond infinity. The code for a black hole.

Thirty minutes later, the cab arrived at the gates to the sprawling base. Caspian could make out the tip of a launch pad, beyond a vast hangar. It looked grim, and grey, lit by a blaring white light. Signs showing stick figures in the throes of electrocution were pinned to the fence.

Two guards sauntered out of their box, holding back two slathering dogs. Caspian had been impatient to jump out to explain. Noticing the dogs, he rolled down the window.

'My name is Caspian Baraban!' he shouted through the snow-stinging wind. 'My father wants to see me. Let me in at once.'

'Baraban?' said the first guard.

'Call him!' Caspian almost screamed. 'Get on your radio and call him now!'

'All right, all right,' said the second guard. 'Calm down now. There's somewhere warm in here where you can wait—'

'I cannot wait!' Caspian interjected. 'It is inconceivable!'

'—Where you can wait while we contact your father,' the first guard finished, nodding at the second. Whatever secret meaning passed between them Caspian missed. At least, he did at the time.

But two hours later, when he was still locked inside the freezing cell, the memory of the taxi driver's curses blistering his eardrums, he realized full well what they had done. Fury coursed through his body. Here he was, at the base, with the code, and these two imbeciles were *punishing him*!

Live a new day. Translate your dreams.
Live a new life. Love's what it seems.

The woman's voice rattled from the car radio. Outside, the snow-grey suburbs of St Petersburg swept past.

'What is this?' Vanya cried.

Andrew pressed his hands to his ears. For Will, the tune brought back memories of his mother. Often, she had played Russian music while she worked. Not that he'd exactly forgotten her, of course. She was there inside him, hiding around the corner of every next thought. As soon as this mission was completed – as soon as they had destroyed the black hole generator – he would find her.

Open your heart. Happiness screams.
Love a new life, go to extremes!

'Rubbish!' Vanya said to Elena. 'I lend a neighbour my

car, and this is what happens!' And he yanked out the tape.

But now Will heard only his own thoughts.

Cutler, he was thinking.

Could Cutler really have some part to play in the plot to destroy the hotel? But *why*? And who was he? Had he really known Will's parents? Did Natalia know about Cutler? Was she somehow in league with him?

I've been stupid, Will thought. I thought Cutler was well-meaning . . . But if he's working on the weapon, what was he doing in London, talking to me? Did Cutler abduct Vassily Baraban?

Nothing made sense. And Will felt a dull ache in his guts. First his father, then his mother. Now even Roden Cutler. He'd thought Cutler was all right. And Cutler had betrayed him.

Unless . . . Unless Cutler was also there against his will?

Then Will thought back, even further, to the first evening with Andrew, in the basement.

At the time, Will had thought Andrew naive. Now, in Vanya's car, clutching his rucksacks, Gaia beside him cradling her sash of explosive, Andrew silent and composed, he believed the truth of those words. And he felt uncertainty, apprehension, all those familiar things. But also camaraderie. Friendship. Even belief.

'I believe you will succeed,' his grandmother had said, as they'd bundled into the car. 'If I was a little younger, a little thinner, I would be going all the way with you – faster than a strangelet! Vanya and I – our hearts are greedy but our bodies are weak!'

'*There*!' Elena cried.

The car skidded to a halt.

'You missed it, Vanya! Back there. Back up!'

'We're here?' Gaia said.

Elena turned to her. 'Look,' she said.

Three sets of eyes blinked at portable streetlights, and an incandescent white glow.

Vanya shot the Lada into reverse. He manoeuvred it so it was parked just off the road, in shadows, beneath pine trees. From this spot, they had a clear view down the hill, to the gates. And beyond those gates, the base.

The complex was huge. A dense-mesh, two-metre high fence and a ring of fir trees surrounded it. Through his grandfather's binoculars, Will studied the three main concrete hangars. Two were to the east, in isolation. The third was to the west, its walls streaked with orange rust, where the reinforcing rods had succumbed to the weather. A lone guard was stationed on the roof. He paced a few metres in one direction then paced back in the other. Attached to this hanger was a lower building with a flat roof and metal roller doors. The unloading depot, Will guessed.

Beyond the western hangar was a launch pad, lit by spotlights. The supports were there, prepped and waiting.

This has to be it, Will thought.

He refocused the binoculars. Rough concrete roads

linked the hangars. To the south, five four-wheel-drives were parked. It was impossible to tell from here where the entrance to the particle collider might be. The tunnels would be well below ground. Somehow they had to find the lift that would take them down.

A flicker of motion made Will shift the binoculars. A stream of men and women in orange uniforms was emerging from behind the western hangar. A bus that had been hidden from his view behind the launch pad edged around them and came to a stop. One by one, they started to board.

'It looks as though the workers are leaving,' Will whispered. His breath froze against the hood of his coat.

Beside him, Vanya nodded and stamped his feet. 'Which might suggest that everything is ready . . . Perhaps only a skeleton team will be kept on.'

As Will watched, the last of the technicians clambered aboard and the bus made its way along the concrete road, to the gates. At once, they were opened. Will and Vanya hurried back inside the car, scraping the worst of the snow from their boots.

'Why the bright light?' Will asked as he squashed in next to Gaia and lifted the rucksacks on to his lap.

'Must be for the security cameras,' Vanya said. 'To help them spot intruders.'

'But we will be in the van,' Andrew said. His exaggerated firmness gave away his anxiety.

'Exactly,' Vanya said. 'Safe in the van, no worries in the world . . .'

Will checked his watch. 'Ten-ten.' He heard brakes screech as the bus disappeared off down the hill.

Vanya nodded. 'We are in good time. I am only sorry that Elena and I cannot go with you. But this plan – it is beyond our strength. We have taken you so far. We are brave enough for that. Now, you have what you need? You want to make one last check through your kit?' And he hauled his body around, so he could look at Will, in the back. 'You going to show me what's in those bags?'

Will held the rucksacks a little tighter. 'Nothing, really,' he said.

Vanya shrugged and turned away.

'Show him,' Elena said. 'Make an old man happy.'

Vanya lowered the window a few centimetres and spat. 'Ha! I am very happy, thank you very much. There is nothing I would rather be doing tonight.'

Gaia nudged Will gently. 'Show him,' she whispered.

Andrew leaned forward. 'I'd rather like to see them all once more.'

Vanya sighed. 'OK, we swap. I will show you something, you will show me something, is it a deal?'

Will shrugged. He nodded.

Vanya reached down underneath the driver's seat and pulled out a red bag. From inside, he withdrew a small hand-held antenna, connected to another device. A receiver.

'I was going to bring this for Elena tomorrow,' he

said. 'Those neighbours of hers, they argue all evening, but we cannot hear what they are saying. This – it's based on microwaves. You hold this up to the wall. It will allow us to listen in.' Vanya turned to Will. 'I can explain—'

'Microwaves?' Will said. '. . . Voices agitate clothing, they modulate the radio beam and you read that with the detector—'

'Well,' Vanya exclaimed, 'my secret is up!'

'It's very clever,' Will said. 'Cleverer than most people would think.'

'Why, thank you, William Knight. I am pleased for the compliment.' Vanya raised an eyebrow at Elena. 'Now, I think it is your turn.'

So, reluctantly, Will opened up the two bags. Vanya caught on quickly. He cut through Will's explanations.

Speak Easy. Vanya nodded. 'Very impressive. I should have thought of this . . .'

Rapid Ascent. 'It is too bulky,' Vanya said. 'Leave it here with me – I will guard it for you.'

Soft Landing. 'Ah, but I recognize this!' Vanya cried. 'For space probes!'

Tooth Talk. 'Ingenious,' he said softly.

'Give one to me,' Vanya said. 'I will wear it. That way, you can communicate with me. If you get in trouble . . .'

'It's a good idea,' Gaia said.

Fly Spy.

'The locust?' Vanya peered at it with interest.

'Switch it on,' Andrew said.

Will held Fly Spy in his palm. He flicked the tiny switch that activated the video camera and the wings, and he took the remote control in the other hand. Gently, he brushed his finger upward across the touch-sensitive pad. The locust trembled. He brushed again.

Gaia looked at him. 'What's wrong?'

Will turned the robot on its back. A tiny red LED was flashing.

He should have known it. 'The battery,' he said. And he cursed himself for forgetting. 'We need this – we need video footage to show what's going on in there, and we need its eyes.'

'You don't have a spare?' Vanya said.

'No.'

'Can you feed it?' Andrew said.

Vanya's eyes widened. 'What is he talking about?'

'It eats leaves,' Gaia said. She glanced at Will. 'Can't we give it leaves? There are trees out there.'

'Yeah, and these are pine trees. My robot doesn't eat needles, they're too tough.'

'Maybe up the road—'

'It's *winter*,' he said grimly. 'I should have brought another battery.'

'You didn't know,' Andrew said. 'We had no idea we'd be here, did we, Will?'

'But now our eyes are gone,' Will said. 'I thought we could use this to get us safely around the base.'

'—What?' Gaia said. Will glanced at her, and realized she was addressing Elena, who was leaning over the gearstick to nudge Vanya hard in the ribs.

'What?' she said again. 'Elena?'

'Yes, yes, I know,' Vanya said. 'Don't make it look as though you force me!'

'Force you to do what?' Andrew said.

'Your video robot is dead?' Vanya said to Will.

'It's *out of power.*'

'Same thing. For current purposes. All right. Maybe I can help.'

Will, Gaia and Andrew watched intently as Vanya reached into his pocket. Before removing his hand, he said: 'I warn you: what you are about to see may seem a little *strange*. But don't go crazy on me. You, girl: no screaming.'

'My *name* is Gaia,' she said. 'And I never scream.' But she'd spoken quietly, tensing, despite herself, as Vanya's delicate hand brought out the thing. It twitched.

'*Ugh!*' Andrew said. 'I'm sorry,' he added quickly.

'No need to be sorry,' Vanya said, a touch of a smile lifting the corners of his mouth. 'When I first showed this to Elena she fainted down flat. I was afraid I had truly scared her to death.'

Abominable. Inconceivable. The same words ran like a stuck angry song through Caspian's head. So much time wasted. Precious time. He glanced at his watch. And he realized his father was wrong when he said only stupid people were governed by the clock. Maybe not wrong, exactly. Maybe he was only idealistic. But what world did he live in . . . ?

And then, at last – at last – came the grate of a key in the lock. Caspian's heart raced, his mouth preparing to form the insults he would let fly the instant—

His mouth hung open.

'*Father!*'

At first, Vassily Baraban did not move. 'They told me you were here,' he said. 'It had been so long I barely hoped it could be true.'

Barely hoped was right. After the stunt with the burning blanket and the broken glass, Vassily Baraban had been hauled into a videoconference meeting with 'the Boss'. Unsurprisingly, his explanation had not been believed. Vassily had been forced to admit the truth: he had contacted his son. He needed him. The Boss had been angry – until Vassily had sworn there was only one person in the world who could create this code – and it was not him. He had not wanted to expose his precious Caspian. But now it was too late.

Under the guards' supervision, Vassily sent Caspian directions to the base. And now, at last, here he was.

'Father!' And Caspian threw himself into the waiting arms.

'My son.' Vassily pressed Caspian's head tight against his chest. 'My son, you came to me.'

'Yes, Father.' Caspian broke back, looked his father full in the face. 'I came – and I brought the code!'

'My Caspian,' Vassily Baraban said, sadly. Gently, he stroked his son's head.

'The code, Father,' Caspian said, his words stumbling. 'I have it. I worked it out!'

'I knew you would,' Vassily said quietly.

'. . . And you are pleased?'

'Of course, my son. Of course I am pleased.'

'Because your life depended on it, didn't you say?' A trace of irritation had crept into Caspian's tone. The fatherly pride he had long anticipated had not materialized. Instead, his father seemed sad, even absent-minded.

Perhaps they had drugged him, Caspian thought. Perhaps he has had no sleep. His father's face did look extremely white, his lips an unnatural pale green.

'Never mind,' he said. 'I have the code, here in my pocket. What do you want me to do?'

'Come with me,' Vassily said. 'There is someone you must meet.'

Caspian kept his eyes peeled as they left the small set of cells. No sign of the guards now, as they passed into a dull, narrow corridor, again lined with cement. At the far end was a steel door. Vassily Baraban bent his face towards a screen. A moment later a green light flashed. The door opened.

'What was that?' Caspian said. 'What biometric, Father?'

'It scans the pattern of blood vessels in my face,' Vassily replied.

'It is interesting security.'

'What would you expect, my son, when here you have a weapon that could swallow up the world.'

Caspian did not like his father's tone – or his implication.

'What do you mean, the world? Father, I have considered—'

'Fundamental physics does not always abide by one's considerations,' said Vassily, who was now pushing open another steel door. It was the third, Caspian noted, on the left, after they'd turned the corner, after the entrance to a lift, and it was labelled *Control*.

At first, Caspian thought the small ante-room they now entered was empty. Then, from behind the door, a middle-aged woman appeared. Behind her, pushed against the left-hand wall, were steel tables. They were topped with cardboard boxes trailing coils of cabling and other bits of kit. The woman didn't seem surprised to see him, Caspian noted. Perhaps she had observed him already using security cameras. Or his father might have told her. Of course, he would have told everyone that his son was bringing the code.

'Through here, Caspian,' his father said. As Caspian glanced back at the woman, she flashed him a curious look.

His father held up his wrist to a scanner fixed to the wall beside another steel door, this time labelled *Operations*. The mechanism clicked. And they were admitted to a narrow space no more than a metre long that led to yet another slab of steel.

Beyond was the inner sanctum. The brain of the entire base. From here, the launch pad could be controlled. And the particle collider, with its stretching tubes and complex cryogenics. Beyond were the final functional rooms of the complex: the *Surveillance* centre, and the *Systems* room, which held a supercomputer.

Caspian peered around him, trying to take it all in. The Operations room was brightly lit. Its high ceilings were of bare concrete, and there were bare concrete walls. A further set of metal tables was strewn with cabling and fuses, light bulbs and manuals written in Russian.

In fact, the room was a mess, Caspian thought. Wires

sprouted from walls and dangled from the ceiling. A large LED monitor was resting on two piles of bricks. The image was fuzzy, but clearly it represented the motion of an object in orbit around Earth.

Now, Caspian shifted his gaze to the man in charge.

He sat in the centre of the room, on a plush red chair, on a circular rich red carpet. Immediately behind him was a desk of moulded plastic. Built into this was a series of three touch screens. The master control centre.

As Vassily approached the chair with his son, he remembered the warning about the 500 volts . . .

The man raised his head slightly as the pair stopped. At once, Caspian took a dislike to him. He noted the wild glint in the yellow eyes. The paleness of the lips. The weakness of the jaw.

'This is Caspian,' Vassily said flatly.

'Indeed,' Roden Cutler answered. He sounded interested, but non-committal. 'You have the code?'

Caspian nodded.

'Well, hand it over,' Cutler said, with impatience.

Caspian glanced at his father. Where was the welcoming party, he thought? The adulation, the honour? But his father only nodded. Slowly, Caspian brought out the notes from his pocket. He looked sullenly at Cutler as he held them out. Instantly, Cutler grabbed them. He scanned the numbers, the equations.

'Does this make sense?' he said to Vassily Baraban.

'I have not read it.'

'Then read it!' Cutler thundered.

Vassily did as he was told. Caspian watched his father carefully as he worked through the notes. He saw realization dawn on his father's features. He saw a shimmer of pride. And then what – surely it couldn't be . . . fear?

'He is right,' Vassily Baraban said, without emotion. 'In that we will have the clumping you demand.'

Cutler clapped his hands together. 'Excellent! Well perhaps now we can get this bloody slow show on the road. What do you say, Vassily? You can tweak the equipment? We can create the weapon at midnight.'

'I believe so.'

'Good. Because as you know, it's really rather vital that we do. Our window is incredibly narrow. And your future does depend on it. As does mine.'

'. . . Yes,' Vassily said, and he let his head hang. 'We can be ready for midnight.'

'Good. Now take your brilliant son away. He probably wants feeding.'

'I would like—' Caspian began, meaning to ask for some proper recognition. But he was silenced by the grip of his father's fingers on the back of his neck. Utterly confused, Caspian let himself be steered back into the other room, under the unpleasant gaze of the woman. She addressed his father, barely concealing her doubt and anticipation:

'The code will work?'

Vassily stopped. 'This is my son,' he said distinctly.

'So it goes ahead tonight?'

'Yes,' he said. 'Midnight. It goes ahead.'

'You know,' she whispered severely, 'what might happen.'

'And what choice do I have?' he murmured.

10.25 p.m.

The car remained beneath the trees, Vanya and Elena inside. Will, Andrew and Gaia were shivering behind two dense pines, planted a little further along the road, close to the gates.

Gaia had the explosive secured across her chest. Andrew carried a torch and a rope. Will wasn't sure they would be much use, but Andrew had wanted to carry something.

Strapped across the Gore-tex covering of Will's jacket was a single backpack. It contained Speak Easy, the empty box for Tooth Talk – the three of them, plus Vanya, had already fitted the tiny devices – and the wall-bugging equipment that Vanya had thrust into Will's hands as he got out of the car. That had been after he'd given him the twitching object. The single strangest gadget, if you could call it that, that Will had ever seen. He could feel it now, in his pocket, still *twitching*.

Andrew stamped his feet. 'If it doesn't come soon I'm going to freeze to death.'

'Shh,' Gaia said. It was an odd sensation, to hear Andrew's voice also through the tooth phone. But so long as he spoke quietly, it wasn't too unpleasant.

'They can't hear me,' he said. 'They're all nicely tucked up inside their little booth.'

Will followed Andrew's gaze. The trees were perhaps five metres from the gates. Just in front was the small guards' Portakabin, and beyond, a concrete road that led directly to the western hangar, with its unloading depot. There were no windows in the hangar but Will guessed it was about seven storeys high. Perhaps here, in this warehouse, the essential parts for the particle collider and the launch pad had been gathered.

The steel roller door to the depot looked extremely strong, Will noted. Far stronger, in fact, than the rust-streaked concrete hull of the hangar. This was a rapid construction, that much was clear.

Despite his layers, Will shivered. The cold was bitter. Will could feel ice crystals even in his eyelashes and the wind burned his cheeks. *Ignore it,* he told himself. The plan was all that mattered.

'I read a theory the other week that a black hole wiped out the dinosaurs,' Andrew said. 'The idea was that one approaches close enough every thirty million years or so to send a shower of comets raining down on Earth.'

No one replied.

'. . . Just out of interest, do we have a Plan B?' Andrew said.

'I know – you sacrifice yourself to the dogs and in the confusion Will and I run in,' Gaia whispered, scowling at him. Her breath clouded the dark air.

'Excellent,' he said and kicked at the frozen ground. 'Just checking.'

'Andrew.'

'I told you: they can't hear us.'

'The van!' Three hands clasped to three heads. Vanya's voice.

'Didn't you tell him to talk quietly?' Andrew groaned.

Will didn't reply. He was watching the flash of headlights as a vehicle approached. The road was windy, and the van would have to snake around a few more bends before it would finally appear.

'I can't believe we're actually going to do this,' Andrew whispered. His tone had previously been light. Now it expressed a mixture of apprehension and dread.

This time, Gaia didn't scowl. 'It'll be all right,' she said.

'It'll be all right – I'm with you, or it'll just be all right?'

'It'll be all right, we're all together. Now be quiet.' And she gave him a faint smile. It was meant to encourage him, but it was for her benefit as well. Gaia was used to having to reassure herself.

At that moment, the van appeared around the last bend in the road. It was white, a Transit type, and it looked brand new. Reinforced wipers were working hard to bat the snow from the windscreen. Alloy wheels skidded to a halt beside the Portakabin.

Will held his breath. Now it was down to Vanya and Elena. The timing was everything.

It took a minute or two for the guards to emerge from their warmth. In that time, the fat van driver had struggled out and opened up the rear doors. Now he was standing, waiting, blowing white breath into the freezing air. He yelled something, which was lost in the wind and the snow. *Hurry up,* Will guessed.

Then the guards were at the van. There were two, as Ivan had promised. Both wore army-style uniforms with handguns on their belts and rifles slung over their shoulders. No dogs. From his position under the tree, Will could almost make out the face of the first as he gave the van driver a friendly slap on the arm and jumped up into the back.

Two seconds more, Will thought. Give him time. Make sure the job's done.

And Will waited . . . And waited.

'*Now, Vanya,*' he hissed.

There was a muffled sound through the tooth phone.

'What are you doing?' Will said. 'Hurry!'

The scuffling stopped. 'It's not working!' came the voice. 'Elena threw it down, it hasn't gone off!'

Will glanced at Gaia. Her face had gone white. Ahead, the first guard was already out of the back of the van. The other was shifting his rifle higher on his shoulder. The inspection was over.

'I might have put in too much stabilizer,' Gaia said quickly. 'Vanya, you'll have to hit it.'

'With what? My *fist*?'

'The cricket bat,' Will said. 'Tell Elena – quick – get the bat.'

'It could go off in her face!'

'There isn't much,' Gaia said. 'It should be all right. Hit it. But tell her to turn her face away.'

Will could feel his heart pounding. If this didn't work, their night – and their mission – was over. 'Do it *now*,' he urged.

He looked up suddenly as Andrew tapped him on the shoulder. The second guard was already striding back towards his booth. The first had his hand on the van door – then *Bang!*

Will jumped. It wasn't the van door slamming shut. There it was, being battered by the wind.

No – Elena had done it.

Will glanced at Gaia, and he grinned. Some of the colour returned to her cheeks. Andrew grabbed Will's arm.

Just as they'd hoped, both guards reacted at once to the explosion. Rifles clenched in their hands, they were practically jogging along the road towards Elena and Vanya.

At first, the van driver did not move. He peered into the darkness, in the direction of the bang. Then, at last, he started to follow the guards. Only a few metres – not all the way to the Lada. But the snow was swirling now. It masked sounds. As Will stepped out from behind the tree, he was relieved to discover his footsteps were silent.

Will didn't have to say anything to Andrew or Gaia. They were at his side. Together, they ran as fast as they could. As they approached the van, Will felt his lungs burning with cold. He glanced back. Andrew and Gaia were still with him. Nothing else mattered. And he could see nothing else, only shadows and snow.

'Well, my dear, they heard it.'

Vanya nodded. As soon as the small pat of explosive had done its job, Elena had thrown Boris's blackened cricket bat into the boot and they had inched the car forward to cover the marks in the snow. Then Vanya switched the engine off, and cranked it up again. Now the two guards were jogging towards them. Vanya could see the black anger on their army-issue faces. Plain, stupid faces.

'You know, I always wanted to be an actor,' Elena said, as she let her features relax into a dullard droop.

'They'll probably imagine we have Alzheimer's,' Vanya said. 'Old age sometimes has its advantages.'

As he finished speaking, the first guard arrived at the car. He was young and sturdy, with a scar through his right eyebrow. He rapped on the roof with his rifle, and both Elena and Vanya looked up, feigning confusion. Fumbling intentionally, Vanya took his time winding down the window. He smiled humbly as the scarred brow rose.

'What was that noise?' the guard demanded.

Vanya looked at Elena. 'The noise?'

'The bang! The explosion. It came from over here. You know what I'm talking about!'

'Oh . . . that!' Elena said, realization apparently dawning. 'The bang – of course. Why didn't you say?'

The guard's face reddened.

His colleague – younger, with sloping shoulders that barely supported his rifle – had arrived by now. 'What is going on?'

'The bang,' Vanya said. 'Oh yes, the bang.'

'What are you saying? Explain yourself, old man!' The second guard was even more irascible than the first. Spit was ejected from his mouth. Vanya could almost see it freezing in a stream, like urine into space.

'Oh, but it happens often,' Elena said. She nodded deeply, up and down. 'We try to fix it – but, what can I say, when it comes to cars, we are useless.'

'Fix *what*?' cried the second guard. His cheeks were throbbing. He reached back for his rifle—

'The exhaust,' Vanya said hurriedly. 'See for yourselves – the car is very old. The engine stalled here on this road. I restarted it and it happened. All the time, the exhaust does this.'

'. . . A backfire?' The first guard rolled his eyes at his colleague.

'Yes, yes, of course, a backfire, ' Elena said, smiling. 'What can I say? I apologize if we disturbed you.'

'*Chert!*' the second guard swore. 'We should take you in for wasting our time.'

And Vanya glanced past him, past the rifle, past the first guard who was kicking his feet in the snow. Beyond them, Vanya could see the van driver, who was keeping a close eye on the interrogation.

'In where? In there?' Vanya jerked his head towards the base. 'What is in there, anyway?'

'None of your business, old man,' the second guard said quickly, and he spat. Then to his friend: 'Come, we waste our own time with these seniles.'

'That's right, sir,' Elena said. 'It is fair, you know. Once we were young and had minds like yours, but now—'

'Silence!' The first guard thundered. 'Hurry now – leave!'

And Vanya and Elena watched as the pair stamped off back towards the van. The snow fell more thickly than ever, enveloping their bodies in white.

'. . . Now what?' Elena said, in her normal voice.

Vanya rubbed his eyes. The wind had made them sting. 'We wait a few minutes, make sure things seem all right. Then we drive along a bit and we park and wait.'

Elena nodded. As Vanya coaxed the Lada into a

forward judder, he said: 'You know, Elena, you were impressive with that bat. If that explosive had been a ball, it would have been a six, for sure.'

Elena's face fell – which hadn't been Vanya's intended effect. 'The bat was to be only for protection. Boris would never forgive me. His son-in-law's gift – he treasured it, and I have destroyed it.'

'And with it saved the skin of your grandson,' Vanya pointed out. 'Not even old Boris, God rest his soul, could complain about that.'

While Vanya and Elena created the diversion, Will, Andrew and Gaia had not hung around.

With a quick leap, Will was in the back of the van. Immediately, he edged between two towers of cardboard boxes. He had no idea if the guards had seen them but if they had, there was no point looking back to find out. He'd know soon enough.

Inside the van, the sudden absence of wind and snow dulled Will's hearing. Blood washed through his ears. It took him a second to get used to it.

'Go on!' Gaia hissed and he felt her hand on his back.

Will couldn't see, but Andrew was right up behind her.

Quickly, Will crept around another pile of boxes. He

found himself faced with a stack of bedding. Clean sheets, neatly folded. Grey army blankets.

'Under here,' he said.

He crouched down, shaking out a blanket. Instantly, Gaia and Andrew were beside him. Will passed another blanket to Andrew. 'Throw it over you,' he whispered.

Andrew did as he was told. The blanket was coarse against Will's face. Fibres scratched his cheeks. He lifted it slightly so he could see out, but Gaia took it gently and tugged it back down. She didn't say a word, but he understood.

Will could hear her breathing, rapid and tense. Next to her, Andrew made himself as small as possible. His arm was wedged against Gaia's leg and his heavy gold watch dug into his flesh. He longed to move it. But he forbade himself to even try.

Staying absolutely still, Andrew decided, was their only chance.

'What was it?'

The shout sounded desperately close. And Will froze as he realized the van driver was back, followed by the two guards.

'An old couple in an excuse for a car,' came the voice of the first guard.

So – it had worked. The guards had believed Elena and Vanya. And no one had seen them enter the van.

Then – silence. Will could see nothing, could only guess what the men were doing. He forced himself to breathe slowly, as he had beneath the table in Vassily Baraban's lab. Impossible to believe that had been only a few days ago. Beside him, Gaia did the same. Will counted his breaths, marking time since the voices ceased.

Four, five, six, seven . . .

Slam.

Will's body shook. Blood shot through his heart. Then the van rumbled into life.

The slam had been the sound of the rear door shutting.

The rumble was the engine.

And the van was moving.

Sudden euphoria made Will grin. He pushed down the blanket. In the blackness he couldn't see Gaia's face, or Andrew's. He didn't need to. He could sense their excitement.

The first phase of their plan had worked. They were in.

The man in the red chair permitted himself a thin smile. Already, he had dispatched Vassily Baraban underground to tweak the beam generators. The next step was for the boy to rewrite the software that would control the energies, and the mass of gold matter that would be released.

It was perfect, he reflected. His plan. At last, coming to devastating fruition. They would create the black hole inside the chamber devised by Vassily Baraban, launch that chamber and time it to open up at the precise moment the hotel passed overhead. The hotel would be destroyed at once. Obliterated. Absolutely. Without trace.

Cutler smiled again. Caspian Baraban was standing in front of him. He had just been fed by Anna, the scientist. He'd had her make up a packet chocolate cake to go with the beans. He wanted to make sure the precocious little brain was well fuelled. The last thing he needed now was further mistakes, or delays.

As soon as Anna had finished, he'd sent her to the Surveillance room. The base was down-staffing. Now that construction was complete there was need only for a few technicians and three or four guards. The external security would be enough. Those gates, and the guards in their Portakabin, could keep anyone out. But what to do with Anna? She had been unable to help Vassily Baraban – unable to come up with the Infinity Code. He knew what he ought to do . . .

Now, the boy was staring at him sulkily. Perhaps a little buttering up was in order, Cutler decided. And, it was true, the brat's achievement was phenomenally impressive. Cutler had believed it was possible. This boy would prove him right.

'You feel better after eating?' Cutler said. 'I asked for the cake to be baked especially. Was it good?'

'It was all right,' Caspian replied. Cake was nothing. What did he care about food? 'Who are you?'

Cutler's thin upper lip curled. 'Oh, you can call me Boss. How about that?'

Caspian only shrugged. Still sulky.

'You know, what you have done really is quite extraordinary,' Cutler said, resisting the urge to slap the boy. 'Your old dad couldn't make the grade, could he? Not that your old dad is a dunce,' he added quickly. 'We all know how many brain cells are packed into that vast skull. But you – you are really something quite different, aren't you?'

Caspian was still frowning, but some of the sullenness started to ebb away.

'How long did it take you to write that code? Go on, let me guess? Two weeks?'

'Twenty hours.'

'Twenty hours! Unbelievable.' Cutler smiled again, revealing his pointed white teeth. 'I knew it could be done. That's something we struggle with, us visionaries. Normal people just don't understand. My own boss—' And Cutler hesitated. 'No, let's talk about you. You're the one who's done it. And tonight, you shall see the fruits of your efforts. The weapon will be created at midnight, right on schedule. We will transfer it to the rocket, which is waiting in the hangar, and at one a.m., we shall launch.'

And Caspian, who had been basking in this inclusive praise, felt his soaring pleasure stagger a little. 'This is necessary?' he said. 'You really want to destroy this hotel?'

'That's right.'

'But I hoped—'

Cutler's yellow eyes narrowed. 'Hoped what? That we would create a black hole and leave it at that? Thought we would generate the most perfect force imaginable – and not harness it? Tell me, Caspian, doesn't it make your heart swell? The greatest power in the universe and we – you and I – *we* shall possess it!'

'But—'

'But nothing,' Cutler said.

'But – if it is really necessary, I *would* like to see it,' Caspian said, and his eyes became a little wistful. '. . . It would be so elegant a weapon. So beautiful.'

Cutler nodded. 'Exactly.' He wasn't really sure whether the kid was serious, or whether he was trying to con him with his apparent change of heart.

'It has always been my dream to bring the perfection of the universe to Earth,' Caspian continued. 'I never thought about weapons – but yes, a black hole, enveloping so absolutely – no mess, no trace.'

'Exactly,' Cutler repeated. There was a glint in the kid's eyes that really was quite convincing. But Cutler was cautious. Again, why risk it? 'Now, we're up against the clock, Caspian,' he said briskly. 'See that door over there – it says "Systems". There's a computer in there just for you. What I need is for you to go in there and use your brilliant code to rewrite our software, so our project will actually work. Your father is sorting out the hardware, but the software is all yours. That is, if you really can do it?' Cutler raised a thin eyebrow.

'Of course I can do it,' Caspian said with indignation.

Cutler nodded. A brilliant mind, yet still so easy to manipulate. 'Excellent,' he said. 'Then off you pop. Close the door behind you.'

As soon as Caspian had gone, Cutler bent forward to his console. Here was the black button that would initiate the weapon in just – and he glanced at the clock – fifty minutes. Fifty minutes until the crowning glory of his life.

At the far right of the console was a green transmission button, which he now pressed.

'Sir—?' Cutler said.

A pause. And then a disembodied voice. It was deep and polished, smooth as leather. 'Well? Get on with it.'

'We're all set, sir. The weapon will be created as planned at twenty-four hundred. The launch pad is ready. Unless—'

'No,' the voice said. 'There has been no response to my demands.'

'Then we will show them, sir.'

'When they see this,' came the voice, 'I will have the planet at my feet.'

'The *universe*, sir.'

'No need to go over the top. Now get on with it.' The voice had stiffened. 'Nothing must go wrong.'

And the green transmission light flicked off. Cutler leaned back in his soft red chair and he smiled. He had the Infinity Code. He had Vassily Baraban to tweak the equipment, and Baraban Jr to rewrite the software. What could go wrong . . . ?

Fifty metres from the Operations room, through five steel doors and a lift shaft, was the arrivals depot. Breeze blocks and a locked door screened it off from the vast assembly hangar and the now disused workshops. Another steel door at the rear opened into the corridor that led ultimately to the Control room.

Inside the arrivals depot was a jumble of open and half-empty boxes, dirty washing, a broken TV, a pool table and the food delivery van.

Vladimir was not impressed. Shifting food was beneath him. He was a henchman. An enforcer, a kidnapper, a sharpshooter, a criminal. And this was the work of a *pridurok*. An idiot.

With a lazy swipe of his hand, he flicked open the van's double doors. Twin towers of cardboard boxes stared him blankly in the face. Just a tenth of the usual food order, as most of the base staff had now left. But still, too much for Vladimir. Screwing up his eyes, he slowly read the words printed on the side.

'More beans. I don't believe it,' he groaned.

As he concentrated on the letters, a small creature scurried out of the back of the van. Vladimir barely noticed.

The van had been parked for five minutes. Its driver, Illyr, had gone inside to hunt out his pay (*Good luck to you,* Vladimir had murmured). This was Illyr's final delivery, and the van belonged to the base. When he had his money, Illyr would take one of the four-wheel-drives back to the city. Now he, Vladimir, was supposed to unload the van. But the night was freezing, and he was tired. Only three more days and at last this contract would end. He would be glad, he thought. The boss was a psychiatric case – and Vladimir had no knowledge of the true function of the base.

'Hey!'

The shout had come from Sergei. He'd appeared from the direction of the Control room. Now he seemed to be digging in among the abandoned boxes.

'Vlad, come here. I saw something move.'

Slowly, Vladimir trundled over to his friend. 'It is nothing, Sergei – some vermin. They are welcome to the beans.'

Inside the van, Will, Andrew and Gaia reacted at once.

Perhaps there was a marines signal that meant 'exit now', but Will did not know it. Instead he pointed hard towards the two open doors and he rolled out from under the blanket. In his hand he carried a screen. It was bulkier than Fly Spy's but it did the job. The streaming video showed snatches of the faces of the two Russians. Will flinched as Vladimir's hand reared in the screen. Instantly, he manoeuvred the device so that it backed up and hid beneath a cardboard box.

Vanya's gift was doing an excellent job at keeping the two men occupied. In the meantime, Will, Andrew and Gaia removed their outer coats and stashed them underneath the bedding. The coats would be discovered, of course, but they were too warm and unwieldy. Anyone who found them would think they were extra supplies – Will hoped.

Then, together, they leaped out of the van and ran around the back. Will glanced to his right. He could see a shaft of electric light released by the half-open door that led into the base. Sergei had been slack.

Again, Will pointed hard, this time towards the shaft of light. First Andrew and then Gaia sprinted from behind the van and through the door, taking care not to touch it. Will hesitated a moment. The controls were awkward, but he managed to make Vanya's device be still. Then he too made a dash for the door, crouched behind it and waited.

After a few moments, Sergei became bored.

'Maybe it was nothing,' he said and kicked at the boxes, making Will flinch. 'Hurry with this unloading. I will clear some room.' And with a boot he began to push aside the pile of dirty bedding.

As soon as the Russians' heads were turned away

from the door and from the boxes, Will guided Vanya's gift across the floor to him. It scurried so fast its legs and its fur were a blur.

Andrew screwed up his face in disgust as it jumped onto Will's hand.

It stood there, motionless, wires sticking out above its ears, like antennae. Attached to its head strap were a tiny video camera and microphone.

A neuroscientist, a friend of Vanya's, had done the brain surgery. He'd implanted the wireless electrodes, which allowed the rat to be remote-controlled. This had been part of a serious project, aimed at using the rats to find people trapped in collapsed buildings. But when the project was over, Vanya had said, the surgeon had given the animal to him. Will, while a little unnerved, was impressed. It was fast, obedient and – so far – reliable.

'Good job, Ratty,' Will said to himself. Quickly, he switched the rat to standby and slipped it into his jacket pocket, on top of his father's cricket ball. He took a good look at their new surroundings.

The corridor was made of concrete, and wires dangled down here and there, like tree roots. Fixed at regular intervals along the wall were rectangular orange lights, each protected with a cage. The lights were effective and they showed, about twenty metres away, a closed steel door with a control panel in the wall.

Will glanced at his watch. The LED was flashing. *Bugs*. Perhaps they'd already been heard . . . Or seen.

Will showed the bad news to Andrew and Gaia. Silently, he removed the tooth phone from his mouth and slipped it into the top front pocket of his fleece jacket. He motioned for them to do the same. Will didn't want the risk of a question from Vanya and then someone's instinctive reply.

'If you have to talk, do it like you're only breathing,' he whispered.

Andrew nodded. He pointed along the corridor, mouthing, *'Come on.'*

Before following, Gaia glanced back at the open door behind her. She didn't lack courage. But this was no game. And this wasn't Andrew's basement. They were here in St Petersburg. In an illicit research base. Somewhere beneath them were two long tunnels, was cutting-edge equipment to make a *black hole*.

Andrew was trying to hide his nervousness by being a little blasé, she thought. Will just looked focused. His eyes were almost glazed.

Very gently, she touched the small pouches of explosive that were strapped across her chest. Six freezer bags, each containing a few tablespoons of the mix and then tied up tight. Quick-release figure-of-eight knots attached the packages to a rope strung from a belt loop at the back of her jeans, over her shoulder, and then tied to another loop at the front. Six little bombs. One timer.

If necessary, they could be defensive, she decided.

Getting safely in and out of the van hadn't been easy. But it was nothing next to what lay ahead.

'Well?' They had reached the steel door, and Andrew was frowning at the control panel. Clearly, this was a biometric access point.

'Looks like it's for a face,' Will said, very quietly. 'Maybe it senses heat.'

Gaia glanced at him. 'We can't trick it.'

Will shook his head. No – they couldn't trick it. But what could they do? Somehow they had to get through. 'Andrew, where's that screwdriver you use for your glasses?'

Andrew touched his pocket. He reached inside, pulled out a zip-up bag and withdrew the miniature tool. 'What are you going to do?'

In response, Will started to undo the tiny screws that held the face of the control panel in place.

Andrew pushed his glasses up along his nose. 'You know that if we cut those, (a) – it might not work and, (b) – an alarm might go off.'

Will didn't take his eyes from his task. 'You have any other ideas? Gaia?'

She shook her head. The second tiny screw fell into Will's hand. Two more to go. Gently he lifted the plate away from the wall. A mass of wiring was revealed. Red, green, yellow, brown . . .

'What a mess,' Andrew breathed. And he glanced up. Wires were dangling all over the place. This hangar was a disaster waiting to happen.

Will was still holding on to the plate. He had no idea which to cut. 'Who's got the knife?'

'What knife?' Gaia said.

Will frowned. 'Andrew?'

'*I* didn't bring one,' Andrew said quickly. 'You're *The Maker*. You're the one with all the *things*.'

Will scowled at Andrew. 'I'm not The Maker.' He held his breath for a moment. Then he looked at Gaia. 'Hold this a minute.'

As she took the plate in her hands, Will brought Ratty out from his pocket. He activated the control screen and flicked through the Russian menu. *Forward, back, 20 degrees east* . . . every possible direction and even speed was available, but not what Will wanted. He'd have to trust that the rat retained some of its natural habits.

Will set Ratty to 'Normal' mode. It sat in his hand, alert, and waiting for instructions. Slowly, Will brought the rat's head towards the mass of wiring. For a moment, nothing happened.

'You're going to make it eat through them?' Andrew said, incredulous.

'I can't force it to,' Will said. But as he spoke, the rat jerked its head and its jaws opened. At once, it started to gnaw on the wires.

Gaia smiled. Noticing, Will smiled faintly too. A

small success, but it was worth recognizing. The nearest red wire was already stripped of plastic and sliced in two. Then the green, and three brown ones – and then the door flicked open.

Andrew leaped up. His back to the wall, he peered through. The high-ceilinged corridor ran ahead for about five metres and then took a ninety-degree cut to the right. It was cold here still, but there was sweat on Andrew's palms.

Will set Ratty down on the floor. As they inched forward, closing the primary access door behind them, Ratty scurried ahead and into the unknown. Will glanced at his watch. The LED wasn't flashing. No audio in this stretch of the base.

Ratty moved according to Will's instructions, but, as they had discovered, his normal behaviour was not totally suppressed. Every so often, the rat paused and sniffed the air, his whiskers twitching. When he reached what was obviously a lift shaft, Will made him stop.

'There,' Will said. 'That lift must go down to the collider . . .'

And then Ratty moved on. His head jerked up – and the three pairs of eyes clearly made out a miniature video camera mounted on the wall. Instinctively, Will glanced around the corridor. There was nothing here that he could see. But then cameras, as he knew, could be made so small as to be invisible.

'That camera will have picked up the rat,' Andrew said.

'So what?' Will replied. 'They're not going to send out security guards for a rat.'

'It's got wires coming out of his head!'

'They won't see that,' Will insisted. He had to believe it.

'But what about us – they'll see us when we follow him in.'

'Shh,' Will said. 'Look.'

Ratty's video footage was showing three doors beyond the lift shaft. The first two were unmarked. In white letters on the third was the word 'Control'. It was slightly ajar. Did no one close doors around here?

'Go back!' Andrew hissed. 'What was that? To the left? There.'

'Where?' But the cyborg animal was already turning its head.

'What's it doing?' Gaia said.

And Andrew smiled. 'Look.'

Rearing large on the video screen was the face of another animal. Whiskers twitched. Tiny black eyes flashed.

'Another rat!' Andrew said. 'I wonder what it's making of our little friend . . .'

'We should go down to the collider,' Gaia said. 'We don't know how much time we've got.'

Will nodded. 'But maybe we could learn something useful first. Come on, Ratty – back to the Control room . . .' He brushed the touch pad to move the rat on. The animal didn't respond.

'We might have a problem,' Andrew whispered. 'What if it's a lady rat?'

'What if Ratty's a lady rat?' Gaia hissed.

But then Vanya's device obeyed. The video screen showed the other rat turning and vanishing, away along the corridor.

Andrew and Gaia close behind, Will edged forward and around the corner. He stopped abruptly. Another glance at his watch showed bugs were active in this strip. The camera was mounted high on the wall, pointing away from them, but beyond their reach. Ratty was pretty useful, but he couldn't scurry up there.

'We need to take it out,' Andrew whispered.

Will nodded. 'You'll have to help me – I'm going to knock it.'

'You won't reach it.'

'Just help lift me up.' And Will wished for his trainers, with their soles inspired by gecko skin.

Andrew interlinked his fingers and waited for Will, who took a couple of steps to build momentum, before landing his right foot hard on Andrew's hands. With surprising strength for his size, Andrew lifted Will – just high enough for him to reach the camera and slap the rear end down, nosing the lens towards the ceiling. Noiselessly, Will's feet reconnected with the floor.

Will felt the pressure of Andrew's hand patting his back. Andrew was grinning. But Will didn't respond. He was still afraid the change in the image would alert security. Ten seconds passed. Twenty. Thirty . . .

They could not know it, but the video in the Surveillance room went unattended. Anna had no interest in being a security guard. Other things were on her mind.

'OK,' Will breathed. 'We'll listen at the door that says "Control". We'll just see if anyone's in there, then we'll go down.'

Andrew held his thumb and forefinger together in the sign for OK.

Gaia nodded reluctantly. The explosives against her body made her nervous. She was keen to be rid of them. And where better than around the collider?

Once Ratty was safely back in his pocket, Will extracted Vanya's wall-bugging kit from his rucksack. He held the antenna in the air as they advanced towards the Control room and he set the speaker volume to low. Nothing.

There was no sound from inside. Will knew what he had to do. And he knew it meant risking being discovered. Sweat prickling on the back of his neck, he pushed the door gently – just enough for him to catch his first glimpse of the dimly lit ante-room, with its steel tables and boxes of left-over kit. He breathed again – there was no one there. Gaia and Andrew immediately behind, Will dashed beneath the steel table that was shoved against the far wall, and once again, he tried the antenna, this time beside the Operations door.

At first, there was nothing. Slowly, Will tracked the antenna back along the wall. That was it. *Reception.*

A man was talking. Muffled, but just clear enough to make out.

'*No,*' the voice said. '*There has been no response to my demands.*'

Will frowned. Who was speaking?

'*Then we will show them, sir.*'

Cutler.

And he still had no idea why.

But who was Cutler talking to. Who was 'sir' – who was his boss?

'*When they see this,*' came the voice, '*I will have the planet at my feet.*'

'*The universe, sir.*'

'*No need to go over the top. Now get on with it.*' The voice had stiffened. '*Nothing must go wrong.*'

Andrew's eyes were wide. 'They are talking about the *weapon.*'

'We have to get down there *now,*' Gaia mouthed.

Will nodded. And if he'd had doubts, now it was clear: Cutler really was part of the plot. And he didn't sound as though he were under duress. Quite the opposite. So Cutler was an enemy. Why didn't I know, Will thought. There should have been some *clue* in his behaviour. But it was too late to think about that now.

Will turned to Andrew. 'Stay here, and keep listening. We'll go down with the explosive.'

Andrew's face blanched. 'What if someone comes in?'

'You'll be all right. Just stay down. Put some of those

boxes in front of you. And put your tooth phone in. Here–' and he took Ratty from his pocket. 'He's not too bad to use. Don't go through the menu, it's all in Russian. Just use the touch screen to control him. You can't change the speed that way but you can change his direction. All right?'

Andrew nodded. He screwed up his face at the rodent that sat obediently in his hand. His blue eyes looked faint. 'How long will you be?'

How could Will answer that? 'Not long,' he promised.

Anna could not hear Roden Cutler talking in the neighbouring room. The connecting door was too thick – and in any case, she knew what he'd be saying. And she had some important thinking to do.

She slumped in the black chair in the Surveillance room, twirling a pen, hoping the repetitive motion would help her think. Her ankle ached, but she ignored it. Beside her, the silent bank of video screens flickered. Anna took no interest. She was thinking about Caspian Baraban. It was hard to believe that he'd really succeeded. But he was a prodigy, that much was for sure. Brighter than his famous father. Brighter than her. And she clasped her hand angrily around the radio-tracking bracelet on her wrist. What could she do? What *should* she do?

Anna let her head fall to one side. And something caught her eye. Her relaxed spine snapped to steel. Her eyes flicked from the third video screen to the fourth – and then to the fifth. Hidden cameras implanted in the ante-room were transmitting fuzzy images that she couldn't quite believe. A child. A boy. And then a girl. And then –

The door to the Surveillance room slammed open. Cutler stood there, his lip curling. His yellow eyes gleamed. Anna rose and moved away from the bank of screens, towards him. It was the only thing for it.

'Anna,' Cutler crooned. This voice in particular she hated. It was oozy, sticky-sweet. And it was practically obscene, coming from those bloodless sharp lips. 'Despite your failings, the project goes on,' Cutler continued. He raised a hand. Reached for her hair. It took all her willpower not to flinch. Anger and disgust, with herself and with Roden, made her cheeks burn. 'Yes, all your mistakes, I forgive. I am a generous man. And tonight, our dreams will come true. The universe, Anna, the absolute power of creation, of destruction – it is ours.'

Anna had to listen. The odious hand was reaching for her cheek. Bony fingers with overgrown nails scraped her skin. And she had the sensation of leaving her body. Her flesh and blood was there, being touched by this man, but she, Anna, was outside this room, racing into the ante-room. Trying for a better look at that girl. And those boys.

*

'It's a long way down,' Gaia said. 'We'll be too deep to use the tooth phones to talk to Andrew.'

Will steadied himself as the lift cage juddered a little, and moved on, ever further underground, deep beneath the frozen Russian soil.

He wasn't thinking about Andrew. He was thinking about Cutler – and what he was doing. And who his boss might be. And the plot, and the question that bothered him almost most of all – *why would anyone want to take out a hotel?*

He glanced at Gaia. She looked tense, which was understandable. So was he, and he wasn't the one with explosive strapped around his chest.

With a jolt, the lift stopped. Hesitant, Gaia led the way out, and into a vast chamber. Dim orange lights cast an eerie glow.

At first they did nothing. Only stared.

Will blinked. It was an odd sensation.

Here they were, face to face with equipment that could obliterate their world.

On the table at his grandmother's house, they had sketched out the likely spec for a collider that might create a black hole. Caspian's diagram in the lab at Imperial College had shown two straight tunnels – so it wasn't a synchrotron, which sped its particles round and round, ever faster, through a circular high-tech doughnut. This collider shot the inner parts of heavy gold atoms right at each other. Head on.

Will could hear Andrew's voice. After helping Gaia with the explosive, he'd gone online to find out details about current colliders, in reputable laboratories. The fundamental technology would be similar.

'In each tunnel there will be a tube,' Andrew had told them. 'These tubes will be made of hundreds of magnets. And these magnets will be super-cooled with liquid helium – the cryogenics. This helium will be surrounded with a vacuum. At these very low temperatures, electricity flows with almost no resistance, creating the most powerful of all magnetic fields. And it is these fields that will let them speed those gold nuclei to incredible energies . . .'

The nuclei themselves would travel down a copper pipe. It would be narrow – just a few centimetres in diameter – and it would run through the heart of these shiny white tubes.

The reality sent prickles down Will's spine. Deep below the western hangar, he was staring at the cylindrical magnets. They rested on regularly spaced plastic supports, and they disappeared into shadows to the left and to the right.

Will shifted his gaze to the point where they met. To a yellow metal chamber. Here, in this chamber, the nuclei would be smashed – a colossal cataclysm, amid the sorts of temperatures and pressures not seen since the universe began.

He shuddered. It wasn't just the sight of the equipment. It was the fact that stopping this madness was down to them.

Will turned to Gaia. Her arms hung heavy at her sides. Her eyes glinted in the sulphurous light.

'We have to find a good weak point,' Will said at last. 'We don't have much explosive – we'll have to choose carefully. Maybe if we can put explosive against a join in the vacuum shield.'

'Or a magnet support.'

'No, the vacuum shield would be best.' He glanced cautiously along the right-hand tunnel, missing the expression of annoyance that flashed across Gaia's face. They could see no one. Hear nothing, only the hum of the equipment. 'We should split up,' he whispered. 'Put your tooth phone in. If I find a good spot first, I'll let you know. Which do you want – right or left?'

In a voice tight with sarcasm, she replied: 'Since you're always right, I'll take left.'

'What do you think is happening?' Elena peered at her watch. Radioactive specks showed her it was thirty-five minutes to midnight.

Vanya shrugged. 'Who knows?' He put his tooth phone in, tried again. 'Hello? Hello? Will? Andrew? Girl? . . . Nothing,' he said.

After the successful encounter with the guards, Vanya had driven the car a little further along the road. He'd parked just off it, underneath more pines. Here, they were invisible, but they had a good view of the base. The white light burned. But it showed nothing. No one moved outside.

'You have the medicine?' Elena said.

Vanya pulled the bottle of vodka from his shirt pocket. As he was passing it to Elena, he froze. 'Look.'

In the darkness of the trees, about twenty metres from the car in the direction of the base, a man had stopped. He was dressed in Russian outdoor gear. A black hat and a black puffa jacket. In his hands, he gripped a pair of standard binoculars. Now he raised them. He seemed to be inspecting the base.

The bottle midway to her mouth, Elena stared. 'Who do you think he is?'

Vanya shrugged. 'A mad man, to be out in this cold.'

In fact, the man was thinking pretty much the same thing. Without knowing it, he'd parked his stolen car within shouting distance of Vanya and Elena. Now he was making one last shivering inspection of the base before his boss arrived. The puffa jacket worked well. But the hat did little to stop the sensation that his scalp was shrivelling.

The man let the binoculars dangle around his neck.

Taking off a glove, he dug around in his pocket. At last, he found what he wanted. Inside the small black case was the device. Awkwardly, he slotted it over his rear molar. The unpleasant sensation reminded him of his childhood braces. But he was within distance of his contact and supposedly operating in silence, so obliged to use it. Quickly, he slipped his glove back on and clenched his numb fingers.

'It's me,' he said, very quietly. 'There's no change. What do you want to do?'

Gaia walked slowly, her hands firmly in her pockets. So far, she'd seen no particular weakness worth further inspection. While the rest of the base was shoddy, the same was not true for the particle collider. The walls and floor were spotless. The tubes themselves really were shiny – brilliant white and cool to the touch.

Like Gaia, Will was wearing boots with soft soles. The sound of his footsteps had quickly vanished as he strode away in the opposite direction. She'd waited a few minutes to see if he'd glance back, or if he'd tell her to be careful, or wish her good luck.

He had not.

Now Gaia felt acutely alone. The only noise was a faint hum of the equipment, the only movement the occasional flicker of the orange bulbs. She felt the weight of the pats of explosive against her stomach and chest. And, like Will, she felt the responsibility of what they *had* to do. Blood throbbed through her neck.

Not long after leaving Will, Gaia passed a quad bike

– minus the key. Technicians must use them to speed along the tunnels, she guessed. Every so often, she noticed, there were steel doors set into the white-painted wall. They would lead into a parallel access tunnel, she thought.

Gaia glanced back. The yellow metal chamber was in the distance now. She must have walked a kilometre, maybe more.

And then, she saw her spot. A plastic support that wasn't properly attached. If she could take this magnet out of action, that should be enough for tonight.

Gingerly, Gaia peeled off her fleece jacket. The sash rested against her T-shirt. Cradling one of the bags with her left hand, she used her right to undo the knot. Her fingers trembled, and she forced herself to stop for a moment, to get her breathing back under control. *Think of school,* she told herself. *You're back in the staff room at school . . .*

Three minutes later, Gaia had a pile of four bags of explosive on the floor. Four should be enough. Best to keep the other two in case anyone spotted her. In case she needed them for self-defence.

Very gently, she placed the bags together around the top of the plastic magnet support. The fuse went in next, and she attached it to the timer – the keypad from the dismembered microwave. Her heart pounding, Gaia keyed in a fifteen-minute delay. Then she pressed the button that Will had told her was marked with the Russian for 'Start'.

15.00. 14.59. 14.58 . . .

Time to get out.

Gaia was about to put in her tooth phone to whisper to Will to meet her back at the lift – and her head jerked. Out of the corner of her eye, she'd seen something move. The last steel door she had just passed, ten metres or so behind – it was opening.

Instantly, Gaia dropped to the floor. She crouched, and she managed to squeeze most of her body beneath the tube. Her breath was coming quick and fast.

She watched as two men emerged in full protective suits with broad black belts with tools dangling. They were carrying a vat. Liquid helium, she realized. For the cryogenic cooling system. Luckily the light was dim and they didn't seem to have noticed her. Still, she was close enough to hear every word they said, and to make out the features of their exhausted faces.

The first man, who had a snub nose and a black moustache, rubbed his back as soon as they had set down their load. He staggered over to the white accelerator tube. The other, who had white hair, was waiting. His eyes looked bloodshot, and he yawned.

Gaia felt a shot of pain in her thigh. Cramp. She arched her body very slightly, so she could move her leg, and as she angled back, the metal box she'd used to carry the keypad and the fuse clattered from her pocket and on to the floor.

Tin on concrete.

Razors sliced up her spine.

Her heart raced. *Had they heard?*

At once, the desperate question was answered.

The man at the tube yelled something in Russian. His elderly colleague turned sharply. He squinted in her direction. Options raced through her mind. If she stayed where she was, she'd be caught. But if she ran away, she'd be running towards the beam generator – away from the lift and from Will – towards a dead end. Gaia touched the pats of explosive that remained against her stomach. There was only one thing she could do.

Quickly, she shuffled from beneath the tube and she stood up. She edged out into the tunnel, into their full view. Again, the snub-nosed technician called out in astonished Russian.

'English,' Gaia said, pointing at herself. 'No Russian.'

'English?' The second one said. Lines furrowed across his old forehead. 'Who are you, English? What are you doing here?'

'I am working here,' she said, improvising. 'I was sent down to check the magnet casings.'

The man frowned. 'You are a child.'

'I am eighteen,' she lied. 'I work at Imperial College with Professor Vassily Baraban.'

For a moment, the man hesitated.

Did he believe her?

'Where is your uniform?' he said. 'And why are you not on the register? We have not seen you before.'

With one hand, the second technician jerked off his

face mask. With the other he reached for his belt. Instantly, he raised what was obviously a weapon. Gaia stared back at him defiantly. She had to keep up the act. It was her only hope.

'You are a child so I will not kill you at once,' he continued. 'This weapon is electric. I will only stun you. We will take you with us. But you will be all right.'

This was too much. Her brain reeled. Being stunned would mean death. Strapped around her chest were two bags of extremely flammable triacetone triperoxide. One spark could set it all off. And this man was pointing the electric weapon right at her heart.

A plan half-formed in her mind. She had no time to think of others.

'Don't be afraid,' the technician said, squinting. 'It will just take a moment—' And, as he shot, she ran.

He missed her. Just. Gaia headed straight for the gap between the two men. She was fast, and she was agile. The gun-toting technician was still aiming when suddenly she was in between them and clear out the other side. If she ducked alongside the tube for cover, she could be at the lift well before—

'Halt!' the technician yelled, spinning on his heels. 'I have you in my sights! No more stupid moves or perhaps I will kill you right now.'

Very slowly, each muscle resisting, Gaia turned. The technician's face was bright red. His chest was heaving.

'Stand still,' he ordered.

Gaia hesitated. There was just no way she could

obey. She realized what she had to do. And she didn't think about it. She ran. Forward this time, sending confusion skidding through the technician's round eyes. What was the girl doing?

In a moment, it was clear. Gaia headed straight for the vat. She reached for the release valve and she pushed at the container with all her strength. As she felt it topple, she turned and she ran, back in the direction of Will, and the lift. From behind, she heard a shout, and then a scream. Then nothing.

Tears formed in her eyes, but she'd had *no choice*. If she hadn't pushed over that vat, they'd have killed her. Had she killed them? She had to hope with all her heart she had not. Perhaps the liquid had simply caught their feet. It would be like frostbite. They'd be hurt. But they'd survive.

After leaving Gaia, Will also walked slowly. He wasn't sure exactly what he was looking for. The vacuum shield was the best bet, he thought – but the outer layer of the tube seemed tough. Would it be susceptible to Gaia's home-made explosive?

Keep looking, he told himself. *There'll be something. You'll find it.* And he thought of his grandmother and Vanya, waiting in the car, and Andrew, back up at ground level, alone. Gaia had been right: they were too deep for Tooth Talk's transmissions to reach the surface.

If anything happened to Andrew, neither he nor Gaia would know a thing about it. Perhaps he should have brought Andrew with him. Down into this dull-orange tunnel, with its cool walls and stale air.

Like Gaia, he noticed the steel doors. And he passed a black quad bike, squat and gleaming. This time, the keys were in the ignition. Will was about to jump on it when he heard a low engine noise advancing from the far end of the tunnel. *Another bike.*

He needed a hiding place. And fast. At once, Will dropped to his hands and he slipped underneath the tube, between two of the plastic support posts. He held his breath, and he waited.

The wait wasn't long. And when the bike appeared, Will's pulse raced along with it. He knew the man driving it. At least, he'd seen his picture in the paper, beside the story about the abduction. *Vassily Baraban.*

In fact, Baraban was returning from modifying the left-hand beam generator. He'd already done the right. He glanced at his watch. Twenty-five minutes. He shook his head. He was a scientist, not a killer. It had been an impossible choice: cooperate and perhaps live, or refuse and surely die. But the responsibility would lie with him, not his son.

Will could only watch as the bike sped past and skidded to a halt along the tunnel, beside the lift. Baraban leaped off and punched his fist against the call button. Will hesitated. Then he made up his mind. He edged out from underneath the tube, and he started to run, towards the lift, towards Baraban. This man had been abducted. He was here against his will. Perhaps he would help. Perhaps he'd have some ideas about sabotage.

Will was a fast runner, and he felt the air whip through his hair. But while he was still a good thirty metres away, the lift arrived. Its passenger was swallowed up. Will yanked out the tooth phone. He shouted: '*Wait.*'

Too late. Baraban was gone. And with him, their first real break? He hoped not.

Will slowed to a walk, breathing hard. He'd missed the chance to talk to Baraban alone. And his tunnel search had been fruitless. He was about to replace his tooth phone to ask Gaia if she'd had better luck. Then he noticed that someone – *Gaia* – was running from the opposite direction. They reached the lift at the same time. She almost collided with him. Tears were streaked down her face.

'*What's happened?*'

She shook her head. 'We have to get out of here. There were two men. They saw me. I—' and she hesitated. Angrily, she wiped away the tears. 'I tipped liquid helium over them.'

'*What?*'

Gaia met Will's horrified stare. 'I had no choice. Will, they were going to kill me.'

'But you set the explosive?'

She nodded. 'It'll go off in . . . eleven minutes.'

With a thump, Will hit the button for the lift. Men were down. The odds were that the security systems had already detected them. For whatever reason, Vassily Baraban had been in a hurry. Time was running out.

Gaia was first in the lift. She rested her back and her head against the metal cage. Will slotted in his tooth phone. 'Andrew? Andrew can you hear me? We're coming back up.' No answer.

As at last they made their unsteady way back to the surface, Will also tried to rouse Vanya. No response. At the top, he was about to attempt Andrew once more. But as the lift door opened, there he was, Ratty twitching in his palm.

'*Andrew.*'

Andrew's face was white. His phone was in his hand. 'I can't get a connection,' he stumbled. 'Either they've got signal blockers or we're in a Faraday cage.'

'What connection?' Gaia said. 'Who are you trying to call?'

'Why didn't you wait for us?' Will whispered harshly.

'I heard something.' Andrew's eyes were empty, all expression gone. Then he held Ratty out to Will, giving him a quick parting stroke. 'He's a good rat,' he said.

'He does what he's told,' Will replied. 'Maybe we should put electrodes in your head.'

'What did you hear?' Gaia said.

Andrew looked at her. 'I've been trying to call – I can't get a connection—'

'*Call who?*' Gaia demanded.

'Elena,' he said. 'Anyone. To get the police. They have to come now. Have you planted the bombs?'

She nodded.

Andrew fixed his eyes on hers. 'Well I hope they work. Because we don't have any time. I heard your friend talking,' he said to Will. 'That hotel isn't actually a hotel. And they're going to make the black hole to destroy it at *midnight*.'

'What do you mean it isn't a hotel?' Will was staring hard at Andrew.

'It's code – that's what they've been calling it. But I heard your friend talking.'

'So what is it?' Gaia demanded.

'Listen for yourself. Ratty's mike picked up the signal from the wall-bugging kit. Your friend was talking to someone else – a woman, I think. I couldn't really hear what she was saying.'

Quickly, Andrew fiddled with the control unit. He backed up through the audio recording. And hit play:

Cutler's voice.

'Now we're so close to the culmination of all our dreams, I can tell you this much. It isn't a hotel at all . . .'

Muffled words in response. There was static, and then the recording continued.

'. . . Right now, who'd police you? Up in space, you can do what you like . . . The UN Security Council sent

it up last week. It's equipped with interception and surveillance devices. The plan, I believe, is to keep it all under wraps until the legalese to support it is sorted out. The grand unveiling was set to be after the UN conference in New York. That security station would have the power to patrol space . . . My patron – he cannot allow that to happen.'

Will frowned. 'A police station in space?'

Andrew nodded quickly. 'It makes more sense. Why would Esmee Templeton be in a hotel?'

'Shh,' Gaia said.

There was another muffled question. More static.

'But who's the patron?' Will said, almost to himself. Whose was the voice they'd heard while hiding outside the Operations room?

Will frowned. He'd heard about the UN meeting somewhere. There was going to be a special assembly to discuss space laws and methods to enforce them. But the mystery still remained: why would Cutler's patron – whoever he was – want to take out an orbiting police station?

Andrew was fiddling with the unit. 'I couldn't hear much more,' he said hurriedly. 'And then he was talking to someone else – Caspian, I think. And he said they're going to use the weapon at midnight. That's in *twenty-five minutes.'* Andrew held up his wrist, his gold watch flashing. 'There's a rocket all ready. We have to stop them.'

'That *is* the plan, Andrew,' Will said. He glanced at Gaia, but she seemed absorbed.

So that's why Baraban had been in such a hurry. And that's why the staff had left on the bus – and perhaps why he, Andrew and Gaia hadn't already been stopped by security.

'There are only eight minutes until Gaia's explosives go off,' Will said. 'It'll be OK.'

Now Andrew's pale eyes met his. 'So what do we do?'

'We wait.'

'Where?' Andrew said.

'With the van. We'll wait there. As soon as the bombs go off, we can run out and call Vanya.'

'What about the room I was in?' Andrew said. 'Then we can hear your friend and hear his reaction when it all goes up.'

The wall-bugging kit in his arms, Andrew turned and strode off, towards the Control room.

'He's not my friend,' Will hissed. But he touched Gaia's arm. At least they'd get to listen in. 'Come on.'

As they raced along the corridor towards the Control room, Will noticed that the surveillance camera was still pointing uselessly up at the ceiling.

Someone must have noticed, Will thought. But if they had, evidently they didn't care enough to check it out – or to get it fixed. That was good news.

In fact, Sergei and Vladimir had noticed the camera. And the chewed wires of the primary access panel. Right at the moment that Will, Andrew and Gaia threw themselves underneath the table in the ante-room, they were facing the red chair, sharing their discoveries with Roden Cutler.

'Rats,' Sergei was saying. 'Vlad and I, we saw them in the depot. This place is falling apart! They are eating it to pieces. Even the wires for the cameras!'

Cutler might have asked how rats could undo screws. But he was far too preoccupied with his weapon. Besides, the external security was tight – or so he thought. 'Rats mean nothing to me,' Cutler said.

'And nor do you, Sergei. Get out. Go and pick up your pay and leave. Vladimir, you stay here in case I need you.'

Sergei gave a quick upward kink of his blond eyebrows. Mad, he was thinking – it was as clear as Russian vodka. There would be no complaint from him. Sergei nodded at Vladimir, and stomped his way through the inner door of the Operations room.

Sergei waited in the narrow quarantine zone for the mechanism's click of recognition. Then with a push, he was half-out into the ante-room.

Underneath the steel table, Will, Andrew and Gaia could do nothing. Except hold their breath. Sergei's hulking legs were right next to them, an electric gun dangling down from his belt. Will recognized it at once. This gun had been among the last batch of patents he'd read before his father died. *Electric bullets.* And Will was thinking of the space police station. What weapons would they use? Not electric bullets. Sonic bullets? Perhaps. It was an extraordinary idea, to think there were law-enforcement agents orbiting Earth . . .

Still Sergei did not move. Will wished he didn't have to breathe. Gaia, who had learned her lesson, did not even dare to. And cramp could kill her, she thought, before she'd move. Andrew kept his head down. Noiselessly, he switched off the wall-bugging mike, and he waited . . .

Sergei had been hovering, using his black-booted foot to keep the door open. He was trying to get his walkie-talkie to work. Trying to call the pay office, to check someone was there. If not, he'd head right back in and demand the cash – without giving Cutler a chance to remotely change the settings of his radio tracking bracelet. Sergei had no faith in the man. But someone must have answered, because he spoke rapidly: 'All right. I'm coming. Get it ready.' And he blundered away, out along the corridor.

Instantly, Will reached out to catch the door before it closed. He pulled a glove from his pocket and placed it around the jamb. 'Just in case . . .' he whispered to Andrew.

Again, he glanced at his watch. Three minutes now until the explosion. Andrew switched the mike back on but no one was talking. At least, not that they could hear.

Two minutes.

'See – it'll be fine,' Will said. He closed his eyes. And his mind flickered with the eerie orange light and the deadly white tubes.

One minute.

Gaia tensed. Her head was aching, her body trembling. She couldn't get rid of the faces of those two technicians. She should have checked they were all right. She should have helped them . . .

Twenty seconds. And Andrew waved the mike. Someone was talking. Cutler.

'All right, systems check. And—'

Ten seconds. Will kept his eyes fixed on his father's watch.

Five. Four. Three. Two. One . . .

'All looking good. Excellent.'

In the ante-room, no one said a word.

'Now, I wonder how that boy's getting on. We're almost ready,' said Cutler.

Will glanced at Gaia. Her face had gone deathly white. Will took hold of her wrist to look at her watch. The time matched his. Beside him, Andrew was intensely still. *No. It had to work.*

At last, Andrew took a breath. But it was more like a gasp. Like a person recovering from drowning.

'So, actually it didn't go off,' he said, very quietly.

Gaia said nothing. Her fingernails were short but still she could feel them digging harder and harder into her palms.

'It doesn't look like it,' Will agreed.

And Andrew rounded on him. 'Now what are we going to do?'

Gaia looked down. But she was thinking, how *could* it not have worked? Did the age of Elena's chemicals have anything to do with it? No, she could only blame herself. Why hadn't she tested it? Just this once. Elena had had to smash her bomb with a bat, and still she'd trusted it – trusted that the fuse would ignite her explosive.

The faces of the technicians vanished. Instead she saw only a swelling black hole tunnelling its way out of the accelerator, down underneath St Petersburg, deeper and deeper until it reached the centre of their world . . .

'Maybe we can do something in there,' Will said, and he jerked his head towards the Operations room. 'There must be a central control system. Maybe we can still stop it.'

He glanced at Gaia, whose facial muscles felt paralysed. 'I might have put too much stabilizer in,' she said very quietly.

'I might have damaged the timer,' Will replied. There was no point in making her feel bad. 'The circuit was really delicate.'

It was counting down, she thought. But she said nothing. And she thought furiously. It was her fault. She'd have to come up with another plan . . . And something struck her.

There was no time to explain. Already, Andrew was standing up. 'I don't care who did what. Now we have no choice,' he said. With his forefinger he jabbed in the direction of Cutler. 'We go in there.'

'*STORM* the place?' Will said.

Andrew flushed. 'I don't think, Will, that now is the time for any jokes.'

Of course, storming their way into the Operations room was out of the question. If they wanted any kind of a shot at success, they'd have to use stealth.

Taking a deep breath, Will put a hand on the steel inner door. Andrew and Gaia were right up behind him, breathing, quite literally, down his neck. And he turned his head. He asked, wordlessly, if they really agreed. This would be the biggest risk so far. Both heads nodded.

After setting Ratty down on the floor, Will pushed. The steel gave way a few centimetres. He waited, his heart racing. Now they could hear the voice – more voices – from inside. But the tones did not change. No one had noticed the door shift.

Gripping the control pad tight in his hand, Will sent Ratty scurrying in. Andrew and Gaia crowded round even tighter to watch.

At first, the screen showed only blackness. Then Ratty inched forward, and the room opened up. He was peeking out from what seemed to be a free-standing monitor, broad and low. Beyond that was a blood-red carpet and a man. He was sprawling on a red chair, one arm on a desk. *Cutler.*

Behind Cutler was a shaved-headed guard. Vladimir – though, of course, Will did not know it. To Cutler's right were Vassily Baraban and Caspian. Andrew gripped Will's arm. And Will could guess why. Caspian's expression was bizarre. He looked both confident and terrified. His sweatshirt was crumpled. Black hair stuck up all over the place.

Eight years. They hadn't been close friends. But Andrew knew Caspian. At least, he knew the person Caspian had been. And now he was betraying them. Betraying all that STORM stood for.

Cutler barked an order. At once, Vassily and his son moved into a room marked 'Systems'. The shaved-headed guard waited outside, a plastic weapon hanging from his belt. Was something wrong? Or was the father-and-son team simply performing final checks?

A quick right–left manoeuvre by Ratty revealed one other person in the room. A woman. She had long, dark hair and an ankle in plaster. Her back was to the camera. Afraid Ratty might be noticed, Will withdrew him to a spot behind the screen.

Will turned to Gaia and Andrew. He mouthed: 'We go out. We hide where Ratty is.' The screen looked wide enough to give them cover. And it seemed pretty clear to Will that if there was a master control system in there, it was located at the desk with Cutler's skinny arm draped across it.

Exactly what they'd do once inside the room, he wasn't sure. Yet.

Gaia nodded quickly. Andrew made the sign for A-OK. Will could read the apprehension in both pairs of eyes. Strangely, he felt calm. Perhaps it was because he knew what they had to do. The only thing that made him uncomfortable was indecision.

Will went first. Gaia and Andrew were noiseless behind him. Gaia let the inner door close around one of her gloves. And then they crouched together, behind the screen. An LED monitor, as it turned out.

At last, they had entered the world hinted at by Ratty and the wall-bugging mike. Now they could hear everything. They could see everything in vivid, stained colour. The concrete was cracking, Andrew noticed. Multicoloured wires sprouted from the walls like robot hair. Their bare metal ends gleamed.

Cutler was mumbling. He ran his bony finger down a list on the first touch screen. 'Beam position. Cryogenics. Check. Automatic timer – check.'

Will glanced at his watch. The LED was going crazy. The room was riddled with microphones. But far worse was the time. *Ten minutes* to midnight.

Cautiously, Will manoeuvred Ratty out from behind the screen. He wanted a better look at the control panel. They *needed* a better look. Perhaps Ratty could find a clue. No self-destruct button, of course. Just *something.*

But to get Ratty to the screen, Will had to send him scurrying behind the woman with the long hair. And, as he pattered along behind her, she turned her head.

She stared at the rat – *right at him.* Her astonishment leaped out of the video screen. Will stared back.

It took all his self-control not to cry out. She was looking into his eyes. It was as though she could see him. Will felt blood throb hard in his neck. It felt as though a vice were squeezing his head. All that pressure building up in his body, and he could not shout.

Then she glanced away. And Will let the screen drop to his lap. Andrew touched his arm. His eyes asked: *what?*

Will shook his head. Everything was wrong. First Cutler.

Now his *mother.*

His mother. She *was* here in St Petersburg. But she was right here – in the base. Here with Cutler. With Baraban. With the *weapon.*

Will's brain was scrambling, thoughts burning red hot. What was she doing *here*? There were no answers, only a raging vortex of questions. They displaced everything. He was trying – really trying – to put everything but the weapon out of his mind. Now this was plain impossible.

On automatic pilot, Will ordered Ratty to retreat underneath a chair. Very slowly, as if on some different plane of time, his consciousness returned to the room.

Ratty's video camera was still pointing right at his mother. But she was looking everywhere but behind her. She seemed somehow to refuse to see the rat with the electrodes in its head. And as Will struggled with what he was seeing, into the picture walked Roden Cutler.

With a stiff hand, Cutler touched his mother's hair. Will's whole body clenched.

If seeing his mother was inconceivable, this was a thousand times worse. She was working with *him*.

Will shook his head. It was as though he'd entered another, inverted, universe. *Nothing* made sense. But there was one thing he was glad of: she was all right. She was alive.

Beside him, Andrew and Gaia exchanged a glance. Will missed it. He saw only Anna. And Roden, whose hand was now touching her cheek. His mouth was close to her ear, but Will could still hear what he was saying: 'You should have come away with me, all those years ago, Anna. Together, imagine, what we could have been!'

Everything faded. Will's hand went to his head. It was black. His vision blurred.

Will wasn't in this room, wasn't here in St Petersburg.

He was in Dorset. It was twelve years ago. He was curled up on the old velvet sofa in the kitchen. It was pleasant here, warm by the fire. His mother was resting her elbows on the table, reading a novel. His father was pulling on his old green boots, preparing to burn the rubbish in the garden. Will was nearly asleep.

This time, it wasn't a dream. Through half-shut eyes, Will saw his father stride outside. And he saw, slipping in through the kitchen door, Roden Cutler.

Cutler. In his house. He'd told Will he'd visited. When he was young. Will probably wouldn't remember. But he did. Because now he remembered something that for twelve years his brain had rejected. Kept locked up in his unconscious, with no chance of parole.

Seeing his mother – seeing Cutler touch her – it flooded out.

There, in the kitchen, he had kissed her. Roden had kissed her, right on the lips. And she – *his mother* – she had not pushed him back.

Anger blazed. Will felt dizzy, hot and cold. Gaia touched his arm. He stared at her with unseeing eyes. '*My mother,*' he mouthed.

Her eyes widened. She pointed to the image of Anna on the video screen. Will could say nothing, do nothing. *Yes,* he wanted to shout.

Gaia hesitated. Then she bent her head to his. She whispered into his ear: 'OK. But now get yourself together.' A pause. 'I mean it. Will. You can't crack up on us now. *Will.*'

Will forced himself to listen. Deep down, he knew she was right. He dragged his eyes back to the screen, which showed Cutler moving away, back to his precious desk. His vision still blurred, Will tried to concentrate. He had lost his focus. He had to get it back.

And then, Anna spoke.

The security footage had been far from clear. But she was his mother. The rat with the miniature video camera and the wires sticking out of its head only confirmed it. *Vanya,* she guessed. Her son was here. He had found her. Pride, despair, both competed in her chest.

'Perhaps you are right, Roden,' she said.

The voice electrified Will. He watched, entranced, as Cutler pursed his lips and nodded.

'Perhaps I should have gone with you then,' she said, in her soft, low voice. 'But you have been with me in spirit. It reminds me of a song my mother used to sing to me: *As you sleep, I hold you dear. As you dream I'm always near.* It meant that she was on my side. That no matter how things might seem – how *confusing* things might appear – she was there, and she would do everything she could to make everything all right. But sometimes I had to realize that my mother was not omnipotent. Sometimes, she could not act – sometimes there were *physical* reasons that she could not—' and

Anna fiddled with her radio-tracking bracelet – 'and perhaps she needed a little assistance from me.'

'Hmm,' said Roden.

Instantly, Will realized this odd little speech was not directed at Cutler. She knew. Somehow, his mother knew he was here. Confusion fell away from his brain. Could he trust her? And what did she mean, she needed help? And what about the kiss. The memory? Her lies?

Will glanced at Gaia. Beside her, Andrew waited, trembling, for direction. They had no choice. And they needed help. *Seven minutes* until the test. All those questions could wait. He had to risk it. And crouching behind this screen was killing him. He wanted to *do* something. But he had to know if he could trust her.

Silently, Will handed the video screen to Andrew. He eased the backpack from his shoulders, and he dug out Speak Easy. Whispering into the microphone, he said:

'Cutler wants to destroy the new space station with a black hole. We have to stop him.'

With extreme caution, Will stuck one eye and his arm beyond the edge of the screen. He aimed the device at the ceiling above his mother's head and he hit send. Andrew was staring at him. 'My mother,' Will whispered, and got an astonished expression in response.

A moment later he also got his reply. His mother's voice: 'I know. You're right.'

Will took a deep breath. Really, could he really trust

her? What if she was pretending? He shook his head. No.

He thought about the particle collider. And the black hole, which would burrow like an evil parasite right to the heart of their Earth. But their timing would be vital. They'd have to wait for the right moment . . .

'Right about what?' Cutler said.

Anna only shrugged. 'Everything, Roden. Everything.' But she was glancing towards Ratty.

Six minutes. The door to the Systems room banged open. 'We are ready,' Caspian announced.

Cutler fixed his gleaming, yellow eyes first on the father then on the son. 'This is true?'

'Yes,' Caspian replied.

He was like a zombie now, Will thought. His black eyes seemed unseeing. His face pale and drawn. What must be going through his mind? Surely he realized what he was doing.

'Very well. Then, Caspian, you go back in and wait a few minutes. I'll call you out when I need you.'

'Why can't I stay here?'

'Do. As. I. Say.' The words were loaded with raw threat. Cutler's yellow eyes shot lightning. 'I want to talk to your father.'

As soon as Vladimir had slammed the door on a reluctant Caspian, Cutler leaped up. He faced Vassily.

Behind the screen, Andrew touched Will's arm. He held up his skinny wrist with its oversized watch. *Five and a half minutes.*

'We have to do something now,' he mouthed.

Will nodded. But he held up a hand. 'Wait,' he whispered. We need a plan, he thought. But what could they do? The guard was armed.

'Well,' Cutler said to Vassily, 'I'm of a mind to let you go. On one condition: your son stays with me.'

Vassily's mouth gaped. 'Why?' he managed to whisper.

'I should have thought that was obvious. He's brilliant. The two of us – we would be invincible.'

'Never,' Vassily rasped. 'Never—'

Cutler shook his head. 'I did anticipate this response. And so, Vassily, I'm afraid you are finished. In all senses.' And he reached out to Vladimir's belt and quick-released the electric gun.

Vassily stared at Cutler with alarm. He raised his hands in token defence. 'But I will leave peacefully. There is no need for the stun – I remember what it was like.'

'Stun?' Cutler said. He spat the word, and he clicked a dial on the side of the weapon. 'Who said anything about stun? You know too much too live. And, unlike your son, you are not too valuable to die.'

'*Roden—*' Anna's voice, fast and urgent.

'Quiet now, Anna.' Cutler spoke with absolute calm. And, with absolute calm, he now raised the gun to the astonished Vassily Baraban. There was no more time for protest.

'*Dosvidanya,*' Roden said. And he fired.

Behind the screen, Will almost dropped Ratty's monitor. Gaia's hands shot to her face. She'd seen the body fall. Heavy. Lifeless. She couldn't quite form the word in her mind, but Vassily Baraban was *dead.* Her eyes were wide. Anger coursed through her. While they had watched, Vassily had died. They could wait no longer.

'*Will,*' she said, barely taking care to whisper. 'Will, we have to do it now. Otherwise we've got no chance! I have to get to that desk. Get out your ball.'

She stood. Three heads turned. Vladimir's. Anna's. And Cutler's.

Cutler's expression rippled. Surprise. Disbelief. While Cutler struggled with what he saw, Gaia gestured violently at Will. Beside him, Andrew cried out in alarm: '*Gaia!*'

Recovering, Roden lifted his gun.

'Wait!' she cried. She pulled back the flaps of her jacket. 'I'm strapped with explosive. If you shoot at me, this whole room will go up.'

There was silence. For one whole second. Then:

'What the hell are you doing here?' The girl from Covent Garden. Will's date. *Will's date.* Cutler glanced from her to the LED screen, which showed the rapidly approaching target. In just a few minutes the hotel would pass over St Petersburg . . .

'*Will.*' Gaia's voice. 'I need an impact.'

And she loosed the little pat that had been sitting on her stomach. Pulling back her arm, she yelled again to Will, and she let it fly, right at Roden Cutler.

As Gaia had prepared to throw, Will jumped up from behind the screen. He grabbed the leather ball from his pocket. He knew what she wanted. And he could think of no alternative. He felt anger flaming in his chest. At Cutler, at Baraban's death. And he thought of his father as he kept his eyes on that flying pat of explosive and sent his ball spinning. If he could pull it off . . . but he had no doubts. There was no room for them.

Smack. The ball collided with the explosive. It sent the pat smashing against the wall above Cutler's head. Instantly, flames erupted. The impact sent Cutler and Vladimir sprawling. Will's ball dropped, blackened.

At once, Gaia was at Cutler's desk.

'The cryogenics!' Anna shouted, her eyes on her son. 'I can't approach the desk – I'll get electrocuted. It's the first touch screen!'

'I'm on it,' Gaia yelled. She knew exactly what to do. The realization had come immediately after the knowledge her explosive had failed. Will had been right, in a sense. If she could cut the insulation to the reservoirs of liquid helium, the pressure inside would rocket. A few minutes later, those shiny white tubes would explode.

Andrew ran to her. Already Gaia had called up the operations control. But the menus made no sense. His fingers trembling, Andrew reached over. He knew the operating system. In a few moments, he brought up the menu that regulated the vacuum skin of the colliders. And he changed the setting – from 'absolute vacuum' to 'none'.

Instantly, Gaia pulled the last pat of explosive from her body. She slapped it down on the console. Andrew grabbed Roden's chair, and he raised it high.

'Look away!' he yelled as he brought it down with a slam, triggering the explosion.

At once, the desk became a mass of flames and smouldering plastic. Sparks caught the red carpet, which began to burn. Others leaped to the monitor, and to the plastic casings of the dangling wires. Now the setting could not be changed.

A siren blitzed the room. '*Evacuate the building,*' blared a calm, pre-recorded woman's voice. '*Evacuate the building—*'

'It's done,' Gaia shouted. 'In a few minutes, those tubes will go.' She turned to Andrew, eyes shining. Without thinking, he hugged her.

Neither of them saw that *at that very moment,* two things happened.

Anna was holding out her arms to Will, who stumbled towards her, the retrieved ball hot in his hand. 'What are you doing here?' he demanded.

She grabbed his arms. 'However did you find me?' she whispered fiercely, scanning his face. 'I will explain everything, I promise.'

At that very moment, on the other side of the flaming desk, Caspian Baraban emerged from the Systems room to discover Vassily on the floor. Before dropping to his father's side, his stunned mind half-registered the presence of Will, Andrew and Gaia.

He saw Roden Cutler, flat on his back. Not moving.

Beside Vassily and Caspian, Vladmir was stumbling to his feet.

And Cutler twitched. His body was racked through with pain. Splinters of plastic had penetrated his right bicep and tricep. The muscles ached. And realization exploded inside his head.

'No,' he whispered. '*No!* What have you done! *What have you done?*' Cutler stared wildly at his desk. The sight was impossible to take in. Had they really stopped the black hole? The flames told him: yes. If so, they had ruined everything. Destroyed his glory. Guaranteed his death. Pain blazed through his veins. Cutler cried out in frustration and anger.

When he'd finished, he saw Vladimir up on his feet, staggering. 'Where are *you* going?' Cutler snarled.

The bitter voice made Will turn from his mother at once. Gaia and Andrew watched as Cutler slowly got up. Blood trickled down his forehead and his hair was singed. But he was standing, barely a metre from Vassily's body. And now he reached out for Caspian. Cutler grabbed him roughly by the collar, yanking him up from beside his father. Uncomprehending, Caspian gaped like a fish on a line. He noticed Andrew.

'*Andrew,*' Caspian murmured, as though just remembering. '*STORM . . .?*'

Andrew nodded. 'Caspian—' *Come with us,* he

wanted to say. *Come back*. But emotion tied his tongue and he could not speak.

Cutler was shaking Caspian, and then he saw Will. And Andrew and Gaia by the remains of his desk. Flames and the smoke made him blink. He eyed them in disbelief. But first things first. 'Vladimir! *Ty, pridurok! Where are you going?*'

'I am evacuating!' came the reply as Vladimir stumbled at last from the room.

'Idiot!' Cutler's face was blazing. He picked up the electric gun that he'd dropped to the floor when he'd been knocked by the blast from the bomb. Cutler's cheeks were streaked with soot, his eyebrows gone. Caspian writhed in his grasp. 'Be still!' Cutler hissed.

Caspian was not slight, but Cutler's thin arms were strong. Caspian's struggles were in vain.

Andrew dodged the blazing carpet and ran to Will. 'We have to get out.'

Will thrust a hand into his pocket. He found the tooth phone, slotted it in.

'Vanya? Vanya are you there? *We're ready*.'

Nothing. The Faraday cage, he remembered.

And he coughed. The room was filling with smoke. Cutler's red carpet and chair were burning hard, sparks leaping two metres into the air. Cables were withering, plastic melting and dripping to the ground.

'Gaia!' Will's voice cut through the flames that now burst from the LED monitor. And she coughed as smoke hit her lungs.

'We have to get out!' Anna shouted. 'You – Will's friend – come and help me.' Shooting a glance at Will, Andrew ran to join her at the door.

'You!' The voice was muffled. With a lunge, Cutler made a grab through the smoke. 'You – girl – I haven't finished with you.'

Gaia tried to yell. But it was hard even to breathe. Bony fingers were suddenly digging into her neck. Words came blasting into her ear: 'I remember you. I do hope you enjoyed the opera. Now, come quietly, or you'll be a fitting subject for one yourself. A perfect tragedy.'

The voice was harsh, hurting her ear. Cutler's spit hit her flesh. 'Will!' she spluttered. She'd tried to shout. But it was more like a wheeze.

Caspian also was yelling, as he dangled from Cutler's other hand. Tears were streaked down his cheeks. 'My father! My father—'

Will had seen it happen. He'd seen Cutler reach out, grab Gaia. Now Cutler glowered at Will, who'd made his way towards them through the smoke. Caspian and Gaia were enough to manage, he decided. And why would he want this boy now?

Behind Will, his mother was already at the outer door. 'My tag,' she was shouting. She'd fallen in the explosion that stunned Cutler and the device no longer seemed to work.

Will's eyes were on Gaia. Cutler's yellow eyes gleamed.

'Let her go,' Will said.

'You,' Cutler snarled. 'You make a demand of me. *You?*'

Gaia was biting the arm that held her against his body. The injured muscle screamed. Angling his gun hand awkwardly, Cutler, wild and angry, pulled the trigger.

The electric buzz was like a kick through Will's guts. Gaia crumpled at once.

'*Gaia.*' Will darted forward, then stopped. Cutler was waving the gun.

Will's stomach turned. Gaia was dangling in Cutler's hand, Caspian limp now beside her. '*Gaia.*' Everything around him blanked. The fire faded. Will was vaguely aware that, behind him, his mother was shouting. He could not move.

And then – she coughed.

Gaia's eyes opened. Her muscles felt loose, her limbs desperately weak. But she was alive. Cutler looked surprised, his yellow eyes rimmed with red. The setting must have been knocked in the explosion. 'Well, look at that,' he said. Pulling Gaia up underneath his arm, and still waving the gun at Will, Cutler voice-activated his mobile phone. 'Helicopter evacuation. *Now.*'

'Evacuate the building,' the voice insisted. And there was a crash as the LED monitor collapsed. Wires behind Cutler's head had caught fire, and now flames spewed high above their heads. With one last glance at Will, Cutler dragged Gaia and Caspian with him into the Systems room and slammed the door shut.

Will turned. His mother was hauling the body of

Vassily Baraban – with his intact radio tag – towards the outer door. Andrew was trying to help her. But he could not touch him. His stomach revolted. Andrew vomited in the corner. He retched again and again. No time, he thought. Get hold of yourself.

'Will,' Andrew said thankfully, as Will ran to them, 'where's Gaia – we're getting out of here. Can you hear me? Will—' Because Andrew could barely see Will now through the smoke. He wiped his mouth.

'Here!' his mother yelled. She had opened the outer door. 'Will – now.'

'Is there another exit?' Will demanded. 'Through the Systems room?'

She nodded. 'It leads to the roof.' She tried to peer past him. 'Where's Roden?'

'He's gone. He's taken Caspian and Gaia. I'm going after them.'

Andrew looked horrified. 'What do you mean, he's taken Gaia?'

'Maybe he thinks it'll stop us trying to stop him.' But there was no time to talk. Will turned to his mother. 'Elena is waiting with a friend. Andrew's got a tooth phone. As soon as you get outside, he can call them – they'll meet you.'

Her black eyes widened. 'My mother? . . . No, Will, you are coming with us.'

'I have to get Gaia.'

'*Gaia?* The girl? No, Will. Roden is armed. He is insane. There is no time for heroics.'

Will blinked at her. In leaving, in lying, she'd surrendered her right to tell him what to do. 'I have to try,' he said simply.

He looked at Andrew. Andrew squinted back. His glasses were filthy, coated with soot. He nodded.

'Will – no – I will not allow it!' his mother cried. 'You come with us – now.' She reached out – and stumbled. Her ankle was stabbed through with pain, re-broken as she'd fallen.

Now the smoke was thickening, making it harder to breathe.

Will hitched his rucksack higher up his back. 'You left me to live my own life. That's what I'm doing. Get out and get Vanya.'

'I should come with you.' Andrew's hesitation was written all over his face. Yes, he cared about Gaia. Very much, in fact. No, he wasn't a hero. But neither was he weak.

Will let him off the hook. 'I need you to get to Vanya,' he said urgently. 'And to look after my mother – look at her, she can hardly stand, she won't get out of here alive without you.'

Andrew nodded.

'*Will!*' His mother limped angrily towards him.

But Will was already halfway to the Systems room. As he ran after Roden, he yelled back: 'And Andrew, tell my mother: no risks, no life.'

Gaia's head was splitting. Her vision was blurring. All she wanted to do was collapse in a corner, smoke or no smoke. But Cutler was half-dragging her through the Systems room and on, towards a narrow flight of stairs.

She was vaguely aware of heavy footsteps above them. A man appeared from there and barged down past them. He was wearing an orange uniform complete with a black plastic gun: the guard that was usually posted on the roof.

Cutler glowered as he was pushed back against the wall. 'Where do you think you're going?' he demanded.

The roof guard glanced at Cutler as though the question was insane. 'Evacuate!' he replied, in a thick Russian accent. 'The building will come down!'

Cutler glanced up at the shoddy ceiling, and the cracks in the walls. He shook Gaia.

'Walk!' he commanded.

'I can't,' she muttered.

Cutler's bony hand was gripping her collar, digging

into her neck. She craned her head to try to get a glimpse of Caspian. She could hear his whimpering.

'Caspian—' she called.

'Shut up!' cried Cutler. They were at the top of the stairs now and he was banging with his elbow on the call button for a lift.

This was a different shaft from the one that accessed the particle collider. Gaia glanced up at a panel fixed above the twin steel doors. Two words were outlined. Ground. *Roof.* Illuminated. They were going up.

She struggled in Cutler's grasp. 'What do you want us for anyway?' she said. And she coughed. Smoke was beginning to swirl up the staircase.

'Well, Caspian Baraban is easy,' Cutler hissed. 'He's got brains. You—' and he shook her slightly – 'are my utterly dispensable hostage. In case any of your little friends think they might like to try to prevent my escape. Now they have ruined everything, I won't let them ruin that.'

We, she thought, *we* ruined everything. And a smile flickered across her lips.

There was a ping from the lift. The doors juddered open.

'In,' Cutler ordered, as he dragged at their collars.

Now, Gaia thought. She twisted in his grip and she bit him hard, chewing down on his arm. Cutler yelled. And, as she'd hoped, this time he dropped the gun. Immediately, Gaia kicked it. She sent it skidding out along the corridor and she heard it clatter as it dropped down the stairwell.

Cutler yelled. But the lift doors were closing. His helicopter would be waiting. There was no time to go after the gun.

Instead, he grabbed harder at Gaia's neck and he shook her violently. He hissed: 'I will punish you later for that.'

At the moment the lift doors closed, Will was at the bottom of the stairs. He'd seen something drop. But he had no time to investigate. The roof guard, who was in the process of rushing down, was grabbing Will's arm. He yelled in Russian:

'Get out, if you want to live!'

Then he was off. But not before Will had reached out with his free hand to the black belt. He'd seen Cutler do it. Now he effortlessly released the plastic gun and he gripped it tightly behind his back.

The oblivious guard vanished into the smoke. Coughing, Will ran up the stairs. He punched at the button and looked up.

Roof.

Where, he realized, Cutler would wait for his helicopter. Will glanced at his new weapon. It didn't look like much. Like a toy, in fact. A horrendous toy that had left Vassily Baraban dead.

Come on. Will urged the lift down. The smoke was building and he lifted the flap of his jacket up over his mouth. From below, he could feel heat. The Operations room was well and truly on fire. Who knew what was happening down in the particle collider. The cryogenic reservoirs would be exploding all over the place. This base itself had been put up too fast. It had the build quality of a shanty hut. How long could it last?

Up on the roof, Roden Cutler watched the flames that billowed out of the arrivals depot below. Unnerving sounds rumbled from what felt like the centre of the Earth. Explosions in the particle collider.

Cutler himself was burning up with anger. His plans. His weapon. Destroyed. And by what? Not just kids – not just by *Will Knight* – he was sure about that. They were working for someone. *Vanya,* Will had said. Who was Vanya? Russian military. Secret service? He scoured his brain for an answer. And found none. It could be anyone, he thought. The CIA. Mongolian intelligence. Anyone. Everyone. Who wouldn't try to stop him?

And who had? *Anna's son.* Disbelief swept along with the anger. He'd tried so hard, and for what? Her husband was dead. Cutler had hoped that once the weapon had been perfected, at last she would come to him. She would be swept away by his vision, his brilliance. The old attraction would bloom. He'd been in London to supervise the abduction of Vassily Baraban, and the timing was perfect – he could also spend time with Will, to win him over. With the kid on his side, Anna could not refuse . . .

Now everything was wrong.

Cutler shook Gaia. Partly to try to relieve some of his anger. Partly to try to make her keep still. It was freezing out here. Where was the helicopter?

The pilot was an ex-military professional bodyguard. He lived less than a kilometre away, and he was on a very healthy retainer. Cutler could rely on him. And he'd be safe. Whoever these kids – whoever *Will Knight* – was working for would be expecting him to come out on the ground.

These thoughts filled Cutler's head. He grasped the collars hard and didn't hear that Gaia was trying to speak . . .

'Caspian . . . Caspian?' she murmured.

No answer. Caspian seemed stunned. He was slumping towards the ground, making strange whining noises. Perhaps he was crying. Impossible to tell. Perhaps he was being strangled. The grip around her own neck was uncomfortably tight.

'Caspian,' she hissed. 'We have to get away!'

No response.

And then Cutler's head shot round. Gaia jerked in his

grasp. She felt him tense. Furious shudders shot through his body. And she saw the reason.

Will Knight.

He was there on the roof. And he was brandishing a gun.

'What now, Vanya?'

Elena stood at the side of the road, staring down at the base. Smoke was pouring out through every orifice of the building. Clear through the still night, they could hear the surreally calm voice: *Evacuate* . . .

Vanya jiggled his tooth phone nervously. 'Will? Anyone? Hello?'

Nothing.

'Do you think we should go down there?' Elena said.

The four perimeter guards had already taken off on two quad bikes. Now the pair watched as the Portakabin guards ran to a four-wheel-drive parked beneath the white spotlight. A few moments later, the vehicle raced out of the gates, brakes screeching as it cornered the first bend. A stocky man had emerged and tried to run after it. Sergei . . . And then Vladimir. Too late. They set off down the hill at a run.

'What do you think is happening?' she said.

'I don't know. I don't know. I don't know!' Vanya

said, with irritation. But more at the situation than at Elena. '. . . The place is burning. That is good news.'

'I suppose so.'

'The explosions have worked. They are evacuating. This is all good news.'

'Yes, but where are they!'

'Who am I, that I have all the answers?' Vanya sighed. And then he straightened. 'Look—' And he slapped a hand to his hear. 'Ow!'

Elena fixed her sparkling black eyes on her friend. 'What? Vanya, what?'

Vanya looked up again at the piercing white spotlights of the helicopter that had appeared over the trees. His hearing was not first-rate but he could make out the sinister whoosh-whoosh-whoosh of the rotor. It wasn't this, though, that had caught his ear. He looked at Elena. And he tapped his jaw.

'That was Andrew . . . He has just left the building – and he is with *Anna*! He wants us to come with the car.'

'*Anna*! But—' A hundred buts. At this second, only one mattered. 'But surely it is safer if they come to us.'

'He says she has been injured . . . He does not say how badly.'

Elena grasped Vanya's shoulder. 'Come, my dear. Now the children – they need us.'

Cutler and Will heard the helicopter at exactly the same moment. Will's eyes shot up.

He recognized it. A camouflage-painted Tiger. Mean-looking. Perfect for Cutler.

Wind blasted through Will's hair. He had to keep his legs well apart to maintain his balance. The wind stung his face. Still snowing, he realized. He blinked and white flecks fell on to his cheeks.

Then Will looked back at Gaia. Twenty metres separated them. Beyond Cutler was the helipad. 'Are you all right?' he shouted.

She tried to nod.

Cutler gave a thin laugh. 'So your Will Knight in shining armour has arrived. Too late.'

'Let her go, Cutler.'

'Let her go? Let me think . . . *No*!'

Will thought quickly. He had to get Gaia. But he also had questions. And he needed answers. Will glanced at the gun in his hand. He tried to level it.

'At least tell me why,' Will yelled. 'Why did you want to destroy the police station? Why risk the planet?'

Cutler's eyes widened. 'The station? What do you know about that?'

'Who's behind this? Tell me why!'

Cutler scoffed. 'Why, why, why – a typical child! You would not understand. You would have no concept.'

'Why create a black hole?'

'Why? Why not? There was one man with the vision. He believed in me.'

'And he wanted to destroy the station? Why?'

Cutler shook his head. 'What does it matter? I told him it was possible, and he believed me. He gave me the money, and I found Caspian Baraban!'

Will blinked. The Tiger was descending now. The four blades of the main rotor sliced through the snow, stirring up the sky. And Will noticed that, despite this machine's attack capabilities, it did not appear to be missile-loaded. Of course the pilot wouldn't have been expecting the urgent evacuation call.

'Let Gaia go,' Will called.

'This girl is a hostage,' Cutler was saying. 'She comes with me.'

'*Why?*' Will shouted.

'Because I say so. Because she may be useful.' Cutler glanced at the gun in Will's hand. His lips twisted into a bitter smile. 'Why not throw that down? You won't use it, boy.'

The helicopter's engine almost obliterated Cutler's words. It was ten seconds from landing, if that. The landing gear was hovering above the roof.

Quickly, his eyes never leaving Cutler, Will let the rucksack slide from his back. With his free hand, he reached inside.

'Gaia—' he called. 'Remember what I have. Remember the *silk*.' Will clutched the soft fabric to his side. And he raised the gun at Cutler.

Cutler's expression was scornful. 'Don't be ridiculous.'

Will took a deep breath. It was hard to keep his arm straight. The wind was buffeting against his body as the helicopter descended. Smoke swirled through the air. From behind, flames suddenly burst from the lift shaft.

Will staggered. But he did not fall.

'You're weak!' Cutler shouted. 'You could never kill me.'

'I read the patent,' Will yelled back. 'Who said anything about *kill*?'

And he pulled the trigger. Twin flaring pulses shot across the roof. He'd fired his air rifle plenty of times, but this was different. His aim hadn't been quite right. Rather than hitting Cutler in the chest, just above Caspian's head, as he'd intended, the electric bullets collided with Cutler's thigh.

But it was enough. Cutler fell backwards. He let go of Gaia but somehow kept Caspian in his clutches. Behind the sprawling pair, the helicopter landed. Will squinted against the wind from the rotor.

Already, Gaia was on her feet. Will shouted to her. And he ducked as another burst of flame erupted from behind him. The concrete beneath his feet was hot. 'Here!' he shouted. And he threw Soft Landing.

She caught it neatly.

'Go now! Vanya's waiting.'

She stared at him, hair flying about her face. 'What about you?'

'I have a plan. Go!'

With one last glance at Will, Gaia strapped on the

backpack and pulled the cord – and she leaped from the burning roof.

Will dropped the gun. He dashed away from the flames. He could only watch as the helicopter pilot jumped out and pulled Caspian inside. The pilot got back into his seat. And waited. Because Cutler was peering in Will's direction. He was blinking through the snow and the smoke.

'Where are you?'

Inside the chopper, the pilot was gesticulating hard. Clearly he wanted to get off the roof. Will heard the man's voice, in Russian, cut through the air: 'Now! We leave.'

And Will made out the grim face of that pilot as suddenly something else came into view. *Thing* was the wrong word for it. It rose like a terrible giant insect from behind the hangar. Another helicopter. And it was armed to the hilt.

The noise was incredible. The five-blade main rotor and the three-blade tail rotor were churning the atmosphere. Fixed beneath the shortened stub wings was an arsenal. Eighty-millimetre rockets were packed into the twin launchers. Beside these were 16 laser-guided missiles and a set of 9 M-120 anti-tank missiles. A 23-millimetre twin barrel gun poked out menacingly from the nose turret.

Will recognized a mounted FLIR – Forward-Looking Infra Red – ball for night vision. On the starboard side was a loudspeaker pack. And there was another gun, mounted underneath the port wing, which he didn't recognize. But he knew the aircraft. A Russian Mi-35M Hind. An assault helicopter – and, in his father's view, the most dangerous ever created.

It had been one of his father's games, on winter nights. To sketch a helicopter or plane, and challenge Will to identify it.

Will's mouth became dry. Was this Cutler's escort? What did he plan to do? Evacuate and then drop missiles for good measure?

But Will didn't have to wait long to find out the truth. That starboard loudspeaker burst into life.

'Target on roof: attention. Target on roof: board the Tiger. Pilot: return to your base and land. We will be in pursuit. Repeat: return to your base.'

The voice spoke in English, without a trace of an accent. Who was this?

Will could imagine the thoughts going through the pilot's head. Why should he return to base? And then the answer, staring him right in the face: because if he didn't, he'd be blasted right out of the sky.

Cutler stared up at the Hind in disbelief. Will was crouching now and through the snow, he could see Cutler raising his fist.

The speaker cut in again:

'Repeat. Target on roof: Roden Cutler, board the Tiger. Now.'

Stumbling, Cutler backed away from the Tiger. Will was astonished. What was he thinking? Where else could he go? The hangar was on fire. Flames were billowing out of the lift shaft. There was nowhere else to go . . . And who was on this Hind? Who was talking to Cutler?

Still Cutler backed away.

His heart pounding, Will waited. Nothing happened. And then the nose of the Hind inched to the left and the 23-millimetre gun in the turret let rip.

The violence of the shells going off shocked through Will's body. He dropped so he was flat on his front on the roof. Icy concrete burned his ear.

The voice again: 'Target, we know all about you and James Parramore. We know exactly who you are. And MI6 makes every effort to recover missing officers. You are coming with us.'

MI6.

Will could hardly believe it. Was that part of Cutler's story half-true? He'd worked with his father, rather than his mother? And Cutler was an MI6 agent *gone bad*?

But Cutler only raised his fist.

The speaker rattled: 'Target, this Hind is equipped with an experimental non-lethal weapon. If you don't board that Tiger now, we will shoot you with a laser pulse. When it hits you, it will generate a burst of expanding plasma. And that plasma will cause you excruciating pain. Then, while you're incapacitated, we'll drop down and pick you up. It's your choice.'

Cutler continued to back away from the Tiger. Will wanted to close his eyes. But he had to watch.

'. . . Tiger: hover NOW. Wait for us to follow. Then return to base,' came the order.

The Tiger obeyed. The engine kicked up a notch, and it began to hover above the roof, before veering away, clear of the building. It waited, as if suspended, its searchlight pointing right at Roden Cutler.

Now the Hind also turned its full, missile-packed, attention to him.

Will raised his head. He'd never heard of a plasma weapon. If it existed, this was something he had to see.

Cutler was staggering across the roof, as if drunk. He glanced back and for a moment Will thought Cutler was looking for him. But then Roden took a few more steps towards the edge of the roof – towards the snow-spattered blackness beyond the hangar.

Will jumped up into a crouch. At that moment, a single laser pulse blasted out of the additional gun on the Hind's port wing. Will saw it fly through the sky – and he saw it hit Roden Cutler full in the chest.

Cutler screamed. He wheeled around and his face seemed torn in half by a hideous grimace. The thin lips were white, the eyes squeezed shut in agony. Once more Cutler stumbled. Now Will knew what was going to happen. Somehow he had known ever since Cutler had begun to stagger. And he watched, helpless, as Roden Cutler clutched at his chest and swayed towards the darkness. He took a few uncertain steps – and was gone.

Seven storeys.

Could he possibly survive?

For a moment, Will could not move. He felt frozen. Trapped. Suddenly the Hind veered away. Will expected to hear it land below, to check on Cutler. Instead the loudspeaker ordered the Tiger to return to base. And as the Tiger swept away, the Hind followed.

Will was stunned. His thoughts swarmed. There was a strange rumbling coming from beneath the roof. The building was about to go, he could feel it. Vassily Baraban was dead. Cutler, probably, was dead. The Hind, and whoever was inside it – *MI6*? – had gone.

There was no way out. He'd told Gaia he had a plan. He had none.

What would Dad do? Will reached into his pocket, ran his fingers across the burned leather. Perhaps Gaia had been right, but he just was not ready to throw the ball away. In the same pocket, he touched metal. Tooth Talk . . . He sat up quickly and slotted it on to his molar. Immediately, he pressed a hand to his ear.

'Ow!'

'Will? Will?' A voice. Andrew's. Yelling. 'Can you hear me?'

'Yeah, I can hear you!' Will rolled over on to his side. Ratty twitched in his pocket, apparently unharmed.

'Will!' Relief lifted Andrew's voice. 'Good – now stay down. We're going to send something up.'

'What?'

'I'm touching your things. I know you said I wasn't to, but I am. Now just stay back from the edge. I don't want to hurt you.'

Deep down, below Will, there was an alarming crashing sound. The roof seemed to lurch. Will rolled, and he was right at the edge. Cracks suddenly zig-zagged through the concrete beneath him.

Will raised his head – just enough to make out Andrew down below, the speargun launcher of Rapid Ascent in hand, and something attached to the end . . .

A moment later, the grappling hook clattered on to the concrete by the helipad. There was no guttering. And Will wasn't close enough to grab it. He ran and he pulled the magnet from his jacket pocket and held it out. It was just enough. The grappling hook trembled in the magnetic field and Will threw himself on it.

At once, he recognized what had been tied to the end.

Soft Landing.

Why hadn't he thought of that?

As Will stood, the roof beneath him started to shake. He wasted no time. He strapped on the backpack and taking Ratty gently from his pocket he threw himself through the air – after Cutler.

The moment Will pulled a ring, the inverted umbrella inflated. Will was on his back, in the centre of the shallow orange cone, its inflated spokes and rim spreading six metres across beneath him. Soft Landing worked well. It slowed his ascent so that he landed, rather than smashed, into the half-frozen ground. Still, Will felt the crunch of his shoulder on a vicious patch of ice.

'*Will*?' His mother's voice.

'Will?' Gaia.

And then Andrew. 'Will – Will – are you hurt?'

The umbrella was flat beneath him. Ratty twitched. 'You're all right,' Will said. And he slipped the animal back into his front pocket.

Unsteadily, he rolled forward into a crouch. His mother was there, right in front of him, grabbing his arms. He winced. Pain shot through his shoulder. Her eyes were wide, black and afraid, scanning him up and down. 'Will – are you all right?'

Behind her, Will noticed Vanya and Elena, her silver hair whipping in the wind. Andrew, with his soot-streaked glasses. Gaia, dirty and shaking, shivering from exhaustion and cold and shock.

Will nodded. 'Cutler?' he whispered.

His mother's wide eyes narrowed. 'Cutler – is dead.' She glanced back towards the hangar. Will could make out a figure underneath a tarpaulin from Vanya's car.

Anna squeezed her son's arms. 'I know you must have a thousand questions,' she said quietly. 'I'll answer them all. And your grandmother's. And I have lots of my own. But first I have to make sure you're safe.' She looked up. 'Vanya, start the car. Let's get out of here.'

With a flourish, Vanya pulled the keys from his pocket. 'At your service! Come Anna, come Elena!'

Vanya and Anna, with her injured ankle, hustled into the front. Into the back stumbled Elena, and then Will, Gaia and Andrew, crushing up against each other. Gaia's leg was pressed into Will's, her head down. Andrew's arm reached past her neck, his hand on the back ledge. The car smelt pleasantly familiar. Old cigarettes and mould.

'Are you all right?' Will said to Gaia.

She didn't speak. She only nodded.

'And so am I,' Andrew said.

Will looked at him.

'We did it,' Andrew said. Tears threatened to roll from his eyes. And this time he had no trouble interpreting his emotion. 'Gaia – we did it.' He touched her arm. 'You hit the cryogenics,' he said warmly. 'You stopped them.'

'Cutler . . .' Will said, frowning. He could still see that laser pulse. And he could see Cutler stagger. And fall.

Andrew nodded. 'Yes. I know. But Roden Cutler was trying to take Gaia. Roden Cutler would have killed us all. Caspian—' And he stopped. Caspian, too, had been willing to kill. Could anything excuse that? Andrew shook his head. The full truth would come later. But for now, the black hole had been prevented. STORM had prevailed.

As Vanya hit the accelerator, Will leaned over his grandmother, craning for a view out of the window. He was looking for the Hind. Just for a trace. For a sign that what he had seen and what he had heard had been real. But he could see nothing. Only smoke and flames.

And then, as the base imploded, huge clouds of snow mixed with dust.

Vanya drove as though the implosion was on their tail.

The streets swept past, dark and foreign. And yet Will's mother was here, and his grandmother. Vanya. Gaia and Andrew. Friends.

Will closed his eyes. He saw Cutler's face, seared with agony. He saw Caspian Baraban, being hauled into the Tiger. Enough. He opened them at once. And he cursed silently as his head collided with the roof.

'Apologies!' Vanya cried. 'Shock-absorbing fluid is not what it used to be!'

By the time they arrived back at Maly Prospect, Will's body was so jolted his vision felt blurred. But it was still sharp enough to spot an unfamiliar car parked up on the pavement outside.

This car was black. With smoked windows and gleaming alloy wheels. Will touched his grandmother's arm. 'Whose is that?'

Vanya cut the Lada's engine and he shrugged. He glanced at Elena, who shook her head.

'We should be careful,' Anna said.

Vanya nodded solemnly.

'Why?' Andrew said.

'What if it's Cutler,' Will said quietly.

'But he's dead,' Gaia said. 'We saw him—'

'—I mean, one of his men,' Will interrupted.

'But why would anyone want us?'

Will raised his eyebrows. It had been a hopeful rather than an honest question.

'What if someone's already upstairs?' Andrew said.

All eyes were raised to the fifth floor. Dim yellow light cut through the darkness.

Anna was first out of the car. Her mother had taken her arm, kissing her daughter's hand, but still she stumbled. 'Will, I need you to help me,' Anna said.

But, as they got out, Vanya noticed the blood on Will's shoulder. Clearly, the fall had been harder than intended. He thought it best to say nothing. Instead, he proffered his shoulder to Anna. 'Allow me, my child,' he said.

'You two know each other then?' Andrew said, as they cleared the graffittied entrance hall and started up the stairs.

Vanya smiled faintly. 'All her life, eh, Anna? My wife was best friends with her mother before this lady was born.' And there was a sadness in his voice that forestalled further questions.

Instead, Andrew switched his attention to Will, who

was immediately behind him. 'What happened to your shoulder?'

Anna heard. She peered and she saw blood. 'Will?'

'It's all right.'

She looked disbelieving.

'He'll be all right,' Elena whispered. 'He is tough, this grandson of mine.'

At the top of the staircase, Vanya made them wait while he checked out the corridor. 'All clear,' he murmured and pressed a delicate finger to his lips.

Vanya went first, followed by Anna and then Elena. Will, Gaia and Andrew followed in single file, hugging the puce-coloured wall. Vague scents of urine made Will's nostrils curl.

'Will.' A whisper, from behind. Gaia. 'Thank you for coming after me.'

Will didn't know what to say. He nodded slightly. And he stopped. Weak yellow light slanted out from beneath his grandmother's door. Above them, a single bulb illuminated the gate and the grimy floor.

Vanya was looking around for a weapon. Leaning against the opposite wall was an ancient fire extinguisher. Rust spread like mould around the nozzle, puckering the metal. But Vanya wanted it in case he had to fight a person, not a fire. He raised it and nodded to Elena.

'That really won't be necessary.'

Will froze. The clear English voice had come from the ceiling. There, fixed to the light bulb, he saw a tiny video camera and a speaker. This was surprising enough. But then his mother gave a quick cry of recognition and hopped forward.

One person was waiting inside the apartment. A man. In his late thirties. Tall and well-built. Slouching at the dining table in a neat, black suit, his black shirt open at the collar. His thinning brown hair was slightly curly. Intelligent blue eyes smiled faintly. He put down his tiny mike.

'Anna,' he said with feeling, as she broke away from her mother and came to sit beside him. And he flashed her a warm smile.

Behind them, Elena pulled Gaia and Andrew to the heater. Vanya looked on, one eyebrow raised, as though this man's presence wasn't exactly welcome, nor totally unexpected.

'Anna, how relieved I am to see you. I was worried. We all were. And this—' and the man turned to Will, who was watching with curiosity – 'must be your son.'

She nodded. 'This is Will.'

'Will, I have something you might like to see,' the man said. He pulled a slim black object from his inner jacket pocket and flicked the lid open.

His mind full of questions – not least: who are you? – Will went closer to look. On the ten-centimetre screen, video footage kicked in. It showed the Tiger, veering away from the roof of the western hangar. Will took the screen and gripped it. He watched the Tiger land on a clearing beside a farmhouse. Two men dashed in front of the camera, which he realized must have been mounted on the Hind. They seized the pilot and pulled Caspian out on to the grass. A moment later, Caspian's wrists were shown, bound with what looked like plastic twine.

Then the scene changed. The camera was hand-mounted now. It bounced up and down, with the jogging motion of the operator. And it picked out what Will knew was the outline of Roden Cutler's body beneath the blue tarpaulin.

'Now press the back button,' the man said. 'It's on the top there.'

Will did as he was told. A new video sequence cut in. This showed the corridor that led from the arrivals depot. He saw the door to the Operations room. And Ratty, wires protruding, legs scurrying.

Will looked up sharply. 'Who are you? Who was in that Hind? How did you get this?'

Blue eyes fixed on Will. 'The truth is, I've had a man following you – and he was on that helicopter. The idea was that he'd make sure you were all right, while your mother was away. Her request. And it was quite fair. We had no idea that you'd end up in St Petersburg. In fact, we were struggling slightly in the ideas department. We didn't know the location of your mother – or the black hole base. We knew it was somewhere in Russia. But your mother was on her own and unfortunately she wasn't able to get in touch with us for oh – what is it now? – *six weeks.*'

'A Faraday cage,' she said. 'And I had this.' She touched her radio-tracking tag. 'Before Gaia blew up the central control, I'd have been electrocuted if I'd tried to get near that panel, or if I'd tried to leave. I tried to sabotage the equipment, and I almost did it. I made explosives from supplies – from washing powder – but when I was climbing up to the top of the collision chamber one of the guards saw me. I tried to hide – I wasn't sure if he'd seen my face – and I slipped. That's how I broke my ankle. I tried to persuade Roden I was in there because I was worried Vassily might be having second thoughts, and *he* might be trying sabotage . . . And if I'd set off the explosions, I'd have blamed Vassily – I'd have had no choice. But Roden didn't quite believe me.'

Questions were flooding Will's brain. He had to order them. He had to make some kind of logical sense of all that had happened.

'What were you doing there in the first place?' Will said to her.

'Your mother – code-name Beryllium – works with me,' the man said. 'At least, she did on this occasion. We couldn't send anyone else in after her, because, as I said, we were in the slightly embarrassing position of not knowing where she was. But then one of my men followed you and your friends all the way here to St Petersburg.' And Barrington smiled faintly at Will. 'I flew in this evening. I didn't manage to get to you before you entered the base, but we did get a swarm of recon-bots in behind you – they sent back the footage from the corridors. And I did manage to borrow that Hind and that rather interesting new weapon . . .'

Needs refinement, Will thought.

'But that's really all the credit I can take. You did all the hard work. Without you and your friends, Roden Cutler would have tried to make a black hole tonight.'

'But who are you?' Gaia's voice. Will turned. She and Andrew had gathered behind him and were listening intently.

The man shifted his gaze to Gaia and Andrew, then back to Will. 'My name is Shute Barrington. I am head of STASIS – the Science and Technology Arm of the Secret Intelligence Service – which is, of course, the original name for MI6. I have to say, STASIS doesn't have quite the ring of *STORM*.'

'MI6?' Andrew's mouth dropped open. '. . . But how do you know about STORM?'

'It *is* my business to know that sort of thing.'

'Yes, but *how*?'

'Well, now that would be telling.'

'Well, we helped you,' Gaia said. Soot streaked her face. Her clothes were black and torn. Beside her, Andrew's blue eyes were determined. He pushed his filthy glasses up along the bridge of his nose.

'Yes,' Andrew said. 'We did help you. So talk.'

Frost made the fields glisten. From the wooden bench at the far end of the orchard, Will had a clear view across the valley. He saw bare trees and huddling sheep, the flocks separated by tangled lines of hedgerow. English hedgerows. English fields. In English cold. He was back in Dorset. Home.

They'd arrived two days ago. His mother had spent the morning removing dust sheets and making the beds, lighting fires, talking on the phone to Natalia (who said she'd always been suspicious of Roden – Will hadn't been convinced), and cleaning out her workshop. Will found it hard to be inside. Everything reminded him of his father. His old life.

Instead, he walked across the fields, and he read emails from Andrew and Gaia. Andrew had found a news-in-brief in a back issue of the *Standard.* The headline ran: '*Poltergeist Restaurant Calls in Ghostbusters.*' And then: '*American exorcist flown in to deal with mysterious voices at the Nebuchadnezzar.*'

Below, Andrew had written: 'Sorry – have to confess that I borrowed Speak Easy to have some fun, after they were so rude. Looks like it worked . . . It's good to be back. But the basement's not the same without you. When you coming home? STORM awaits . . . By the way, in the light of our first major victory, I'm suggesting a temporary renaming: Society for Taking Out Renegade Madmen ☺.'

Gaia had sent an email the evening after they parted at Heathrow Airport, Andrew and Gaia into the SmarTruck with Sean, Will and his mother into a hire car organized by Shute Barrington.

It had been an awkward moment. On the plane, there had been lots to talk about. Various crucial details to go over. Including perhaps the most amazing details of all – the truth about the law-enforcement station and Cutler's boss.

Gaia, Andrew and Will had sat together on his grandmother's flowery sofa while Barrington filled them in. Will already knew that Cutler was an MI6 officer, clearly doing some work 'on the side'.

And the man funding that project was Sir James Parramore, a shadowy British billionaire.

He had all sorts of interests, Barrington said. Oil, uranium, software, pharmaceuticals.

'Parramore's new business is in space. He's put up a number of satellites and now he's got plans for half a dozen space hotels. He's already got a few hundred handsomely paid-up customers, in part because he's been promising pure lawlessness. You have to understand that Parramore doesn't play by normal rules,' Barrington said. 'He sees himself as above the law. He operates internationally, he covers himself in layers of false businesses, lawyers, accountants. He demanded exemption from the new space laws. Of course this was rejected. But he'd already met someone who had enough belief in his own crazy ideas to convince him to pay for the development of an entirely new type of weapon. In theory, an anonymous weapon – take something out with a black hole, and what's left to investigate? The new outpost was the perfect target. Parramore wanted rid of it. For Roden Cutler, it was probably just a test.'

'And the whole black hole weapon idea was Cutler's?' Will said.

'Cutler used to work for us,' Barrington said. 'He still does, technically. But he lost the plot. He was coming up with all these outrageous, unethical ideas, and of course I knocked them all down. Then I heard he was talking to someone with money. We didn't know exactly who, or what they were planning, but we had to find out. I don't know if you know, Will—' and Barrington glanced at Anna – 'but your mother has long been an adviser to STASIS. We had no one else with the right knowledge. She agreed to pretend to be recruited by Cutler.'

Will stared at his mother. Should he have suspected

it? His father worked for MI6. Why shouldn't his mother?

'I'm sorry, Will,' she said. 'I wanted to tell you, but I couldn't.'

Will still wasn't sure how to behave around her. Or how to react. So much had changed. 'But Roden must have known you worked for MI6,' Will said. 'Why would he believe in you?'

'I've known Roden a long time,' his mother said. She would have preferred to talk to Will alone, but Gaia and Andrew were watching. And behind, Elena and Vanya. Though she owed them an explanation too.

She fixed her eyes on her son. 'When your father died, it wasn't hard to convince Roden that I hated MI6 for taking him from us. I didn't want to do the job, but I felt I had to. Do you understand, Will? We weren't sure what he was doing, but we knew it was dangerous. He could have destroyed the planet, let alone this new station, and that would have meant he'd destroy you . . .'

She looked down. 'In the end, Roden believed me. He needed my knowledge – he came up with the theory but he knows almost nothing about black holes. He thought he was recruiting me. But it was meant to be my job to keep an eye on the project and report back to Shute. Or to sabotage it, if it seemed to be going somewhere. But then the sabotage didn't work. And Roden didn't trust me and he changed the settings on my radio bracelet. I couldn't even get into the workshop to find tools to get rid of it! And then he brought in Caspian.' She turned to her son. 'And then you came . . . I thought I saw you on the surveillance monitor. And then I saw the rat – I knew that had to be you, or Vanya – more likely Vanya.'

'Why Vanya?' Will glanced round. Vanya was standing quietly, his huge face impassive.

'That is classified,' Barrington said. 'And not by me.'

'Nor by me,' came Vanya's gruff voice. 'I used to be Barrington's opposite number here in Russia. Until I retired.'

Kicked out more like, Barrington thought, but he kept his mouth shut.

'You always liked the weirder stuff, didn't you, Vanya?' Anna turned back to Will. She smiled slightly. 'While I know you're very talented, brain surgery does take a bit of learning, and I haven't been gone that long . . .' Her soft expression hit Will hard. It was so strange to be with her. And there was still so much to find out. 'So how did you do it?' she said. 'How did you find me?'

There wasn't really a lot to explain, Will decided. He glanced at Andrew and at Gaia. 'We broke into Vassily's lab and we saw what he was working on. We knew we had to stop it. So we followed Caspian Baraban.'

'So we both had the same aim – but you succeeded . . . Your father would be so proud of you, Will.'

At Heathrow, none of them had really known what to do, or what to say. Andrew had held out his hand. Gaia had only nodded at Will and avoided his gaze. Anna and Shute Barrington hovered in the background.

Gaia's email later was more conversational.

'Andrew says to tell you we need you. I think he's worried there'll be no STORM unless you come back. And he says we need to come up with some way of making our mobiles secure so Barrington and his friends can't call up transcripts of our conversations whenever they want them . . .

'Barrington came to the basement last night. He said Caspian's been admitted to a secure psychiatric hospital. Andrew thinks maybe he'll get better and he can join STORM again. I told him not to get too optimistic. And Barrington said local police picked up two men in a hospital in St Petersburg. One had frost damage to his foot and the other had lost four fingers but they were OK. Andrew asked if Barrington could somehow let Esmee Templeton know that he saved her life . . .

'School has been asking where we've been. I said you had a nervous breakdown and ran off to Russia, so I had to try to save you ;)'

Will smiled.

As well as reading their emails, he tried to get everything clear in his mind.

Between them, Barrington and his mother had explained a great deal. Asking about Cutler had been the hardest. At the same time, it was impossible to wait.

On the motorway out of Heathrow, Will had brought up his memory. His dream.

Anna went very white. Her hands gripped the steering wheel. Her eyes darted to him and instantly away, as if burned. 'I can't tell you it isn't true.'

And all the disbelief and hope that had been building fell away. Will focused on the hire company carpet below his feet. He couldn't look at her. There was a long pause.

'I don't know if you can understand, but I'm going to tell you. That was a very long time ago. I loved your father totally. Completely. But. Well there are no buts. I wasn't very happy when you were very young. Your father was away all the time. I never knew if he'd come back. Roden was a good friend to me then. But that – your memory – it happened only that once, I promise you. It meant nothing, Will. Nothing.' She looked at him. For so long, Will was forced to say:

'Watch the road!'

She slapped the wheel. 'But this is more important, Will. It meant nothing. I love and I loved your father and you – that's it. The end.'

It wasn't satisfactory. And Will wasn't really sure what to think. This would take a lot more assimilation than some of the other new details he'd learned about her life.

In St Petersburg, squashed up against the heater long after everyone else had gone to bed, his mother told him more about her consultancy work with STASIS.

'And your tooth phone – you remember, you made it when you were ten. It's standard issue now,' she'd said, with pride. 'All field officers get one. And the techies who sometimes have to go out in the field – like me. It's not always desk work. Sometimes the regular field operatives just don't have the necessary knowledge. I had to go. Do you understand, Will? I *had* to.'

Will kicked at the ground. Frozen leaves crumpled and fell apart. He watched the fragments merge with the frost. From across the fields came the melodic chime of church bells.

The church, and the village, was a twenty-minute walk from the house. How many times had he travelled that road. Will pictured the rows of fresh bread rolls in the bakery. The post office with its summer baskets of plums. Everything that had once belonged to him. His memories. His birthright. And he reached into his jacket pocket and touched soft fur. A twitch told him Ratty was all right. Told him how much had changed.

Like his feelings about his mother. He could forgive her for leaving him. She'd done what she had to. In her position, he would, he realized, have felt forced to do the same. Bitterness lingered – but he'd get over it.

But Roden? He could never forgive her for that. He'd never trust her in quite the same way. Then, perhaps, St Petersburg had taught him he didn't have to. He'd been all right. More than all right. Looked at in this way, it made him free.

'Will!'

His mother's voice, ringing across the lawn, through the orchard.

'Shute's leaving!' she called. 'He wants to say good-bye.'

Barrington had arrived at eleven and stayed for lunch. Afterwards, Will had looked out over the fields, while Barrington further 'debriefed' his mother.

Now, Barrington was waiting around the front of the cottage, his silver E-type Jaguar gleaming on the gravel drive.

Barrington was wearing jeans this time. And a leather jacket over a black T-shirt. As he held out his hand to shake Will's, the leather creaked.

'Now all this is over, I should really tell you that you should never have followed Caspian Baraban – you should have gone to the police. Though I can see that breaking into his father's office and intercepting his email might have been a little tricky to explain.' Barrington smiled slightly.

'Or,' he continued, 'I should tell you that it was insanity for three fourteen-year-olds to actually think they could get inside the base and destroy the black hole weapon. I should tell you that by not telling the proper authorities, you risked Cutler actually succeeding and causing potentially enormous damage. Quite how enormous, thankfully we'll never know. And that's really the main point. Which is why I'm not going to tell you any of those things. You did it – that's all that matters in the end.'

Barrington pressed a button on his key fob. He followed Will's eyes, to his car.

'Yes, I have made some modifications. But I'll have to show you those next time we meet.'

'Next time?'

Barrington fixed Will with his gaze. 'I was thinking we might work with you in future. STASIS and STORM. That's if STORM continues, of course. What do you think?'

It took Will a moment to recover from his surprise. He nodded quickly. Then Barrington slipped into the driver's seat and with a final wave, he was gone.

Will watched the dust settle. So Barrington wanted to work with them. *MI6*. With STORM.

He turned to his mother. She wore an odd expression. Almost a smile.

The snow had cleared and the sky was clear blue. Ice-fresh. Anna wrapped her arms around herself.

'Will, I think you have to tell me what you'd like to do,' she said. 'I was thinking you would want the two of us to be back here, in Dorset. But if you like, we can move to London. Before you were born, your father and I lived there for ten years. We were very happy. It would be nice for me to show you the city. And Imperial has been on the phone – they're in need of a new professor of astrophysics . . . I could take that job, and leave STASIS behind. We could get a new house, near Natalia, if you like. I know it's a risk. But we don't have to sell up. We could rent. If you wanted, we could come back any time.'

Will nodded. He was thinking of Barrington, and Gaia and Andrew.

This had been his home. And that was the point. *Had been.* Dorset and all that happiness was in the past.

In London, he had new friends. New possibilities. STORM.

His mother's face was pale, he noticed. Was she worried about what he was thinking? Or was it just the December cold?

'You always used to say it,' Will said. 'No risks, no life. Let's go to London.'

Author's Note

All the gadgets in this book are based on genuine research and inventions.

1. Rapid Ascent is based on PowerQuick, developed by the company Quoin International, Nevada.
2. Double Entry is based on patent application GB 2393479.
3. Ear print recognition and facial blood-vessel pattern recognition are both genuine biometric identification devices.
4. A fog computer screen has been developed by Finnish company FogScreen and the Tampere University of Technology.
5. Guns that fire electric bullets are being developed in the US, under a Homeland Security Advanced Research Projects Agency program.

6. The technique for capturing words on a computer screen using the electromagnetic radiation from that screen is sometimes known as TEMPEST monitoring.

7. Soft Landing is based on a product developed by the Lavochkin Association, an aerospace firm located near Moscow.

8. Speak Easy is loosely based on a device patented by Seiko Epson of Japan.

9. Tooth Talk is based on a concept developed by students at the Royal College of Art, London.

10. Fly Spy is loosely based on an insect-cam invented at the University of California, Berkeley. This robot is the size of a locust and uses flapping wings to fly.

11. Vanya's wall-beating bugging is based on a NASA invention.

12. Remote-controlled rats have been created at the State University of New York.

13. A genetically modified plant that glows when it needs water has been created by researchers in Singapore.

14. A remote lie detector (known as the Remote

Personnel Assessment device) is being developed by the US Department of Defense.

15. Development of a non-lethal laser weapon that delivers a bout of pain from up to two kilometres away is being funded by the US military.

Notes on the science:

Black holes and strangelets are poorly understood. General comments about the nature of black holes and strangelets in this book are intended to reflect mainstream thinking – except when it comes to the idea of a black hole eating the Earth. Some scientists do think this is possible, but they are in the minority.

Could a black hole be created in a particle collider? It is thought to be possible (and collisions of two beams of gold nuclei might do it). Could this be dangerous? Depending on the conditions, some scientists think so. In the past, some have argued that, in theory, a black hole generated in a lab might start 'eating' the matter around it, and then fall to the centre of the Earth, where it would slowly 'eat' the planet.

However, most believe that any black holes created in a particle collider would be simply too short-lived to pose any threat to Earth.

The concept of creating a black hole and then

blasting it into space to engulf a satellite is fiction. According to current thinking, a black hole weapon is not feasible – at least not yet . . .

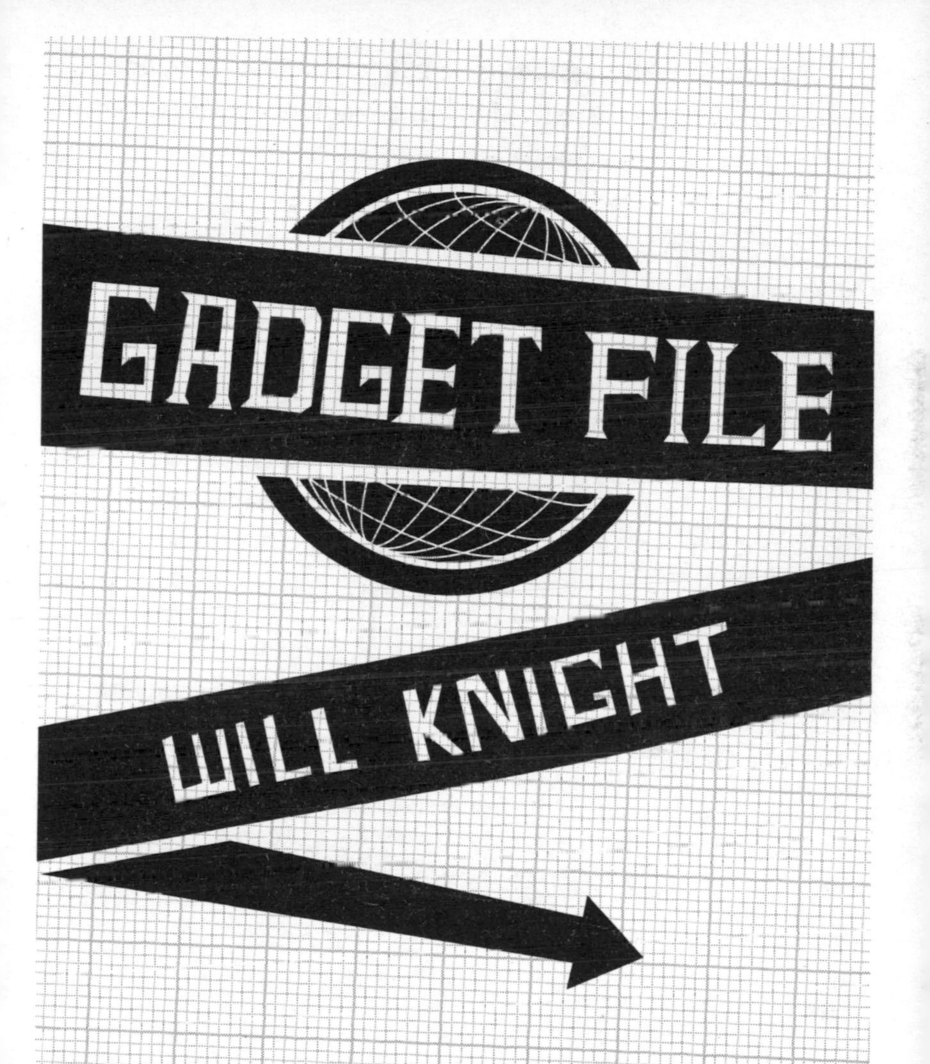
GADGET FILE
WILL KNIGHT

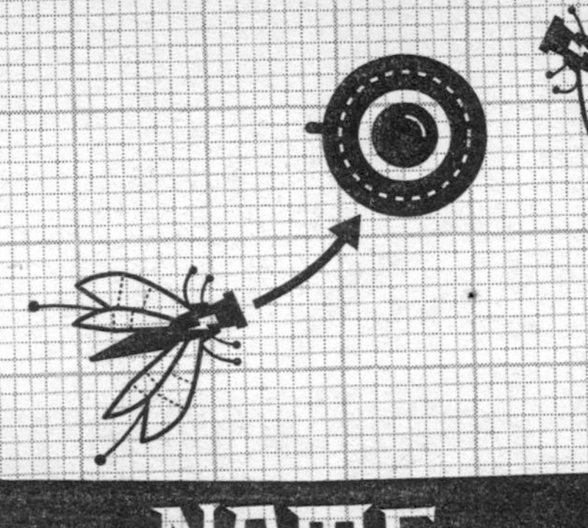

NAME

FLY SPY

INTENTION:
Surveillance

TESTED:
School trip to Houses of Parliament, London

SPECS:

Body made from honeycomb of carbon fibre (light and strong). Flapping wings. Current from battery runs to strips of piezoelectric crystal. Crystal connects to wings via carbon-fibre cranks. Current causes crystals to flex. Cranks amplify motion. Wings flap – at 160 times/second. Change wing angle to change direction.

CREATED: Workshop, Dorset

POTENTIAL MODIFICATIONS:

Better batteries? Eats flies for power?? (Robot digests flies in a microbial fuel cell. Fuel cell contains bacteria from sewage. These bacteria break down sugars in exoskeleton of a fly, releasing electrons. These electrons drive a current.)

(Modify so that your friends can actually use it? Maybe that will involve modifying your head, though, rather than your invention . . . Andrew)

INTENTION:

Protection for marines jumping from buildings (quicker than abseiling)

SPECS:

Toughened silk. Inflatable spokes. Inflatable outer ring. Diameter of cone: six metres. Deceleration in final 0.5 seconds no more than 12 G (military requires force of no more than 12.1 x gravity). Fits into backpack. Works for a drop of five metres or over.

CREATED:

Workshop, Dorset

TESTED:

From bell-tower of local church (night)

POTENTIAL MODIFICATIONS:

Use fire-resistant material?

(Rename 'Hard Landing' or make soft landing actually soft?? - saw your shoulder. Andrew)

RAPID ASCENT

INTENTION:

Scale buildings fast (marines).
Get up cliff faces?

SPECS:

Battery-powered. Cogs and wheels lift person at rate of 1m/second.

Operate: By firing rope to top of building using harpoon gun. Attach rope to device, which attaches to harness.
Cogs and wheels push rope through the body of the device, lifting the load.

CREATED:

Bedroom of Natalia's house,
Bloomsbury, London

POTENTIAL MODIFICATIONS:

Use solid fuel for power instead of battery?

NAME

RATTY

Gift from Vanya

CREATED:

Illyr Ruskin Private Hospital for Injured Mafia Hoods

Use remote computer to activate electrodes, which stimulate parts of the rat's brain to give it the sensation that e.g. its whiskers are being touched. Use these stimulations to control rat's movement.

Rat must be trained to e.g move to the right when you stimulate its brain so that it 'feels' that its right-side whiskers are being touched.

Species: Rattus norvegicus (brown rat). Fitted with video camera and microphone. Miniature microprocessor and electrode system is implanted. Remote-controlled, with a range of 750 metres.

TESTED:

Secret weapon base, outskirts of St Petersburg

POTENTIAL MODIFICATIONS:

remove excess electrode length (Ratty doesn't have to have electrodes sticking out of his head)

(Modify him to handle vertical surfaces? - would mean you don't have to jump on me to get up walls. Andrew)

FUTURE INVENTIONS ?

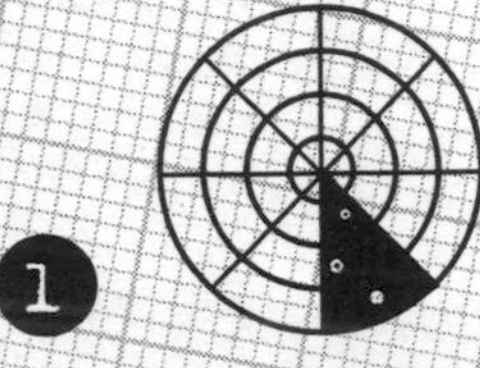

1

Listening through walls is useful. What if you could see through walls? How? Use radar??

2

Ratty can't run up walls. Solution??

3

Retrieval robot. Send it into dangerous situations to pick up and retrieve objects. Based on human hand? (No . . . too complicated – so based on what?)

(4. Remote-controlled Will - we still have use of his brain, but he always agrees with Andrew and does what he says ;) - Andrew)

Acknowledgements

Thank you to James, my first reader. And to Sarah Molloy, my agent, and Harriet Wilson and Lauren Buckland, my editors at Macmillan. Thanks also to Dr Terry Percival of National ICT Australia, Professor Peter Dyson of La Trobe University and Dr Larissa Koroleva of the University of New South Wales for valuable technical comments and suggestions. I would also like to acknowledge the work of journalist Barry Fox, who regularly identifies gems among international patent applications. Some of the new inventions highlighted by Barry have found their way into this book.